A Hacker a Vampire & a Chimera Walk Into a Bar

Warning: Author is dyslexic as hell.

The editing and beta reading team: Martha Collins and Lauren Meghoo

Profession Editing: Jenny Sliger, Owl Eyes Proofs

Cover Illustration: Ryn Katryn Book Covers

Feel free to contact me with questions, requests, or comments: author@rk-munin.com

-There is cussing throughout this book and two scenes with derogatory statements concerning one or more of the following: transgender-phobia, plus-sized body shaming, misogyny, and poverty. (Don't worry. Everyone who's mean in this book gets what they deserve!)

-Several chapters include graphic descriptions of violence/fight scenes. During some of the fight scenes, bad guys end up dying/being killed.

-There is a description of a motorcycle crash on page.

-There is mention of a past suicide, nothing on page.

-One scene contains several characters smoking cigarettes.

-There are several scenes of alcohol consumption.

-This novel is an **MMF**. That means there will be crossed swords (descriptions of MM sexual activity).

-This book is meant for mature audiences, 18+ readers only.

To every author who wrote the books I've enjoyed. Those stories kept me going and eventually gave me the courage to write my own.

Do not go gentle into that good night
Dylan Thomas, 1914-1953

Do not go gentle into that good night,
Old age should burn and rave at close of day;
Rage, rage against the dying of the light.

Though wise men at their end know dark is right,
Because their words had forked no lightning they
Do not go gentle into that good night.

Good men, the last wave by, crying how bright
Their frail deeds might have danced in a green bay,
Rage, rage against the dying of the light.

Wild men who caught and sang the sun in flight,
And learn, too late, they grieved it on its way,
Do not go gentle into that good night.

Grave men, near death, who see with blinding sight
Blind eyes could blaze like meteors and be gay,
Rage, rage against the dying of the light.

And you, my father, there on the sad height,
Curse, bless, me now with your fierce tears, I pray.
Do not go gentle into that good night.
Rage, rage against the dying of the light.

DOWNWARD
DOG

"Oh yeah? Well, fuck you!" Briar regretted the words the minute they were out of her mouth. The guy she cussed at was massive, tall, and with a beer gut that made him look nine months pregnant with at least ten sets of twins. Then the scent of stale sweat hit her nose as he moved to loom over her. At least he wasn't sneering at her anymore. He looked pissed, but not so arrogant.

"What the fuck did you say to me, you fat dike bitch?" God, this man's breath could fell a tree.

Briar got the impression that was a rhetorical question, so instead of answering, she took in the bar around her.

Negatives: the guy came in with four of his buddies, all as big and as nasty looking as him.

Positives: she'd decided to wear her steel toe boots today.

"I said fuck you," Briar repeated loud and slow, as if speaking to someone hard of hearing.

"Are you looking to get knocked around?" one of the guys behind Bad Breath asks. He looked eager to abuse anyone smaller than him.

Hmmm, that could be a name for a bad country western band: Bad Breath and the Eager-to-Abuse.

She felt Maddy cringe behind her, her tall body pressed against Briar's back. Her friend's long fingers tugged at her arm. "Oh, chica, we need to get out of here."

Briar could tell by the tone of Maddy's voice that she was on the cusp of a meltdown. Maddy didn't do confrontations. Unfortunately for her best friend, that was one of Briar's most fluent forms of communication.

And her love language was defending the few people she cared about, so there was no way in hell she'd back down from any of these assholes.

"Me and my friend were sitting here first," Briar pointed out, giving these guys a chance to back off. "We didn't look at you guys, didn't talk to you, and sure as hell didn't invite you to walk over here and start harassing us. So why don't you do the gentlemanly thing and fuck off?"

"This isn't some gay bar," the guy behind Bad Breath announced. "Dikes like you and she-men like that twink behind you shouldn't be here. This is a bar for men and women, not fucked-up freaks."

"Then what are you doing here?" she snapped back. She must have talked a little too quickly because Bad Breath seemed to struggle to understand what she said. Or maybe he really was hearing impaired.

"Briar, please," Maddy begged, tugging with more vigor.

Unwilling to take her eyes off this group, Briar reached around to pat Maddy's hand soothingly. "Go in the back and find Mikey," she instructed. "Everything's going to be fine."

"Briar you can't do this, not again," Maddy insisted and tugged at her arm with a little more force. Briar's ancient shirt rips a little at the neckline.

She threw Maddy a frustrated look over her shoulder. "Hey! This is one of my favorite shirts," she grumbled.

Maddy wasn't intimidated by her at all. "They're all your favorite shirts," she retorted.

Bad Breath used Maddy's distraction to shove Briar. Hard.

Trying to keep from knocking Maddy down, Briar ended up stumbling into a bar stool and falling on her ass. Bad Breath and his village of idiots started laughing as she scrambled to her feet.

Maddy threw them a terrified look. "Oh no, you've done it now," she whispered, then looked down at Briar. "Please be smart about this, Briar. You're barely off probation."

That comment made the guys stop laughing. "Probation?" Bad Breath asked, looking down at her with condescension. "What, did you slap some poor guy 'cus he wasn't willing to drill that ugly cunt of yours?"

"That's it, I'm getting Mikey," Maddy declared as she fled. Her six-foot frame came with a set of long legs that practically flew over the dirty floor of Downward Dog in search of the owner, Mikey Short.

"Now that the lady has left," Briar said as she made a show of dusting herself off, "I think we can finish our conversation."

"You're honestly calling that freak a lady?" Bad-Breath asked, glancing over to where Maddy disappeared through an employee's only door. "Neither of you counts as female. The guy's got a dick, and you might as well have one."

"Then can I have yours? I could add it to my miniatures collection." Before he can react to her words, she swung her leg. Her steel toe boot impacted Bad Breath's crotch with a satisfying sound. The guy's eyes rolled back in his head as he went down with a squeak.

She didn't get time to gloat. Eager-to-Abuse was on her in a hot second.

At five-foot-ten, she was not as tall as any of these guys, but she was far from intimidated. Eager-to-Abuse managed to come in with a fast jab that she mostly avoided. It clipped her temple and sent her stumbling, but when he tried to follow up with an upper cut, she grabbed the barstool next to her and put it in the way of his fist.

The barstool took the hit without even a creak from the blow because Mikey bought sturdy furniture. Eager-to-Abuse howled in pain and clutched his hand to his chest.

One of the other guys wearing a shirt with armpit stains hotfooted it forward, already drawing back for a punch. With the barstool still in her hand, Briar simply swung it up to take the hit.

The guy tried to pull his punch as soon as he saw what was about to happen but didn't manage it. He ended up tearing the stool from her grip and sending it skittering off.

A few patrons gasped and moved to get away from the widening battlefield. Good, that would help her in the long run. While she might feel bad if innocent bystanders got hurt, she was pretty sure none of these guys would care.

Pit-Stains ended up shoved out of the way as Never-Bothers-to-Bathe snatched up an empty beer bottle from a nearby abandoned table and came at her with it held high over his head.

A beer bottle as a club? Really? What did he think this was, some kind of movie?

With practiced ease, Briar also grabbed a beer bottle, but she didn't hold it like a club and waited for the guy. She pulled back her hand and let it fly. Years of softball made her accurate and it pegged Never-Bothers-to-Bathe right in the nose. He went to his knees, dazed.

Three down, two to go.

Adrenaline and righteous anger were pumping through her system, making her feel powerful. And virtuously violent.

"Which one of you motherfuckers is next?" she yelled out.

She felt something trickle down her face but ignored it. Her temple was throbbing from where Bad-Breath landed that first punch and probably opened up her skin with one of the heavy silver rings on his beefy fingers. She'd have Maddy put some butterfly band-aids on it later.

Swinging her head around, partially to get her cheekbone length bright blue hair out of her eyes and partially to look dismissive, she glowered at the two guys still standing.

Next time, she'd remember to spike her hair up before she and Maddy went out for drinks. Stiffly spiked hair was a great look for barroom brawls. It's so "in" these days.

"Take this bitch down!" Bad-Breath wheezed out. He'd managed to get from a fetal position to his knees, but he didn't look ready to stand yet.

Keeping the two remaining guys in her line of sight, she scoffed at Bad-Breath.

"Aww, look at you, learning to crawl and shit. I think you might be ahead of your learning curve already."

"What the hell is going on out here?" Mikey boomed out as he barreled into the room. The two guys still on their feet used that as their cue to rush her. She was half expecting it, so she wasn't entirely unprepared.

She managed to sidestep one of them entirely, then dodged the first punch from the second guy. But that second guy was quick and caught her in the gut with a lucky second swing.

Her breath whooshed out of her, stunning her for a moment. Before the guy could press his advantage, Mikey was there and grabbing him. The wolf shifter easily flung him halfway across the room.

While that happened, the first guy she'd avoided ignored Mikey and came at her again. She managed to suck in enough air to straighten up and bitch slap him so hard it made his head twist and his legs stumble.

Oh, there's nothing as satisfying as bitch slapping a guy like that.

She managed to land the slap over his ear, which she knew from experience was not only painful but disorientating. She followed up the slap with an upward elbow to the guy's nose, feeling it crunch as he screamed. He went down in a sobbing heap on the floor.

She'd love to stand there triumphantly and intone some witty last line, but the sound of police sirens closing in fast was a clear indication that she was out of time.

Then Mikey was at her side and shoving her hard toward the back of the club.

"Get out of here," the he ordered in a voice too low for anyone else to hear. "I swear to the goddess, you get in as much trouble as a half-grown pup. How the hell can one human female cause this much mayhem? Go!"

He didn't have to tell her again. Rushing through the employee's only door, she was down a short hall and out a back door as fast as her legs could carry her.

Coming to a stumbling halt, she stood for a moment, blinking under the floodlights in the alley. Which direction should she take? It's not like the people in the bar wouldn't be able to easily identify her. Between her height, tattoos, and blue hair, she was hardly discreet.

But she knew Mikey would claim ignorance of her identity and those dicks she fought with would only be able to give a description, not her name. If she could get away from the area, it was unlikely the cops would locate her.

San Diego wasn't a small town. There were plenty of tatted-up, blue-haired women here and enough real problems that the authorities won't bother with much follow-up for a bar fight that didn't end with anyone dead.

A familiar car squealed as it turned down the alley. Briar squeezed against one of the buildings as Maddy screeched to a halt next to her. Oh, it was good to have friends.

"Get your angry ass in here!" Maddy ordered, her head out the window. Grinning, Briar slipped into the passenger side of the non-descript Toyota.

"What bar are we going to hit next?" she asked with a grin, slumping down in the seat.

Maddy shook her head as she drove with just the right amount of caution out of the alley and past the cop cars gathering in front of Downward Dog. Not a single one of them gave the car a second look.

"Girlfriend, you're all kinds of crazy," Maddy commented. "Let's get you home and cleaned up."

"Eh, if you insist," Briar agreed. She let her head fall back against the headrest and closed her eyes. Now that the adrenaline was fading, her head and belly were starting to hurt. But it was worth it. No one was allowed to pick on her family.

Maddy remained quiet as she drove them to the small, two-bedroom home they shared in a not great neighborhood. Briar helped Maddy move in day escrow closed on the property. Then she moved herself in and rented the second bedroom.

There was no way she was going to let Maddy live alone, not in this sketchy area.

Pulling the car into the narrow driveway at the side of the house, she parked behind Briar's ancient Honda Civic. Maddy got out even before the engine had shut down completely to rush around the car and pull the door open for Briar.

"I'm fine," Briar insisted and pushed Maddy away gently.

"You are not fine. You're bleeding all over the place," Maddy countered. Briar looked down at her shirt and frowned. Damn, not only was it torn, but now it was covered in bloodstains.

"Forget the shirt," Maddy said, reading her mind as usual. "Get your ass in that house so I can get you cleaned up. I swear to God, Briar, all I wanted was to have a drink out. Downward Dog should've been safe. How the hell did you get into a bar brawl there?"

Briar shrugged as she let Maddy tug her into the house through the backdoor. "I didn't throw the first punch."

Maddy turned the lights on and snickered. "Nah, you threw the first kick."

The back door led into the house's postage stamp-sized kitchen. Maddy shoved her at the tiny kitchen table. Briar collapsed into one of the only two chairs.

"You're acting like I went out looking for a fight," Briar complained.

"I know you don't look for fights, but you sure seem to find them anyway," Maddy commented, thumping down a box full of bandages and ointments. Taking the other chair, Maddy scooted close and started cleaning the cut on her temple. "It's okay to walk away sometimes. Words are just sound."

"They called you a pervert and a freak," Briar reminded her. "I couldn't let that go."

"I know," Maddy said gently, a wealth of feeling behind those two words.

Madeline Aguilera started out as Mateo Aguilera. She and Briar grew up next door to each other and had become best friends the first day of kindergarten.

When Mateo admitted to her at sixteen that he might like guys more than girls, Briar didn't even blink. All she said was that she liked guys too, so they could go out hunting for dick together.

Briar stood by Mateo's side when he came out as gay to his family. They were all first- and second-generation Mexican American and staunch Catholics, but most continued to associate with Mateo. A few decided homosexuality was something they couldn't handle and refused to have anything to do with him.

Briar told them to fuck off and then used her blossoming hacker skills to ruin their credit.

When Mateo hit twenty and fell into a deep depression, it was Briar who got him to therapy. When therapy started to help, it was Briar who listened to Mateo's confession that he felt like he was born into the wrong body. It was Briar who helped him find a doctor to oversee the transition from Mateo to Madeline.

After all that, Briar refused to stand by and let Maddy take shit from anyone.

Briar might not be able to right all the wrongs in the world, but she could make damn sure that the people in her little corner were taken care of to the best of her ability. If that included kicking some stupid dickhead's ass, then so be it.

That had a ring to it; Kicking Stupid Dickhead's Ass could be the name of Bad-Breath and the Eager-to-Abuse's first album.

"You know Mikey's going to ban us from the bar for a while," Maddy pointed out as she finished cleaning up Briar's face.

She winced. "Ban me, you mean. He'd never ban you."

"If you're banned than I'm not going," Maddy answered promptly.

"Sorry," Briar said, this time meaning it. "But I think I'll be happy staying in for the rest of the weekend. You should go out and hang with Mikey and the pack."

Maddy made a disapproving sound. "You stay in every weekend. Between working from home and being a general shut in, I'm amazed when you remember how to use verbal language skills. Tonight was the first time you've left the house for almost a month!"

"Don't exaggerate. I went out yesterday," Briar retorted.

"Because we were out of coffee," Maddy countered. "If I let you have a coffee maker in your room, I might never see you."

Now Briar was feeling a little picked on. "I leave my room all the time."

"To go to the fridge," Maddy argued. "That hardly counts. Come on, Briar. Tonight was supposed to be about both of us having a few drinks to celebrate. Maybe even find a cute hook-up for the night. You've been whining that you've been wanting to get laid."

"I got to kick some ass, that's almost as good," Briar argued with a grin.

Maddy held up a hand. "Stop right there, I'm not listening to your 'fight or fuck' theory again."

Briar gave her a grumpy look. "I stand by it. Are you done messing with my head yet? I should probably check my message boards and get a little work done."

Standing up, Maddy made a shooing motion with her hands. "I'm done. Go hide in your cave."

Grabbing a beer from the fridge, Briar gave Maddy a grin as she popped the top off using the edge of the counter. "Breakfast at that pancake place in Poway tomorrow?"

Maddy's smile was indulgent. "Sure," she agreed.

"Great!" Briar said before retreating into her room. Once in her cave, she slumped down at her desk with relief. Her head was pounding, and her body ached, but she was nowhere near tired enough to try sleeping. By her standards the day was just getting started.

Time to see if anyone else was awake and online.

Memphis stared at the website, waiting. It was a site the hacker he knew only as Baby Doll set up so they could communicate without anyone being able to find either of them.

To the uneducated, it looked like a page dedicated to poison plants, but if you dove into the menu, you could eventually find a conversation box titled "Ask the Gardener." After Memphis entered the password Baby Doll gave him, a second box opened up, allowing him and Baby Doll to talk.

But Baby Doll wasn't there. He'd been staring at the box for over thirty minutes and still nothing.

He should give up. Baby Doll almost always responded within minutes, so if she hadn't responded yet, she might be asleep. Or maybe hanging out with her friend Maddy. Whatever she was doing, she wasn't online.

He could shut down the computer. Get a few hours of sleep. Get up early and help his brother Nash with the house he was roofing. Call Soren and check in on the Annwyl Pack. Pick up groceries. Clean the house.

There were a lot of things he should be doing instead of staring at a computer screen.

He didn't move to do any of them.

Absently, he finished the beer in his hand and chucked the bottle into a bin a few feet away. The glass shattered when it hit the other bottles in the bin.

"Two points," he called out, bringing both hands up over his head as if in triumph. The laptop started to slide off his lap, and he fumbled to grab it.

Then he went back to staring at the empty box like a looser.

"Come on, Baby Doll," he murmured to the screen encouragingly. "We haven't talked all day. Please come online."

He tried to text her earlier in the day but got nothing. That wasn't surprising. She was constantly going through burner phones. Over the last few months, she'd changed her number at least a dozen times. But she always made sure he had her latest number.

That had to mean something, right?

The ding of a message made Memphis straighten up as a shot of excitement went through him.

Baby Doll: *Memphis Bell, you still up?*

Memphis: *Up and eager to chat, Baby Doll.*

Baby Doll: *You might be the perfect male.*

Memphis: *You know it! Hey, can we do the phone thing? I'm a little too tired to be doing all this typing.*

Baby Doll: *Shit, sorry! Did I catch you about to go to bed? You don't have to stay up to keep me company.*

Memphis: *I'm NEVER too tired for you, sweetness. But my big old fingers are clumsy enough on a good day. Right now, I'm being forced to type with my pinkies to keep from hitting more than one key at a time. Take pity on a guy and call me.*

When someone was typing, there was a small bar at the bottom that lights up in a blue wave from left to right in the chat window. But after his last message, the bar stayed stubbornly white.

Damn it, did he scare her off? He'd been slowly getting her used to talking to him over the phone instead of using this program, but it'd taken almost a month. Baby Doll was the most secretive and reluctant woman he'd ever dealt with.

Memphis: *You still there, darlin'?*

Nothing. She wouldn't sign off without saying goodbye. She always said goodbye in some way. Did something happen? Maybe someone broke into her home. She'd mentioned once that her neighborhood wasn't too classy, which he translated to ghetto.

Worry started churning in his gut as horrible ideas flooded his mind. When his phone rang, he answered it without looking at who was calling, his eyes glued to that little conversation rectangle on the screen.

"What?" he barked out.

There was a sharp intake of breath, and then Baby Doll's voice came through the line. "Whoa there, I thought you wanted to talk."

"Baby Doll? I do want to talk! Sorry, you had me worried there for a minute when you went silent in the chat window," Memphis admitted, slumping back on the couch. He slapped the laptop closed and set it on the cushion next to him. Propping up his feet on the low table in front of him, he let out a deep sigh.

Baby Doll laughed. "Give a girl a minute to find and power up her phone."

"You been busy, Baby Doll? What are you up to down there in sunny San Diego?"

"Maddy got that promotion!"

"That's great! I told you it was a sure thing." Although he'd never talked to Maddy or any of Baby Doll's other friends, he felt like he knew them after listening to Baby Doll talk about them.

"Sure things don't exist," Baby Doll said with a laugh.

"They do," Memphis argued. "They're rare, but I know they're out there."

Like you and me, he thinks. *We're going to be a sure thing once I convince you to meet me.*

"Whatever, old man," she teased back.

"Call me a Boomer one more time and I'm putting you over my knee," he countered.

"Like I'd fit over your knee," she scoffed.

"You'll fit, Baby Doll," Memphis said, his voice turning sensual. "I know you'd fit perfectly draped over my body." There was silence at the other end. Crap, had his little push into seduction had been too blunt?

Finally, Briar spoke. "Yeah, so, uh, we went out to celebrate. Maddy's promotion, I mean. We went out. To a bar."

Memphis was happy to note her voice didn't sound entirely steady and she was stammering a bit. That, coupled with the lack of a snarky response, told him everything he needed to know. She was affected too. Not as much as him, but there was still something there for him to work with.

"Did you go to your friend's place?" Memphis asked, letting her change the subject. "What's it called, The Humping Mutt or something?"

"The Downward Dog," she answered with a soft laugh. He loved that sound. He'd remembered the name but wanted to hear her laugh. Her laugh did strange things to his heart.

"Mikey's the guy that owns it, right?"

"Yeah, Mikey's the alpha of his pack," she said, and he could hear the eagerness in her voice. "We get to drink for free since I cleaned up a credit snafu for him last month."

"I remember you telling me about that credit thing. So what happened after you got there? Was the place crowded? I hate it when there are too many humans stinking up a place."

"I'm human," she reminded him with another chuckle.

"You don't count," Memphis answered. "Some humans are special, and you're one of the special ones."

"I'm special all right," Baby Doll whispered. "But not in the way you think."

If he didn't have chimera hearing, he might have missed the sad note in her tone. Over the months, he'd gotten hints that she didn't think she was worthy of his attention. That pissed him off. He knew his mate was perfect, but how to convince her?

"Invite me down. Meet me. Give me a chance to show you how fucking special you are, Baby Doll."

Her laugh sounded forced this time. "That's a long ass road trip with only disappointment at the end."

"I doubt it," he answered quickly. "But it's on me, right? I come down, we meet at a coffee shop or some shit. Whatever the hell humans do on dates. And we talk. I wanna see your face, Baby Doll. I really do."

Silence met his request.

He debated telling her that the moment he heard her voice, he knew she was his mate match, but to a human that might sound bizarre. She was aware of the hidden magical world all around her, but it was one thing to know and another thing to have a man you've never met declare that the two of you were meant to be together. She'd think he was crazy, even if it was the truth.

Chimeras know the instant they hear or smell whoever is meant to be their mate. Memphis's father was a perfect example.

His father, Hank, met his mother at a Grateful Dead concert in the early 1980s.

Actually, he smelled her first, managing to discern Darlene's scent from the smell of hundreds of humans and all the pot smoke. He tracked her through the venue for nearly an hour until he finally caught up to her. The sound of her voice along with the strong smell of her in his nose when he went up to introduce himself ended up triggering his chimera mating reflex. Without thinking about the wisdom of his actions, he grabbed her and ran.

No sooner did they get to his cabin than she got hold of a plank of wood and knocked him on his ass. The most fascinating part of the story was that after all that, she decided to stay with the "stupid bastard." Memphis and his seven brothers were the result of their happy union.

Because there was some druid blood in her linage, Darlene's family didn't like that she paired up with a chimera. There was a massive fight when she tried to introduce him to her family. Afterwards she'd marched up to Hank, told him to pack up and that they were leaving Tennessee to head west.

Hank didn't question, he obeyed.

Within a few hours they were heading west, and kept driving west for days. Every time they'd stop Darlene would get out, look around and instruct him to keep going.

That didn't stop until they got to Bend, Oregon. She had him pull over in the mountains near an empty lot for sale, got out, and declared that this was their new home.

Would it help or hurt his case with Baby Doll if he told her that story? He wasn't sure.

Fuck, this was frustrating! He needed her to agree to meet. He wouldn't do what his dad did. He never wanted his mate to feel like she needed to knock him out. But his need to find her was coming close to overwhelming his determination to be patient.

"So anyway, we wanted to go out and get a drink," Baby Doll began, as if he hadn't begged her to let him visit. This woman was hard on his ego. "Not anything major. Just hang out and celebrate Maddy getting a promotion."

Allowing her to redirect the conversation, he asked, "Did she get the raise package she wanted too?"

"She sure did! There isn't much of a pay increase, but this position means she can sign up for better medical benefits. That's going to help out a lot."

"That's great, but tell me what happened at Downward Dog," Memphis pressed. He hoped this story was about the bar being out of her favorite beer and not something worse. She'd only recently gotten off probation for assaulting someone who'd been harassing a pixie named Izzy.

Thankfully, the judge had only given her six months' probation instead of jail time. But she wouldn't always be so lucky.

When he finally managed to install himself in her life, he'd make sure she never ran afoul of the authorities again. And if someone thought they could hurt her or someone she cared about, well, he knew how to dispose of a body where it wouldn't be found.

"Right, so what we didn't realize was that tonight was Dumb Bastard Open Mic Night." Her voice was a combination of rueful and upset, making Memphis's skin flush red with anger.

He didn't like where this was going.

"What happened?" It took effort to keep his voice from breaking down into a growl.

"Some assholes decided to pick on Maddy and—"

Memphis's plea cut her off. "Please tell me you didn't get into a bar fight."

"Uh, I could tell you that, if you want me to."

It took several breaths before Memphis could form words again. "Are you hurt?"

"Nah, just a little cut and some bruises. I left all the guys on the floor. Haven't I told you I'm a badass bitch?" Her voice was lighthearted, and Memphis would love to be able to respond in kind, but he couldn't.

"Do you know their names? I can hunt them down for you." There was no mistaking Memphis's tone for anything but deadly serious.

She laughed off his offer. "Thanks, but I'm pretty sure they aren't going to live tonight down any time soon." Then she tried to change the subject. "How's that vamp friend of yours and the two wolf shifters doing?"

He worked on swallowing the fear and anger raging inside him at the thought of anyone laying hands on his mate. "They're settling in well. Kalli's pregnant."

An exclamation of surprise came out of her. "Pregnant? Do they know who the father is? I mean, she's got two guys. Is that going to cause tension?"

"No way, Baby Doll. Triads are pretty common among us non-humans. On top of that, Soren and Quinn don't care who the bio dad is because that baby will belong to all of them. Not just those three, but the entire Annwyl Pack. Everyone's excited about Kalli's baby. It's a sign of prosperity for the pack."

"Huh, I like that," she commented, a wistful note to her voice. "Supportive family is important."

That wistful tone brushed away his earlier anger and made him want to hold his mate close. He didn't know much, but he got the impression that his hacker had a shitty childhood.

A sharp ping in the background came through the phone clearly, interrupting his thoughts.

"Crap, I gotta go," she announced. "I've been waiting for this message. Time to earn the big bucks."

"Do whatever you gotta do, Baby Doll," Memphis said quickly. "But call me any time, you hear? Any time day or night."

"Sure thing," she agreed but he could hear that she was already distracted. "Talk to you later." Then she hung up on him.

"Bye," he said to empty air. "You're my mate. I love you unconditionally. Could you please tell me your real name?"

Fuck!

Memphis was halfway through his fifth beer and not even close to being drunk yet when his phone rang. He'd been playing Call of Duty and the ring of his cell caused him to hit the wrong button and fall into a group of Nazis he was hiding from.

Giving up on that game, he dropped the controller to fish out his phone from under the couch cushion. He'd have been surprised if it was Baby Doll calling him back, but he was hopeful anyway.

The number wasn't Baby Doll, so he answered without any diplomacy as he growled into the phone. "What do you want?"

The caller wasn't thrown off by his attitude. "I've got a job for you."

"Hey, Craig," Memphis grumbled, slumping back on the couch. "Missing persons or skiptrace?"

"Skiptrace," Craig answered. "Guy's a three time loser and probably looking at some heavy time. I shouldn't have bothered with his bail, but his mama cried."

"Softie," Memphis smirked. His bank account was more than healthy, so he wasn't interested in tracking down some idiot. "Not interested. Call if you got a missing person, otherwise I'm taking some time off."

"I figured you wouldn't want it because I'm pretty sure he's all the way down in San Diego," Craig muttered. "But you're not even doing local stuff right now?"

Memphis jerked up straight, causing the controller to fall off his lap. "San Diego?"

"Yeah, San-Fucking-Diego. You interested now? Or should I hand it off to Samantha?"

"This has gotta be fate," Memphis muttered.

"What?"

"I'll take it," Memphis said louder. "Text me what you got on him."

"Great," Craig's rough voice lightened with enthusiasm. "Usual fee?"

"Plus travel expenses," Memphis countered.

"Yeah, sure, but don't be going all crazy with the spending," Craig warned, his voice lowering to the usual grumpy tone.

"Whatever," Memphis countered and hung up.

Skiptrace in San Diego.

Baby Doll was in San Diego.

This had to be a sign. It's not stalking if he's got a job down there, right? And after he turns this loser in, he could spend some time in the area. See if he can talk his Baby Doll into meeting him.

Life was suddenly looking up. Now he just had to figure out which t-shirts and jeans to pack. He wanted to dress to impress after all.

Briar took in the boarded-up front of the old building, then swung her gaze to Mikey. "Really?"

Mikey's grin didn't falter. "I know it doesn't look like much now, but the place has good bones, is in a prime location, and the price was too good to pass up."

Maddy hugged an arm around Mikey as she gazed at the building. "I can already tell it's going to be great! Probably even better than Downward Dog."

"See," Mikey said, "Maddy can tell it has potential."

"Potential as a fire hazard," Briar mumbled.

Everyone around her snickered except for Maddy and Mikey. Mikey gave her a mock scowl, and Maddy rolled her eyes.

In truth, she was happy that the pack's finances were healthy enough to back another business venture, but she didn't think any price other than zero was a good deal for this building. It might have been nice long ago, but years of neglect had taken a toll. Looking around at the busy street, she had to admit it was in a good spot, but was it worth the location to have a building in such disrepair?

"The place was a restaurant before so it'll be easy to set it up as a bar and pack members can use the apartments on the second and third floor," Mikey explained as he pulled Maddy's arm out from around him. He tangled his fingers with hers and led them into the dark building. "Let me show you!"

Briar let the others file in before she followed.

There was one lighting fixture with an intact bulb that barely lit up the place. The main room was filthy with cobwebs and enough dust in the air to make everyone cough. But after she finished sneezing, Briar had to admit the place looked a lot better on the inside than the outside. Unlike the boarded up and badly graffitied storefront, the inside was well preserved, if dirty.

"What kind of restaurant was this?" Maddy asked.

"I'm not sure, something high end," Mikey explained.

"I'm surprised it's been empty so long," Izzy said as she nudged an overturned chair with her Converse-covered foot. If Briar wasn't so attached to her boots, she'd want a pair of those Converse; they were blood red with black thorny vines painted all over them. They paired perfectly with Izzy's ragged netting skirt and overlarge black sweatshirt that had a stylized crow on the front.

Izzy had the best style.

"I looked into it and there was a shooting here," Mikey explained as he led Maddy over to the bar area.

"Shooting?" Izzy asked before Briar could. Now things were getting interesting.

"About ten years ago, this guy came in and unloaded a couple of guns. Killed one of the owners but no one else was even wounded. They never figured out who it was." Mikey pointed to a corner where an old security camera was dangling by a cord. "Even though everything was recorded, and they could clearly see the guy's face."

As everyone thought about what he'd said, Mikey righted a bar stool and presented it to Maddy. "My lady."

She sat with a demur smile. "Thank you, kind sir."

Suddenly, Briar could see how this place would look all cleaned up. Way classier than the Downward Dog, but still comfortable. A place anyone could hang out with a couple of friends. He could have some tables for sit down customers, a few pool tables, and darts. Maybe even an Italian shuffleboard table along one wall. It was going to be a great place to gather.

"So a guy comes in with a bunch of guns, kills one dude on camera, and they never catch him? That's odd," Juan said as he leaned against the counter next to Maddy.

Mikey nodded as he rounded the bar to take a position behind it. Then he leaned against the empty countertop behind him and crossed his arms, it was his typical bartender pose. "It gets weirder. There were two guys who owned it. The same night one of them was murdered, the other one disappeared."

"Disappeared?" Briar echoed, intrigued. "What do you mean?"

"As in no one ever saw him again," Mikey explained with a grin. He loved a good mystery. "Some thought he was murdered, but no body turned up. And if he ran, he must have had cash hidden somewhere because he never used any credit cards or bank accounts. He basically vanished. That's why this place sat empty for so many years, between the murder and disappearance, ownership was a legal mess."

"But now it's yours," Maddy said, looking around with a thoughtful expression. "But we should do something to get rid of the bad juju before you open."

"I think the bigger priority might be cleaning," Juan commented. "I mean sure, get a witch or druid in here to make sure no one's spirit is hanging out, but most humans won't even notice that. They will notice the mess."

"I've got all that figured out," Mikey said with an elaborate sweep of his hands to a far corner. Stacked there were brooms, mops, trashcans, dust cloths, and various jugs of cleaning liquids. "My friends, welcome to your opportunity to earn a future full of free drinks!"

They all groaned, and Briar put her hands on her hips. "Dude, I already did that credit cleanup for you, now you expect me to do actual cleaning?"

Mikey hurried out from behind the bar and drew Briar toward the back of the place. "You're not cleaning. I've got a skilled labor request for you."

Everyone else started for the corner full of cleaning supplies, slinging jokes and comments back and forth as they got to work.

Despite the groans and protests, everyone had known this was a likely outcome of this visit. But they were pack, and this is what you did for the pack.

When Izzy first moved here, a local group of imps had made life difficult for her. Because she was half human, none of the pixie clans would let her join and the imps saw an opportunity for exploitation.

She'd ducked into the Downward Dog one night to get away from a couple of them and ended up confessing all her troubles to Mikey. He'd adopted her into the Lobos Gris. As the Alpha, Mikey could do as he liked and anyone in his pack who didn't like it could leave.

None did. They'd all been outcasts too and accepted that Mikey's generosity to non-shifters came with being a member of Lobos Gris Pack. Briar and Maddy were both honorary members too. This pack was the loving family a lot of them didn't have growing up.

It was for that reason that she followed Mikey down a narrow flight of stairs; otherwise she would've "noped" out halfway down when it got dark and eerie.

Pulling out her phone, she opened the flashlight function to shine it down on the steps so at least she wouldn't trip and break her neck.

"You better not be leading me to my doom," she teased the big shifter.

"Oh shit, sorry," Mikey said as he stopped on the stairs and looked back at her. "I forgot you're human."

"That's probably the nicest thing you've ever said to me," Briar shot back, making Mikey's expression ease.

"You stay here, and I'll run back up for some lights. None of the outlets or fixtures down here work. That's what I wanted you to look at."

She stopped him before he could try to squeeze past her. "You know I'm a hacker, right? I work with computers. I'm not an electrician."

"Yeah, but Maddy told me you fixed some of the outlets of her house and helped Jace rewire the garage. Until Jace gets back from that job in San Jose, you're the best we've got," Mikey explained. "But if you really don't want to, I get it."

It was on the tip of Briar's tongue to turn Mikey down flat. She didn't like dealing with electricity. She'd been shocked enough times to have formed a deep appreciation for the more painful aspects of electrical work.

But she couldn't refuse Mikey. None of them could refuse Mikey. That's how Izzy ended up with four rescue dogs at her place and Juan ended up renting his spare room out to Jaime. Just like them, Briar couldn't stand to say no to the generous alpha.

"I'll look, but there's probably nothing I can do," she warned him.

"Looking is all I ask!" Mikey declared cheerfully as he squeezed past her. "I'll be right back! I've got a lamp and extension cord in the truck."

Between his shifter bulk and her thick frame, it was a tight fit, but he managed to get past her and to run back up the stairs.

"Sure," she grumbled as she made her way down the rest of the stairs. Her phone cast enough light to navigate and then find her way around once she was in the basement.

Thankfully, it was one big room and mostly empty, with only a small pile of broken chairs against one wall. She spied the breaker box and headed for it. Hopefully, the problem would be something that simple.

She wasn't one to freak out easily, but halfway across the room she got an odd feeling. Gooseflesh broke out on her arms, and she swore there was something down there with her.

Freezing in place, she held her breath and listened.

Music started up on the floor above, making it hard to focus her hearing on the room around her. She swept the phone light side to side, looking for movement and expecting a shadow to jump out at her.

The instinct to run was so strong that she turned, only to bump into Mikey's massive chest.

"I thought you were going to wait for me," he said as he set down a portable shop lamp, a bag of tools, and dropped an extension cord slung over his shoulder. "Let me go plug this in, then you'll have light," he said as he plugged one end of the cord into the lamp. Unfurling the cord, he trooped back upstairs, taking three steps at a time. No sooner had he disappeared than the lamp flickered on and filled the room with light.

"Yell if you need me!" he shouted down from upstairs. Then she heard a muted conversation between him and someone else.

Right, she was on her own. The light helped, but Briar still felt like she wanted to yell for Mikey to come back down.

"Put your big girl panties on and get to work," she muttered to herself and focused back on the breaker box.

Of course the thing was at the far end of the basement in an area not well lit by the lamp. Looking down, she tried to move the lamp, but the extension cord was stretched as far as it would go. She was going to have to cross the room into that dark corner.

Fuck!

"Just walk over there and check the box. If all the breakers look good, go upstairs and say you need your tools and you'll come back another day."

Yeah, that sounded good. Come back another day with tools and a few other people. Maybe even Jace would be back from San Jose by then and the two of them could figure this out together.

She'd never walked as slowly as she did when she crossed that room. Her heart was pounding hard in her chest and adrenaline was flooding her system. By the time she got to the breaker box and brushed away the spiderwebs, her hands were shaking.

A quick look told her that none of the breakers had been flipped, but a couple of them looked corroded as hell.

Actually, the whole box looked like it needed to be swapped out. She didn't exactly keep spare braker boxes in her back pocket. Looked like Mikey would need to order one and she'd could come back later to help Jace install it.

She took a picture so she could help Mikey order a new one. Relieved that she could leave now, she turned only to have something behind the pile of broken chairs catch her attention.

Was that a shadow of something? Did it move or was it her imagination?

She froze in place, staring hard at the pile and the wall behind it. Nothing moved, but she was sure something was there.

Out of nowhere, she got the crazy idea that someone close by was in trouble and needed her help.

The Argentinian half of her said to run. Get the fuck out of the basement and send down a dozen beefy shifters to deal with whatever was going on.

The white half of her urged her to investigate, because that always ended well in the movies.

It was probably because she was basically raised by her entirely white half-sister that she started walking to the pile of chairs. She could almost imagine tense music playing in the background.

The closer she got to the pile of chairs, the more she felt something. It was intangible and saturating the surrounding space. All the fine hairs on her body were standing up on end. If her short turquoise hair wasn't already spiked up, it might have stood up on its own too.

Was there some kind of electrical charge in the air? A powerful short that was waiting to arc through her body looking for a ground?

If that was the case, nudging one of the chairs and making the rest of them all topple over was a dumb idea.

But of course she did it anyway.

Putting her phone away so she could have her hands free, she gave the pile a little kick. As the broken furniture tumbled around her feet, she saw something on the wall that made her lean forward for a closer look.

Was that a door? It was roughly four feet by three feet with no knob or visible hinges, made of wood and painted to match the drywall around it, but it wasn't textured like the drywall. Now that the furniture wasn't in a pile hiding that section, it was easy to see the outline of the door.

Her white half was in complete control now and deep curiosity was in the driver seat as she pressed a hand to the door and pushed. It gave a little.

Looking up, she took in the dimensions of the room. If she was right, this room ended about ten feet short of the building itself.

How old was this building? Could this be a left-over crawl space from prohibition? Or something more recent? There was a shooting here. Maybe the owners were drug runners or part of some organized crime family. Bars were great for laundering cash.

There were a lot of illegal activities where having a hidden room would be helpful. And now she wanted in that space despite all the strange tingles running along her skin.

A little more pushing caused the door to swing open, revealing a pitch-black space beyond. She couldn't hear anything or discern any movement.

The smart thing to do would be to get another extension cord and Mikey for back up before exploring the crawl space.

But she'd never done the "smart thing" before, so why start now?

Pulling out her phone, she turned the light function back on, then shone it into the space as she pushed her head and shoulders inside.

Pure white eyes set in a pale, drawn face stared back at her. Bloodless lips pulled back to reveal long, glistening fangs—vampire!

Dirty fingers reached out for her, grabbing an arm before she could even think to move back. She was roughly dragged through that small door. She couldn't see anything beyond the dark, but one thing was for sure; it wasn't Narnia on the other side.

Her fucking white girl curiosity just got her killed.

Even though she was pretty sure she was dead, there was no way Briar was going down without a fight. She managed a strangled scream that was cut off when one of the vampire's hands went over her mouth. The other one effortlessly dragged her the rest of the way into the dark hidey hole.

She punched and kicked, but the creature didn't flinch or release her. Once she was entirely inside the dark, secret room, the thing flipped her around so her back was to him. Wrapping his arms around her, he held her securely to his chest.

Then he went still, even as she kept thrashing in his arms. It took her a moment to realize that he wasn't doing anything but restraining her.

No fangs punctured her skin.

No claws tore into her flesh.

She stopped struggling, her heart beating wildly in her chest and her breathing ragged.

What the hell?

He nuzzled his face into her neck, and she tensed, ready to start fighting again if he tried to sink a fang into her. No one was going to drain her dry without suffering some damage.

This girl wasn't going quietly into that goodnight; she was going to fucking rage against the dying of her light.

But he didn't try to bite her. He made a few inarticulate sounds and put his lips right on the skin above her carotid artery but didn't press fang to flesh.

When he brushed a gentle kiss there, she was confused beyond measure. What was going on here?

He kept nuzzling her neck, and then his hands started petting her. One on her belly and the other on her cheek. If that wasn't weird enough, the electric current-like magic she'd felt in the air earlier now buzzed along her skin. It was intense and uncomfortable but not painful.

Questions filled her. Where was the magic coming from? Him? Why the hell was he down here? And most significant—why was this obviously starved vamp not trying to suck her dry?

When he moved to bring his legs against hers, she heard chains rattle. He didn't stop her when she lifted her head to look down. Enough light was filtering into the cramped room for her to make out the chains around the vampire's ankles. Moving slow, she felt for one of his wrists. There were shackles there too.

Sympathy filled her. Someone had chained this guy up and left him in this tiny, hidden place to die a slow death by starvation. He must have been here a while to have such a drawn appearance. She didn't know much about vampires, but one thing she'd heard was that they're hard to kill, especially the ones with a hundred years or more under their belt.

Touching one of the manacles gave her a slight shock, telling her that there was some heavy magic imbued in the steel. That must be what she was feeling on her skin. She wasn't very sensitive to magic; most humans weren't. If she could feel it, then the spell had to be powerful.

He watched her like a hawk, but once their eyes met again, he tugged her back down and snuggled her back to his front. He made a soft content sound as he held her that broke Briar's heart.

They lay there in silence for a moment as she took stock of her situation. She was being cuddled by a starving vampire chained in a secret room in a building that had been empty for ten years.

"Looks like I stumbled into your Count of Monte Cristo reenactment," she said.

He didn't respond.

They probably weren't the best first words she could have picked, but she'd never been good at filtering her thoughts. She tried again.

"Thanks for not eating me." There, she probably should have led with that one.

He didn't answer. His arms tightened around her for a moment before he went back to nuzzling her neck. That was unexpected. He was cuddling, hugging, and nuzzling her. This was very far from the blood-thirsty soulless monsters Mikey warned her about.

"Is there anyone I can call for help? Maybe a friend or another vampire?"

When he didn't speak, she wiggled as far as his grip would allow, ending up on her back and able to look him in the face.

He regarded her with a curious expression that reminded her of one of Izzy's dogs. Interested but non-comprehending. She was caught by his eyes. The white was so absolute that she couldn't even tell where the pupil and iris should be. Could he even see? Was he born like that or was it a result of being starved of blood?

"Can you tell me your name?"

He didn't respond with words. Instead, he moved his face closer, then slowly put his lips to hers. When she jerked away, he didn't try to follow. But he did look confused and disappointed.

"I don't know how old you are or how long you've been down here, but you can't go around kissing people without permission," she told him.

Part of her was deeply disappointed that he didn't press the issue and try to force the kiss, and the other half was relieved that he backed off without a fight.

She had no idea which emotion came from which side of her heritage, but she needed to focus on making sure both of them made it out of here alive.

"If Mikey finds you down here, he'll kill you," she whispered. "He hates vampires. Hate-hate. It's a set-the-building-on-fire-and-let-you-burn-to-death level of hate."

His brows furrowed and he blinked a few times, as if trying to figure out what she was saying. Maybe he didn't speak English?

"Habla Espanola?" she asked.

Nothing.

"Parlez-vous Francais?"

He didn't respond to that either, which was probably good because all she knew was how to cuss and talk dirty in French.

"That's it for languages," she muttered. "If you don't speak English or Spanish, I can't help."

He opened his mouth as if to form words and worked his jaw a few times. Some sounds came out, but nothing that made any sense. His expression turned frustrated, and he buried his face against her neck.

He reminded her of a diabetic friend when his blood sugar got too low. Robby didn't lose the power of speech, but he did act like he couldn't think straight and wouldn't make sense when he talked. Like Robby, the lack of sustenance could be the reason behind all this vamp's issues.

The poor guy made her heart hurt.

"I'm going to get you out of here," she whispered to him. "I'll take care of you. Promise."

His response was to kiss the skin of her neck.

She thought about everyone upstairs and if they could help. Then dismissed all of them. Most were Lobos Gris wolf shifters and wouldn't be able to lie to Mikey. They wouldn't even be able to tell a half-truth. Mikey's alpha aura would make it impossible for one of his shifters to knowingly mislead him.

What about someone like Izzy? The pixie wouldn't be as affected by Mikey's powerful aura, but that girl didn't have a poker face. And Maddy wouldn't help. She'd take one look at the vamp and yell for Mikey to get Briar free.

She also needed someone who knew about vampires, magical chains, and how to get bagged blood. Really, there was only one person she could call—Memphis.

But he was pretty far away. Still, he might have connections down here. Even if he didn't, his vampire buddy Soren might know what to do.

First, she needed to get her phone. Looking around, she saw it sitting just beyond the door. She tried to sit up to get it, but the vamp made a sad, panicky noise and she relaxed back down.

She met his white eyes. "I need my phone. I'm not going to leave, but I need to get us some help."

As she talked, she felt around with her boot until she made contact with her phone. Hooking her heel against it, she dragged it toward her butt. With a grunt, the vamp sat up to see what she was doing. The flashlight function was still on, and he got a face full of bright, LED light. She half expected him to get upset and try to smash the phone.

Chains rattling, he snatched it up and shoved it into her hand before settling back down next to her and snuggling close. He made a soft content sound and kissed her neck again.

"Thanks," she murmured.

She thought the sound he made was meant to be a "you're welcome."

She did a quick survey of the secret room, her phone lighting up a mostly bare chamber thick with dust. At first, it looked like the chains were attached to a hunk of metal, but then she realized it was a spell anchor.

This anchor looked like an innocent solid piece of iron about a square foot, but she knew better. Spell anchors were nothing but magic and if she tried to touch it, she'd get fried. Anchors feed off the magical creature they were attached to and restricted their movements.

She'd seen it used as punishment or a way to keep a creature restrained. At most, she'd heard of someone being attached to one for a few weeks, a month max. By the poor state of the vamp and the amount of dust in the room, he'd been down here attached to the anchor for years.

And that was the biggest spell anchor she'd ever seen. They were going to need the services of a powerful bruja for this one. Did she even know a bruja strong enough?

"That anchor is step four or five," she muttered as she shut off the flashlight. "Step one is getting help down here and keeping you hidden from Mikey."

She pulled up the contacts on her phone. Although she never used her main phone to call Memphis, she had his contact info programed in. It felt weird to call the guy for help. Usually, people called her because they needed something, not the other way around.

"Let's hope he knows what to do," she told the vamp who was rubbing his face back and forth against her neck.

Right, he was no help. Taking a deep breath, she pressed Memphis's number.

"Go away!" the man screamed as he brandished a gun at Memphis. "Leave, or I'll turn you into a fucking corpse!"

Memphis sighed. A bullet anywhere but straight to the head would hurt but wouldn't kill him. And the gun was only a 9mm, it would take a .40 or bigger to do true damage to a chimera's noggin. Those facts coupled with the way this guy's hand was shaking meant Memphis was more annoyed than worried.

"If you put a hole in my vest, I'll rip your whole arm off," Memphis warned him.

The skiptrace jerked at the threat but didn't lower the gun. "Back off. I'll do it. I'll kill you."

Memphis could hear someone in the kitchen of the small house but other than that, the place was quiet. He didn't want any innocent bystanders to catch a stray bullet, so he stepped sideways until he wasn't in front of the wall between the living room and kitchen. The skiptrace followed Memphis with the gun, eyes wild with fear and body shaking like a leaf.

"Stop fuckin' moving!" the guy screamed, his head twitching a little.

Was it too many drugs or not enough?

"First you say go away and then you tell me not to move? You're not making any sense. Why don't you hand me the pea shooter?" Memphis suggested. "Before I have to hurt you."

The guy blinked at him a few times, as if Memphis had spoken a foreign language. His eyes kept bouncing between Memphis and the front door, probably gauging the distance.

"Give me the keys to your ride," the guy ordered.

"That's not happening," Memphis answered. The sound of something big pulling up outside told him Craig's contact was here to pick up the skiptrace. Memphis had agreed to find the guy but didn't want to escort him all the way back north. The moment Memphis verified the guy was in the house, he'd called Craig to arrange a pickup.

To be polite, he should probably disarm this loser before handing him over.

"Give me your keys!" the skiptrace yelled, spit flying.

Memphis curled his lip in disgust and nodded his head out the front door at the sound of a vehicle door slamming shut. "Company's comin'."

As he expected, the guy looked over his shoulder at the front door. Memphis moved before he'd even finished turning his head. With speed that would make even other shifters envious, Memphis grabbed the guy's wrist with one hand and the gun with the other.

The skiptrace shrieked as Memphis twisted the weapon out of his grip. The guy let go of the weapon then tried to fight.

Balling up his left fist and sending it at Memphis's face, he moved like molasses compared to the chimera. It was easy to tilt his head away and let go of the guy's right wrist. Momentum made the guy stumble and Memphis helped him find the floor with a little shove.

"Motherfucker!" the guy yelled as he scrambled to get back to his feet. A loud knock at the door caused the skiptrace to flinch so violently he knocked himself back down to his hands and knees.

Definitely too many drugs.

Grabbing the guy by the back of his jacket, Memphis effortlessly hauled the skiptrace to his feet then efficiently secured his hands behind his back with a pair of zip-tie cuffs.

"Memphis, you in there?" a voice called out. "Craig told me you had my skiptrace here."

"I got 'em," Memphis yelled back as he hauled the struggling human to the door. When he swung it open, he was startled to have to look up to meet the stranger's gaze. Memphis was a pretty big guy that didn't need to raise his head to meet the eyes of too many people. "Damn boy, what did your mama feed you?"

The guy grinned as he reached out to take the struggling skip trace. "Live rats and beer," the guy answered. "Name's Mac."

Memphis was about to grin back when he caught Mac's scent. Sloth bear. Memphis shoved the skiptrace at him and took a big step back. "Here, he's yours."

The name sloth bear might sound like they'd be slow and cute, but in truth, sloth bear shifters were arguably the most aggressive shifter out there. Memphis might be a big, bad ass chimera shifter, but even he didn't want to tangle with a sloth bear. Once in battle, sloth bears never stopped. They had a reputation of being willing to kill themselves simply to hurt their opponent.

Mac frowned at Memphis's abrupt movements, then sighed. "I'm not going to attack you so chill," he grumbled. Then took a sniff before smirking. "I'd think a chimera would be braver than that."

Memphis didn't take offense. "Brave, yes. Stupid, no. My brother Knox tangled with one of you guys up in Sacramento. Got his arm broken in three places and lost a finger. Finger grew back but the caution stayed."

"How'd the bear do?" Mac asked.

"His foot did not grow back," Memphis informed him.

Mac barked out a laugh. "You know you guys have a rep too, not just my kind."

Memphis was intrigued. He didn't hang out with many shifters other than his family and his buddy Soren's wolves. "Yeah? What do they say about us?"

"Nobody knows what your animal looks like 'cus they don't survive the experience," Mac said.

This time Memphis laughed. "Sounds about right."

Mac narrowed his eyes, studying Memphis. "You know, you look damn familiar."

"Trust me," Memphis said. "I know we haven't met."

"Yeah, but I—" Mac's face lit up as he figured something out. "Memphis, city in Tennessee. You got a brother named Lexington, goes by Lex?"

"I do, you know him?" Memphis asked, surprised.

Lex was a bit of mystery to the rest of the Granger family. No one knew what the middle brother did for a living, but he'd come home a few times with new scars. It took a lot of damage to cause a chimera to scar, so whatever he did was damn dangerous. And now this stranger claimed to know him. Small world.

"We've done some jobs together," Mac said. "Your brother's a good man to have at your back in a bad situation."

"No doubt," Memphis agreed. Before he could start asking Mac what Lex did, the sloth bear shook his head.

"I can't," Mac said simply. "If Lex ain't talking, then I can't talk either. You know how it is."

"I don't," Memphis answered. "But I guess I'll have to accept it."

Mac gave Memphis an apologetic look. "Sorry, man."

The skiptrace made a muffled, whining sound, drawing their attention to him. That's when Mac must have realized he'd been holding the guy by the throat the entire time and the human was having difficulty breathing.

Mac loosened his hold a little and the skiptrace pulled in a ragged breath. "You're gonna kill me!"

"You'll live, but I won't promise it'll be pleasant if you don't behave," Mac warned him in a cheerful voice. "You and I are going to take a little drive," Mac said as he dragged the guy to a battered black SUV.

Memphis followed to watch Mac open the back door and shove the guy into a space that had been modified to carry unwilling passengers with bars over the inside of the windows, bars across the back window, and a heavy-duty grate between the backseat and the front.

A causal look in the back area behind the backseat revealed a locked industrial toolbox. Nothing else back there that a person could use as a weapon. It was a good set-up.

"I'm guessing this isn't your first collection," Memphis commented as Mac secured the skiptrace in a seat with a seatbelt that looked specifically designed not to allow the person to get out. Who knew you could get seatbelts with locking buckles? It was brilliant but probably illegal as hell, especially here in California.

"And you'd be right," Mac agreed as he straightened up. "I was told you were going to hang out down here after you found this guy."

"Now that you have him, I'm on vacation. Going to take in the sights," Memphis told him. He felt his mood lightening as he realized he was now free to start talking Baby Doll into meeting up with him.

"I know that look," Mac drawled. "You got someone down here. Someone special."

Memphis shrugged. "Maybe. We'll see."

"Oh, so it's like that," Mac said with a sympathetic look. "Well, I'm driving this guy north. I'll be back in a few days. I'll give you a call then. If you're still in town, we can hit a few bars."

"Yeah, that sounds good," Memphis agreed and held out a hand.

Mac took it without hesitation. "Those of us with the reps got to stick together 'cus no one else is going to want to get too close."

Suddenly Memphis felt a little lonely. "Ain't that the truth."

Longing for Baby Doll filled him. He loved his family and saw Soren and his flock as his friends, but none of that stopped the ache in his chest. He needed his mate and no one else would do.

Ending the handshake, Mac turned to get into the driver seat. "That your ride over there?" he asked.

Memphis grinned. "If you're referring to one of the sexiest Harleys to ever exist, then yeah, she's mine."

"Then you're really gonna like your vacation. This area is as close to motorcycle mecca as you're gonna get on the west coast." Mac settled himself into the seat and shut the door. "Keep the shiny side up, brother."

"Always," Memphis answered and stepped back as Mac pulled out of the driveway, the skiptrace screeching in the back seat. Memphis was glad he didn't have to deal with that.

A quick text to Craig confirmed Mac had the skiptrace and was heading north. Memphis's part was done.

Strolling over to his bike, Memphis debated what to do next. He should probably find a motel room, and maybe check out the sights. Make himself familiar with the area so he knew where to take Baby Doll once he convinced her to meet with him.

He was slouched on his bike scrolling around his map app when the phone rang. It was a San Diego area code. Maybe Craig gave his number to someone local. He answered, ready to refuse any offer of a job when a familiar voice made the words die in his throat.

"Memphis?" Baby Doll whispered.

"Baby Doll," Memphis murmured, worried by the whisper and the level of tension he could hear in her voice. "What's going on?"

"You know about vampires, right? I mean, you're friends with that Soren guy and he's a vampire."

"Yeah, I know some stuff," Memphis answered cautiously. Then he heard an angry hiss in the background and his hacker said something in a low, soothing voice to someone else. "Baby Doll, where are you? What's wrong? What happened?"

"I think I might have a problem," she whispered to him and fear for his mate roared through Memphis's body.

"Tell me where you are right now!" he demanded. "I'm in San Diego. I'll get to you. Tell me!"

He heard her suck in a surprised breath. "You're down here? I . . . ah, fuck, stop that!" It sounded like she was struggling with someone and then there was a thump.

"Baby Doll!" Memphis yelled into the phone, feeling more helpless than he ever had in his life. "Yell where you are. Give me a clue! Tell me what you see. Anything and I'll find you sweetheart."

"Oh, shit, no," she said, her voice a little breathless. "Sorry, I dropped the phone. I'm not in danger. I don't think. But I've got an, uh, issue. Can you get your buddy Soren to call me? This is my real number, the one I never change."

Memphis wasn't appeased at all. "Tell me where you are. After I see you, I'll put you in contact with Soren. I mean it, Baby Doll. I'm not bending on that."

"This is a mess," she muttered. He heard something in the background that he couldn't identify. Then she huffed out a breath and spoke again. "You've got to promise me you'll do everything I tell you. Right?"

"Absolutely," Memphis lied without guilt.

"Okay, my real name is Briar and here's what I need you to do."

It took Memphis a considerable amount of concentration to keep a pleasant smile on his face when he walked into the run-down building. The place was lively, with a compact Bluetooth stereo blaring out music while a dozen people all worked, talked, and laughed to the beat.

He smelled a variety of species inside—human, pixie, and shifter. But the strongest smell was wolf shifter and the guy that looked down at him from on top of a ladder had a powerful aura declaring him an alpha.

"I'm sorry, we're closed," the guy called out with a smile. Memphis started to speak but the guy caught his scent and his friendly smile turned menacing. "You need to turn and walk away, stranger. No one here has caused you or your kind trouble, so I won't let you hurt any of us."

Memphis had to admire the balls on this wolf shifter. He might be big, but not as massive as Memphis and even with his wolf shifter speed, he didn't stand a chance against a chimera. Few did. And yet he was ready to protect his pack without hesitation. That was something Memphis could respect.

"I'm here at the request of a friend," Memphis said quickly. "Baby—uh, Briar called me. I guess she needs a little help in the basement." It was hard to think of her as Briar after spending so long thinking of her as Baby Doll Hacker.

A tall, colorfully dressed human that smelled both like a male and female stepped up with a cautious smile. "I thought I knew all of Briar's friends, even her hacker ones. But I don't think I've ever met you."

"Maddy, don't get any closer," the wolf said as he jumped down from the ladder and hurried to put himself between Maddy and Memphis.

Memphis was relieved to have her here. "Maddy? It's nice to finally meet you. Briar's told me a lot about you. Congratulations on your promotion."

Maddy smiled broadly at Memphis. "Are you the biker up in Oregon that Briar's been chatting with?"

"That'd be me. The name's Memphis Granger, and I'm here as a friend, nothing more." He gave her a big, open smile. "Briar has helped me out, so it was nothing for me to come on over and lend a hand while I'm in town."

"We don't know you," the wolf said, still frowning. "This is the first time I'm hearing your name or seeing your face."

"Mikey Short, right? Alpha of the Lobos Gris Pack?" Memphis asked.

Still scowling, the wolf answered. "Yeah, that's me."

"Do you know the Annwyl pack up in Bend?"

The shifter blinked at the change of topic, but reluctantly nodded. "New pack mostly made up of wolves from the Volk Pack. I heard their alpha is one hell of a powerful wolf."

"She is. And if it would make you feel better, I can get her on the phone to vouch for me." Chimeras didn't hang out in groups like wolves or nagas did, so Memphis wasn't sure if having another wolf pack vouching for him would do any good.

"Are you a member of her pack?" Mikey asked.

Memphis blinked. "Uh, I'm a chimera if you haven't figure that out."

Mikey gave him a sour look. "Hard not to notice. You stink."

"Gee, thanks," Memphis said, barely keeping from growling. He did not stink. No more than theses wolves did. "Annwyl is a wolf shifter pack."

"So I've heard. But for some packs, species doesn't matter. Community matters. And the rumor says that pack has a bloodsucker as a member. So I ask again, are you in her pack?"

"Sure," Memphis drawled.

The alpha didn't look convinced. "If I call her, will she say the same thing?"

"She'll say I'm family," Memphis declared with confidence because that part was true.

Without taking his eyes off Memphis, Mikey pulled his phone out and handed it to Maddy. "There's a contact in there for Annwyl Pack. Call it and see if they'll let you talk to the alpha or one of the pack members in charge."

"Mikey, I don't think this is necessary," Maddy said as she took the phone. "Let me go get Briar and we'll settle this."

"No one's moving until I know this guy isn't here for nefarious purposes."

"Nefarious purposes? Did you eat a fucking dictionary for breakfast?" Memphis scoffed.

Maddy cast him a disapproving look. "You don't need to be mean."

Memphis was quick to hold up his hands, palms out. He needed to keep Maddy on his side. "Sorry. I guess I'm feeling a little defensive because I came to help, and I'm being treated like some kind of lowlife."

"If the shoe fits," Mikey said without a change of expression.

Memphis flashed a few chimera teeth at the guy, making the alpha hiss out a startled breath and flinch. Unlike wolf shifters, chimera didn't have canines because all their teeth were long and sharp. Instead of white, they looked silver in the light. It was an intimidating sight he'd used often when dealing with aggressive non-humans.

Maddy missed the teeth because she was busy glaring at Mikey. When the wolf met her gaze, she spoke. "And you don't need to be so overprotective. You know Briar doesn't invite people in. If she called this guy, then it means he's good people. Let him go downstairs and help."

It was fascinating to watch the powerful alpha fold under Maddy's stern glare. "But everyone's safety is my responsibility." Mikey's words came out whiny and Memphis had to stifle a laugh.

"You go on down there," Maddy said to Memphis with a wave at a door in the back. "Yell if you need any help."

When Memphis moved to walk past Mikey, Maddy put a hand on the alpha's arm to keep him from blocking Memphis's path.

All eyes were on him as he strode across the room. Maddy and Mikey were whispering to each other but other than that, the room was silent. Someone had even turned the music off.

Honestly, Memphis couldn't blame them. There weren't many shifters more powerful than chimeras. Almost all other non-humans gave his kind a wide berth. He was going to need to work hard to make Briar's friends comfortable with him because he knew these people were her family. It was going to be hard enough to convince a human that she was his mate, but it would be a losing battle if he didn't have the support of Briar's found family.

It was a quick trip down a narrow flight of stairs into a mostly empty basement. He stumbled at the last stair, almost going to his knees when the combined smell of vampire and human hit him.

It wasn't that he was shocked to smell vampire. He wasn't afraid of any fang-face. No, the bigger issue was that both the smells triggered his chimera mating reflex.

The two people in this basement were both his mates.

When the music upstairs suddenly cut off, Briar figured
Memphis must have arrived. She hoped he'd be able to get down
here without Mikey but didn't have much hope. Mikey wasn't
one to trust strangers and the alpha was protective of his pack.
When she heard one set of heavy treads on the stairs, she braced
to protect the vamp from Mikey's rage.

The footsteps stopped and there was silence. What was
going on?

"Mikey?" she called out softly. She didn't need to shout,
all the shifters had amazing hearing. Suddenly, the music started
back up, but she was still able to hear the voice that answered
her.

"It's Memphis," a familiar deep voice responded. Relief
made her slump in the vampire's arms.

"Thank fuck," she muttered as the vampire moved his
head to stare through the small door. A pair of battered
motorcycle boots appeared.

"You in there, Baby Doll?" Memphis asked as he sank
to his knees and brought his head down to peer in. The vampire
holding her remained calm as he stared at the new arrival.

"Yeah, it's me," Briar squeaked as she got her first look
at the man that she'd been chatting with online for almost a year.

God, he was beautiful. It was hard to tell how tall he was
crouched down like that, but his broad shoulders and powerful
chest were hard to miss. He had deep brown, short-cropped hair

and a thick russet-colored beard covering the lower half of his face. The leather vest he was wearing looked old and worn and hung open, so she could see the shirt under it stretched tight across a muscled chest and a collar pulled taut around a thick neck.

But it was his eyes that really captured her attention. They were a deep brown and made her think of mahogany. Briar wasn't a poet, and she wasn't given to lyrical thinking, but Memphis's eyes made her want to be romantic. She wanted to use all kind of flowery language that would compare him to artful things found in nature.

"Fuck, you're pretty." She winced. Had that just come out of her mouth?

Far from being upset, he chuckled at her. "You're gorgeous too, Baby Doll" he answered, then nodded to the vamp. "And he looks like he needs a whole hell of a lot of help."

That statement shook her out of her daze. They had more important things to do than waste time having her stare at Memphis like a hormonal teenager!

"You're not wrong," she answered and glanced back to find the vampire staring unblinkingly at Memphis with an interested expression. That had to be a good thing, right? She didn't want him to see Memphis as a threat. "Is the eye thing normal?"

"Lack of feeding," Memphis answered. "I've never seen it in person, but I've heard of it. Vampires can put themselves in a kind of coma that allows them to go for long periods of time without blood. But if they spend too much time in that state, then that can happen to their eyes."

Memphis's expression turned gentle as he addressed the vampire. "You're safe. We're going to take care of you, okay?"

"He can't talk," Briar explained when the vampire didn't answer.

"Not surprised," Memphis said, and his expression turned angry. "We're going to find out who the fuck did this to him and make them pay."

"I've got a baseball bat and no hesitation," Briar agreed. "But first, we need to get everyone to leave and then we need to get this guy blood."

"Let me get the two of you out of there first," Memphis said as he reached inside. Briar stopped him with a shake of her head.

"He's chained to a spell anchor," she said with a nod of her head in the direction of the magical item.

Memphis hissed out a breath, anger taking over his expression for a moment before he got it back under control.

"Hold tight and close your eyes," Memphis instructed as he stood back up.

"What—" Briar didn't get to finish her question before Memphis was destroying the wall around the door. "That better not be a load bearing wall," she muttered, and she ducked her face down and closed her eyes. The vampire made a soft comforting sound and drew her further away from the wall.

Weak light from the shop lamp filled the space when Briar opened her eyes again. The vampire remained calm as Memphis ducked through the massive hole he'd made in the wall, boots crunching on the debris on the floor.

"That's better," he said as he sank to his knees next to them.

The vampire moved without warning, making Briar gasp. The next thing she knew, she was squished between Memphis and the vampire in a big bear hug.

"Fuck, ouch!" Memphis exclaimed, but he didn't fight the vampire's hold. "Goddamn spell anchor."

Briar was surprised that Memphis wasn't trying to get away from the vampire.

"Image how bad it's been for him," she grumbled and wiggled a little so Memphis's big belt buckle wasn't digging into her skin anymore.

The vampire was trying to crane his neck over Briar so he could nuzzle and kiss Memphis too. After so many stories of violent, merciless vampires, Briar was flummoxed with this guy's overly affectionate attitude.

"Stop that," Memphis said, and she could hear the grin his voice. "Save it for later, fang-face."

It was with obvious reluctance that the vampire moved his face away from the other man.

Memphis pulled out of the vampire's arms to sit up, the vampire mirroring his action without letting go of her. Briar ended up in the vampire's lap facing Memphis.

"Let me have a look at this," Memphis murmured as he gently pulled one of the vamp's arms out from around Briar. The vampire didn't resist, only watched with eager interest as Memphis examined the manacle around his wrist.

When Memphis looked at her, his expression was worried but determined. "I can get these off, but it's going to cost me."

Briar didn't like the sound of that. "Cost you?"

Memphis flashed her a cocky grin. "I might be a little weak after I break these. But they need to come off first." His expression turned fierce. "They're hurting him."

"Okay, sure, what can I do?"

Memphis nodded his head at the vampire behind her. "Will he let you move away? You shouldn't be touching him while I'm breaking them."

"Let's find out," Briar said as she moved off the vampire's lap. He looked sad and disappointed as she moved away but didn't try to stop her.

"It's okay," she whispered to him. "I'm not going far. I'll be right here."

She stopped when her back hit the remains of the wall. "This good?"

"Yeah, that should be far enough," Memphis said.

He took a deep breath and then gripped the manacle in both hands. A deep growling-grunt came out of him as she watched his muscles strain. With a flash of light, the manacle broke in two and fell to the floor.

Memphis rocked back and panted. "That sucked."

"Memphis?" She started to move closer, but he was quick to shake his head.

"Don't get close to me yet. That spell anchor is connected to me now too." Sweat was running down his face and soaking his shirt. He wiped a shaking hand over his forehead and across his eyes to clear some of it off.

Briar's anxiety skyrocketed at the sight. She'd only met Memphis in the flesh minutes ago but felt more connected to him than any other person on the planet. She didn't want to see him in pain. "Should we wait and get someone else to get these off? I don't want you to get hurt."

Memphis scoffed. "I got this. A few little spell anchors aren't going to hurt me none."

The vampire had been staring at his bare wrist the entire time they'd been talking. But now he scooted closer to Memphis and thrust out his other arm, jangling the chain in Memphis's face.

Memphis smiled. "Yup, that one's next." He took hold of the manacle and strained. It took longer for him to break this one apart, but the flash of magic wasn't as bright this time. As the bits of broken restraint fell to the floor, Memphis sat back on his heels and swayed a little.

It took Briar a lot of effort to keep from reaching out to him. "Memphis?"

"I'm good," he said quickly. The vampire was shifting his whole body and ended up with his back to Briar and both feet perched on Memphis's massive thighs. He made an inarticulate sound and wiggled his feet impatiently.

Memphis chuckled and rested his hands on the vamp's legs. "I know you're impatient, sweetheart. But give me a moment."

Sweetheart? Had she read Memphis all wrong when she thought he'd been flirting with her? Was he actually into guys? Or maybe he was into everyone. He could be bi, pan, or demisexual. The way he was looking at the vampire with such tenderness told her that whatever his sexuality was, it included this guy.

His best friend Soren was a vampire who fell in love with a couple of wolves. Could Memphis have silently been pining for a Soren of his own?

Was vampsexual a thing?

And this vampire definitely had a thing for Memphis. He was gazing at the bearded man with total adoration. If Briar wasn't so worried about both of them, she might be a little jealous.

The first leg shackle took almost a full minute of straining for Memphis to break it apart. He'd sweated through his shirt and vest and was dripping sweat on the floor now. His entire body was shaking, and he kept having to blink his eyes to focus.

"One left," he declared through gritted teeth.

"Maybe you should take—" she didn't get a chance to finish that sentence before he'd grabbed the last restraint.

This time, when it broke apart, there was a slight flash of magic and suddenly the air in the room felt cleaner. The strange electric hum against her skin vanished as the entire spell anchor fizzled then crumpled into a small pile of sand.

Memphis sat there, his eyes squeezed shut and his breathing ragged. The vampire pulled his feet off Memphis's lap and crouched closer to the man. Briar moved to kneel next to the vampire, her gaze focused on Memphis.

"Hey, big guy, you okay?"

"No." That one word was said through his clenched jaw. He didn't open his eyes, then his body suddenly went lax and slumped sideways.

The vampire was quick to catch Memphis's bulk and pull him into his lap. Memphis dwarfed him, but the vampire didn't seem to care. Making cooing sounds, he cradled Memphis's large form and rocked him gently as if they'd been lovers for years.

Now she was really jealous.

"Briar, you okay down there?" Mikey called down. Shit, no time to wallow in envy, she needed to stop Mikey before he came all the way down.

"Stay here with him," Briar whispered to the vampire. When she stood up, the vampire made an unhappy sound and reached for her. Hampered by Memphis's bulk, he didn't manage to get a hold of her before she was on her feet.

"I'll be right back," she promised, happy to know she hadn't been entirely thrown over for the big biker in the vampire's affection.

Wait, was she upset that the vampire might like Memphis over her? She'd only met the guy a couple of hours ago. What was wrong with her?

The sound of Mikey's big feet on the stairs forced her to focus on the task at hand. Turning her back on the two males, she hurried to meet the alpha on the stairs.

"Hiya, Mikey," she said breathlessly. "I've got some bad news about this building. You've got a shit-ton of black mold. We need to get everyone out."

Tobias knew how to speak. He was sure he knew how to speak, but he couldn't make the words come out of his mouth.

Even as he watched the human disappear up the stairs, he couldn't figure out how to call her back. She shouldn't be leaving the room yet. He was weak and the chimera was unconscious. This was a disastrous situation. The little human was by far the most vulnerable of the three of them and yet neither he nor the giant shifter could protect her.

He knew he needed blood. The sound of the chimera's heart beating was a steady rhythm in his ears. He could even hear the blood flowing through the shifter's veins.

But he wasn't tempted to feed. He needed so much sustenance right now that if he sunk fangs into either of his flock, he risked losing control and hurting them. Better to starve than hurt his flock.

Flock.

That word bounced around in his head. He tried to get it past his lips, but it wouldn't go. There were things that needed to happen before he bound all three of their souls together, but in his heart, he knew they were his. And he was theirs.

The way both of them cared for him was proof. He hadn't meant to scare the human when he grabbed her. Her movement had woken him from his long sleep. Then the door to his cage had opened and there she'd been. Bright and beautiful.

He'd smelled her at the same time he'd felt her soft, magicless aura.

The scent told him she was human. The aura told him she was his.

And now he had a shifter in his flock also. A male so big and strong that he'd broken the cursed manacles and set Tobias free. Hugging the chimera, Tobias brushed a kiss across the man's bearded cheek. This male was a bit scruffy and in need of new clothes, but it would be Tobias's honor to care for him once he regained his thinking mind.

Tension filled him when he heard the music abruptly stop and then raised voices above. Did he need to go up there to defend his human? He wasn't sure he could walk yet. It was taking a lot of effort for him to remain sitting up, cradling the shifter.

Laying the chimera down on the dirty floor, Tobias tried to stand. It didn't work. He fell hard, hissing in pain. Had he ever been this weak? Even as a human?

How was he going to care for his flock if he couldn't even stand?

He wanted to howl in frustration. He was free and had found the two people more precious to a vampire than anything in the world, and yet he was as helpless as a newborn kitten. He couldn't even talk!

What if his flock decided he was too pathetic and left him? He would have survived all that time in his prison only to have his heart and soul ripped out of his body.

Desperation made him try to stand again. This attempt wasn't any more successful than the previous one. When he hit the floor, he whimpered from both the pain and emotional fear.

"What the hell?" the female's voice was music to his ears. He opened dry, tired eyes to find her leaning over him, her expression worried. "Did you try to stand up? Shit, don't do that."

She rested a hand on his chest. Gently, he covered her hand with his. She felt so warm and vibrant in a cold, gray world. She needed to know how important she was.

"No . . ." He got a word out! He tried again. "N-n-no . . ."

"Hey, you're talking!" she said, leaning her face closer to his. "That's great. Can you tell me your name?"

"N-no . . ." Why couldn't get another word out? Even one more word would suffice. "No-o-o . . ." Now it sounded like he was wailing. He was a vampire, an apex predator, and he couldn't even string two words together?

Her expression turned gentle as she shushed him. "Easy, it'll come. Don't force it. I've got you. Everyone left and won't be back for a few days." She petted his chest as her expression turned regretful.

"Shit, I scared Mikey something awful. Told him the whole place was toxic. He wanted to take everyone to a druid or the ER to get checked. Maddy talked him out of it, but he still insisted everyone go back to his place and hang out to make sure no one was going to get sick." She sighed. "Fuck, I feel guilty as hell."

Tobias wanted to comfort her and promise that once he was better, he'd set everything right with these people. But he was so exhausted that he couldn't even get his one word out. She didn't seem to notice as she kept talking, her expression grim.

"I had to leave with everyone and then double back. I'm going to call Maddy and tell her I'm heading out of town for a few days to meet up with my buddy Yasmine in Santa Barbara. I do that every once in a while, so she shouldn't be suspicious. It's lucky we drove separately, or it would've taken me an hour to get back here."

She glanced over at the shifter lying next to him. "Man, he's out-out."

Tobias wiggled closer to the chimera and tried to tug the human to lay between them. She pulled her hand away with a small smile. "I'm not tired, but you nap with Memphis, okay? I'm going to use his phone and see if I can get us some help."

He didn't like that idea, but as long as she stayed close, he would be content. Rolling on his side, he threw a leg over Memphis. It felt good to be touching him again.

It wasn't enough. Reaching behind him, he hooked a finger in the beltloop of her pants and pulled with steady pressure.

"You want me closer?" she asked. He made a sound and let go of her pants when she scooted up next to him. "How's that?" Her leg was touching his back now. He sighed out a soft breath and draped an arm over the shifter's wide chest, feeling mostly satisfied with the situation.

They were all at least somewhat hidden and sheltered, but that would change if anyone came back. He closed his eyes and let his body slip back into a suspended state. He needed to save what little strength he had for when night fell. His flock would want to get away from this accursed place, and he wasn't going to be left behind.

Memphis didn't have any kind of lock on his phone, so it was easy for Briar to scroll through his meager contact list and find one labeled Fang-Face with an Oregon area code. She hit the call button, put the phone on speaker, then absently rested her hand on the vampire's shoulder. Damn, he and Memphis looked adorable all snuggled up together. If she didn't have a whole hell of a lot to get sorted out, she'd want to wiggle between them and settle down too.

Soren answered the phone on the third ring. "Memphis, it's been while. The pack is having a dinner tonight and you're invited." The vampire's voice was warm and welcoming.

"This isn't Memphis," Briar said quickly. "He's fine, but asleep."

"Baby Doll?" Soren asked, his tone turning serious and cold. She was impressed he remembered her voice from the brief conversation they had last year. "Why do you have Memphis's phone?"

"That's a bit of a story," she said with a wince. "But, uh, look, we need some help."

"Tell me what happened," Soren demanded. She heard a voice in the background ask a question and Soren hushed them, waiting for her response.

Briar jumped in with both booted feet. "I was in the basement of an unoccupied building and ran across a vampire in a hidden room chained to a spell anchor. Memphis showed up and broke the chains, but that knocked him out cold. He's asleep and the vamp is really weak and not able to talk. What do I do?"

There was a moment of silence on the other end as Soren digested the influx of information.

When Soren spoke, his tone was shocked. "He didn't try to attack you or Memphis? The vampire didn't try to drain you before Memphis got there?"

"No," Briar assured him. "He kissed and touched my neck but didn't bite me. And he's snuggled up against Memphis on the floor asleep right now. It's actually really sweet."

Soren sucked in a sharp breath. "The two of you must be the vampire's flock."

"Flock? Isn't that like a shifter pack?"

"It's so much more," Soren said, his voice heavy. "We vampires share a piece of our souls with the members of our flock. It's a connection more intimate than anything you can imagine."

Briar flinched at Soren's words. "Soul? He put a piece of his soul in me? I didn't feel anything, except when Memphis broke the spell anchor and the magic flashed."

"You would know if he'd bound you," Soren assured her. "He would take a piece of your soul also and if it wasn't done carefully, it would hurt badly. If he's as weak as you say, he might not be able to make you flock yet."

Briar wasn't sure if she was relieved or disappointed. "That's good. A girl likes to be asked before exchanging body fluids or bits of soul."

Soren didn't laugh at her humor. That was fine. Most people didn't realize how funny she was.

"I need to know your exact location. I'll get blood to you. Do you know the name of the vampire or how long he's been chained up?"

"No idea on either," Briar admitted. "But the building has been empty for about ten years."

"If he's survived that entire time, he must be powerful," Soren said. His words came out like a warning, making Briar feel a little defensive.

"He's been sweet so far."

"I'm sure," Soren said, his tone more neutral. "Send me a picture of the vampire, let me see if I recognize him. And I'll also see about getting a delivery and guards for you. If Memphis broke a spell anchor powerful enough to bind a vampire, he's going to be unconscious for a while."

"Should I be watching out for anything?" Briar asked. She glanced over at where Memphis lay, his mouth slightly open and his eyes moving rapidly under his closed lids. "Like seizures or something?"

"He'll be fine," Soren promised. "Chimera shifters are some of the toughest creatures out there. As long as he isn't pierced with a silver weapon, he'll be okay after some rest. Stay put until I call you back."

Soren hung up without a goodbye. Shrugging, Briar took a picture of the vampire with Memphis's shitty phone and sent it to Soren. She was going to need to talk to the bearded giant about upgrading.

She hadn't even set it down before it started ringing again. Soren started talking the moment the call connected.

"That's Tobias Becker! We all thought he was dead. He's been down there this entire time? Do you know how much he must have suffered, Baby Doll?"

"The name's Briar," she said sharply. Baby Doll was Memphis's name for her, so no one else was allowed to use it. "And I guess you better send a whole shit ton of blood if this poor guy's been down here that long."

"No, you don't understand," Soren was close to shouting. "It's not only a miracle he's alive, but also that he didn't drain you or attack Memphis."

"You said we were his flock," Briar reminded him.

"But after ten years of starvation, his mind would be nothing but instinct. All he should feel is the driving need to feed. There shouldn't be another thought in his head. But he held back. You can't realize what a colossal feat that is!"

She hadn't before, but she understood it now. "Was he a strong vampire, before he got chained down here?"

"As powerful as me. Perhaps more so if he's survived this." She could hear Soren take a deep breath before he continued. "I don't really know him, but I know of him. He had a reputation for being a good man. I was saddened to hear about his disappearance. I assumed he'd given into the desolation that effects many vampires who don't find their flock. But now I find out he's alive and my good friend is going to be in his flock. It's a storybook ending for both of them."

He sounded so happy that Briar found herself smiling. "Yeah, there's no question this Tobias guy really likes Memphis."

"And you," Soren reminded her. "If you weren't meant to be his flock, then you wouldn't be alive right now. And Memphis was already feeling a mate pull toward you, so this all makes sense."

"Mate?" Briar asked.

Soren cleared his throat uncomfortably. "You should really discuss that with Memphis when he wakes up. People will be there soon with supplies and will stay to guard you. The person in charge is named Jody."

Then he hung up. Briar glared at the phone, then looked over to where Memphis was sleeping—mostly—peacefully.

"Someone's been keeping secrets," she muttered with a small shake of her head. "And someone's going to fess up once he's awake if he knows what's good for him."

Predictably, no one answered her, but Memphis's sleeping form did twitch a little. With a roll of her eyes and a grin, she picked up her phone. Time to do a little research while she waited for Soren's people.

"Briar? I'm Jody. Soren sent me."

A voice shouting from upstairs told Briar that Soren's people had arrived. She looked down to find Tobias's eyes open and his upper lip pulled back in a snarl, revealing a long, glistening fang.

"Easy," she whispered, petting the arm he still had draped over Memphis's chest. "They're supposed to be here. I'm going to go talk to them, you stay here."

When she got up, Tobias tried to follow, but he didn't even make it onto his knees before flopping back down. He made an inarticulate sound and reached for her. His expression was devastated as she moved away.

He was breaking her heart. "I'm only going up stairs and I'll be right back, I promise."

Unable to take the forlorn sounds coming from him, she rushed up the stairs to find a man as big as Memphis taking up a lot of space in the middle of the place. Were all these preternatural guys big? Or were Mikey's pack members on the small size? Sure, Mikey was large, but the rest of the pack were all more average.

Whatever, that was a mystery for another day.

Jody was dressed in black cargo pants and a long sleeved black shirt with a small light gray logo embroidered over the left breast. Stone Protection was written under a stylized image of a closed ornate gate with stone pillars on either side. He was not wearing any obvious weapons, but he looked menacing enough that even most well-armed individuals would think twice about tangling with him. His shaved head, serious expression, and piercing dark brown eyes completed the threatening appearance.

Ignoring how intimidating he looked, she reached for the cooler he was holding. "Hi there, is that the blood?"

He pulled it out of her reach. "Hold on, we need to talk first."

Briar wasn't pleased. "Dude, this isn't some tea party. I've got a starving vampire down there."

Jody cracked a smile. "I like you." He held the cooler by the bottom, then tilted and opened it. She was disappointed to see that there were only three bags of blood in there. That didn't seem like enough.

"Couldn't you get more?"

Jody shook his head. "If he's been starved for as long as you and Soren think, too much blood at once could make him really sick. I looked it up, and this is the max he should have for his first meal. It's the equivalent of a medium human meal."

"Medium human?" She eyed the three bags then looked up at Jody. "I don't want to be ugly, but I'm pretty sure a human body has more blood in it than that."

A grin flashed across the man's face. "Medium meal that lets the human live. Someone who gave this much would be a little woozy for a while, but alive."

Briar decided she wasn't going to think about it anymore. "Right, mid-sized meal first. Super-size it later. He won't get sick if he drinks all this in one go?"

"He shouldn't," Jody said. "But there isn't much known on vampires in his condition. The entry I read only had one paragraph on this topic."

"Entry?" she asked as she reached for the cooler again. "Is there some kind of reference book or website on vampy guys?"

"Vampy guys?" he echoed as he let her take the cooler. "You really are as human as you smell, aren't you?"

"I'm afraid so," she said with a shrug. "But don't judge me too harshly."

"No, I wouldn't," he agreed. "But am I allowed to be impressed? I don't know too many humans who would be handling this situation so well. Even with prior knowledge that magic exists."

Before she could answer, her stomach growled, making Jody grin. "We were prepared for that too. My colleague is bringing pizza and drinks for you and the chimera. He should be here soon."

"I'll just run this downstairs and . . ." she trailed off when Jody shook his head.

"I'd wait to give the vampire that meal until the food arrives."

That made her cautious. "Why?"

Jody looked away; his expression uncomfortable. "Uh, Soren said you and that other guy might be the vampire's flock, right?"

"Yeah, but it's not official or anything," she replied sarcastically. Holding up her left hand, she waved it a bit. "We haven't exchanged rings or announced it on social media yet."

Jody's lips twitched. "Okay, human, here's the deal. Your vampire is going to go from being weak to feeling damn good after getting those bags of blood. He's not going to be in top form yet, but he'll feel well enough to, uh, get frisky."

She blinked at him. Who even used that word anymore? "Frisky? Care to elaborate on that?"

He gave a little sigh and finally met her eyes. "Do I really need to give you the birds and non-humans talk? Once he gets some blood in him, he's going to be horny as hell because he'll be surrounded by his flock. His devotion to the two of you and his lust is going to consume him and he might not have much control."

Fear jolted through her. "Would he try to rape us? Memphis is unconscious!"

"No! That's not what I meant at all," Jody said, eyes wide. "I'm messing this all up. Let me start over." He rubbed a hand over his bald head a few times. She stayed silent, giving the guy time to figure out what he wanted to say.

"Okay, so vampires will claim that not all of them sleep with their flock, but I've never seen it. Every vampire and flock I've met have always slept together. Their bond is so intimate that sex ends up being a natural part of it."

"Right, I got that he wants to have sex with Memphis and me. That one wasn't hard to figure out."

"Yeah, but it's more than that. His happiness will come from your happiness. You don't need to worry about rape because if you're upset, he'll be upset. If you're unhappy, he'll be unhappy. Even if you guys haven't exchanged bits of soul yet, his whole world will revolve around you."

Jody's words made Briar think about the look Tobias gave her as she was standing up. He looked shattered that she was leaving him. She thought it was the starvation making him act weird, but what if the starvation was only accentuating his natural instincts?

That raised the very interesting question of what he'd be like once he was well fed.

"Jody?" a voice called out from the front door. Both of them turned to see another massive guy that looked startlingly like Jody. He was also dressed in the same outfit as Jody, which made them appear even more alike.

"Your brother?" she asked.

"Yeah," Jody said to her before calling out. "Come on in. Blake, this is Briar. Briar this is Blake."

"I've got food!" Blake announced with a cheerful smile that quickly differentiated him from Jody. "There's a pizza, some burgers and fries, soda, and bags of chips."

Jody made a frustrated sound. "You couldn't pick out a single healthy option?"

Blake's grin didn't dim. "Who wants to eat healthy during a stressful time?"

"You'd say the same thing if it wasn't stressful," Jody fired back. She got the feeling this was an old argument between the brothers.

"How about I take the food and head downstairs so you guys can have a little privacy?" she quipped. Blake laughed and Jody grimaced.

"Eat a slice up here and drink some water," he instructed, taking one of the pizza boxes from Blake and opening it up in the same way he opened the cooler earlier. With a shrug, she set down the cooler, grabbed a slice, and took a big bite. Damn, that was good pizza.

After eating the slice, she accepted a bottle of water from Blake and guzzled it down. She'd been hungrier than she realized. "Thanks. That was good."

"We're going to stay up here until all of you are ready to leave. We've got more blood so yell if you need us to toss it down because Tobias won't let you leave the basement. He's going to be overprotective for a while, so don't be surprised if he doesn't want you to leave him, especially while the chimera isn't awake."

She was still half convinced that Tobias was only really interested in Memphis, so she gave Jody an unconcerned grin. "We'll see."

"Shout up if you need anything," he said as he helped her figure out how to carry the cooler and the food.

"Sure thing," she said and let them walk with her to the basement stairs. "Thanks for all the help." She wasn't sure how expensive their services were going to end up being, but it was worth it if both Tobias and Memphis came out of this healthy and whole.

To say Tobias was upset when the human walked up the stairs would be putting it mildly. With both him and the chimera unable to go with her, she was defenseless to all kinds of horrible things. Feeling helpless, he hugged the shifter close, worried that one of his flock might die because he was too feeble to protect them.

If his human made it back to him, he'd never let her out of his sight again!

The sound of footsteps on the stairs told him someone was descending. Joy and relief filled him as the human stepped back down into the basement. But now she was carrying an array of items. He tried to get to his feet to relieve her of the burdens, but only managed to flop down onto his belly.

She hurried over to him. "Easy, I've got you." She dropped to her knees, placing all the items on the floor near him.

He managed to roll onto his back, panting from the effort. His reserves were empty. He didn't think he could even sit up now. He was going to die and leave his beautiful human and handsome shifter unprotected. They would never know how much he wanted to cherish them.

He closed his eyes, too depleted to even cry.

Then his human was leaning over him, pressing something cold to his lips. Under the smell of sanitizing chemicals and plastic, he caught the scent of blood. Running on instinct, he opened his mouth, and his fangs slid out to puncture the plastic being held to his face.

Nourishing blood filled his mouth. He sucked it down greedily, whimpering when it stopped flowing.

"There's more," his sweet human said as the empty bag was pulled away and replaced by another. He consumed that one as rapidly as the first and by the time she pressed the third bag to his lips, he was strong enough to open his eyes and reach up to grasp her wrist as he drained it. All too soon there was nothing left in the bag.

Tugging out of his grip, she tossed the bag away. "There's more coming, but they said you would get sick if I gave you too much in one go." She grimaced, "They said that was the equivalent of drinking from one medium-sized human. Ugg, that's really not the mental image I wanted. Memphis told me Soren's a good guy, so I'm going to assume that blood was sourced from willing people."

He opened his mouth, but no words came out. He knew it would take more than one feeding, but he desperately wanted to talk to his bright-haired human. She leaned in close, and he remained still as she examined his face. Would she find him handsome or at least not ugly?

"The color in your eyes is coming back," she said with a wide smile. "That's good, right?"

Not what he was hoping for, but it was better than fear or disgust. He wanted to assure her that yes, color returning to his eyes was a good sign. So was the vitality spreading through his body.

When she sat back on her heels, he tried sitting up. It was a minor feat, but he managed it, feeling inordinately proud of himself. Especially after not even being able to drag his body across the floor earlier.

Looking down, he took in the state of his body. His clothes were rags; dirty, worn, and far from the fine attire he'd been wearing when he'd been forced into the basement prison. Every inch of him felt gritty and dirty, meaning he must stink even to a human's nose.

Shame filled him. He should apologize to his human. He should promise her that he didn't normally appear this way. Explain that when he was fully himself again, she would never need to coddle him or put up with this kind of disadvantageous situation.

But then his gaze fixed on her face and blood rushed to his groin. His human was beautiful. Dark tan skin, lush full lips, and deep amber eyes he could happily drown in. He couldn't resist any longer. Her colorful hair styled in a spiky mohawk only made her more appealing to him. His own exotic bird.

Wrapping a hand around the back of her neck, he pulled her face close to his.

"Hey, wha—"

He cut off her protest with his lips. He didn't force the kiss, but gently urged her mouth to open to him. When she yielded, the kiss was everything he'd hoped for.

She sighed and melted into him. Her soft, lush body felt good against this own, but there was too much clothing between them. He slipped one hand under her shirt to find a bra cupping those perfect breasts. His hands were shaking a little, so he didn't risk trying to grow a single claw and cut the garment. Instead, he wiggled his hand between the bra and her flesh, luxuriating in the smooth, soft texture of her skin.

When his fingers found her nipple, she moaned softly. Yes, she liked that. It was a good start to finding out all the different ways his human liked to be touched.

Deepening the kiss, he urged her back until she was laying on the floor. He had to let go of her breast for a moment so he could push the bulky shirt up. Worried he might catch the shirt on one of her many ear piercings, he left it bundled under her arms. The only thing left was her bra. He gave the threadbare garment a little jerk and to his delight, the thing broke with a startling snap. Her perfect breasts spilled free, and he took full advantage.

Kissing down her jaw and throat, he worked his way to one breast while caressing the other with his hand. Her dark skin made his hand look far too pale and sickly. He could only hope she kept her eyes closed. After he'd consumed enough blood, his skin would return to the light brown shade of his heritage, but for now, he was as white as a sun-bleached corpse.

To keep her from viewing his ugliness, he flipped the front of her shirt up with one hand, so it covered her face. She laughed and pulled it back down. She started to pull one arm through, probably to take it off, but stopped as he sucked her nipple into his mouth.

"Oh, I like that."

He could smell her arousal. Desperation filled him. Desperation to taste what he could smell. He needed to eat her out. It was an urge as powerful as his thirst for blood.

Rearing up, he tugged at her pants, but the button was stubborn and his hands unsteady.

"Easy," she murmured, covering his hands with her own. He stilled. If his flock didn't want his touch, he wouldn't force it.

Looking up, he met her gaze. Could she see how much he desired her? Was there any chance his eyes could tell her the level of pleasure he wanted to give her?

"Frisky my ass," she muttered after a moment. "He should've said horny as fuck."

Breaking eye contact, she let go of his hands and started undoing her pants herself. She grunted a little as she maneuvered the worn material off her hips. He reached out to help, only to be stopped by her words.

"Be gentle, okay? Don't go pounding me into the floor."

Her comments didn't make sense to him, so he ignored the words and focused on the tone. The fear and trepidation. She must be worried that he'd be too rough. He wished she wasn't concerned. Even in this state, he was not a mindless beast.

Determined to show her how good he could be to his flock; he quickly dragged her pants down. When he was hampered by her shoes she was quick to sit up and remove them.

Once they were gone he was able to pull her pants all the way off and tossed them aside. Her long legs separated with a little pressure from his hands. There was only a scrap of cotton between him and her sex. The scent of her arousal perfumed the air. He needed her in his mouth now!

The cotton ripped under his fingers with ease, eliciting a surprised sound from her.

"I was going to need those later," she grumbled. He ignored the complaint. He'd buy her an entire store full if she wanted.

Or none at all if he could persuade her to never wear them again.

He eagerly ducked his head between her thighs. She jerked when he nuzzled the soft curls there. He wanted to savor his first moments with his human. But her scent was too tantalizing, and he ran his fingers through those curls to find dark, glistening flesh. Holding her pussy lips apart, he ran a tongue over her sex.

Mother of Darkness, she tasted as good as she smelled!

She jolted slightly under him, then made a pleased sound as he licked at her. "That feels nice," she murmured.

Nice? *Nice!*

That word was insulting! She wasn't going to get away with using it to describe his skills!

With a growl, he attacked her sex with his tongue, teeth, and lips. He swiped, nibbled, and sucked, cataloging what reaction each one of his touches caused. Then he focused on the combination that made her writhe under him.

"Oh fuck!" she cried out. Rolling his eyes up, he watched her hands cover her breasts, pinching the dark brown nipples.

He rearranged his body a little so he could push one of her hands away. Cupping her breast and rolled the nipple between his fingers. One of her hands tangled in his hair and the other scrabbled at the floor.

"Please," she sobbed. "More, please!"

That's what he wanted to hear. There was none of the *nice* from earlier in her voice. She sounded desperate—exactly what he wanted.

He pulled at the small magic he had and ran it through his fingers, making her shudder and undulate as warmth ran from his skin to hers.

He focused on working her flesh like a pianist, increasing the tempo until she got close, then slowing slightly so she couldn't peak. She screamed in frustration and yanked at his hair when he did it for the third time.

"I need to come," she ground out. "Let me, or I swear I'll cut your balls off!"

He paused for a moment; his smile hidden by her flesh. As she crested the next time, he kept the same pace. She went perfectly still as her orgasm washed over her. Their souls might not be bound together yet, but he could feel the pleasure coursing through her.

What would it be like when their two souls were connected? Better yet, when all three of their souls were connected? He didn't think there were words expressive enough in any language to describe what their love making would be like then.

He didn't stop until she let go of his hair and urged his head away from between her legs. "Enough," she croaked out. "You're going to wear Little Thorn off if you keep that up."

She referred to her clit as Little Thorn? How adorable!

He grinned up at her as he moved from between her legs and settled on the floor next to her. He felt a little shaky but satisfied beyond measure. Curling his body around hers, he shifted them a little until she was settled between himself and the chimera.

His poor shifter had slept through the whole thing. He'd make it up to the male after they were all recovered.

Closing his eyes, he let his body slip back into a restful state. The last thing he heard was her murmuring in a sleepy but amused voice.

"That's the first time I've ever had a guy give me an orgasm, and then fall sleep."

Memphis had woken up hungover a few times in his life, which was a feat because it took a whole hell of a lot of alcohol to get a chimera drunk enough to feel it the next day.

As he opened his eyes and let the room swim into focus, he tried to remember how much he'd consumed to feel this shitty. His head hurt, his body felt like he went nine rounds with all his brothers at once, and his eyes had more grit in them than the Mojave desert.

Sitting up with a soft groan, he rubbed his hands over his face. Dropping them into his lap, he looked around, trying to figure out where he was. When his gaze fell on Briar and the vampire, it all came back to him.

His heartbeat kicked up a notch and the aches and pains took a backseat as he stared at the two. They were both so beautiful it took his breath away.

The vampire was curled around Briar, still dressed in the rags they'd found him in. Briar was naked with her shirt tangled up around one arm and her neck. By the smell of it, the vampire had shown her a good time.

He checked in with his beast and found the chimera he shared his body with wasn't jealous of the vampire at all. If anything, the chimera was as interested in him as Briar. He'd heard of chimeras choosing more than one mate, but it was so rare that he'd never met anyone who'd done it. But the evidence was irrefutable, he had two mates.

"Leave it to me to end up with a fang-face for a mate," he muttered to himself, running a hand over his beard. Soren was going to tease him mercilessly the next time they got together.

He ran his eyes over the vampire and human slumbering next to him. He took in Briar's lush, tan body, and the vamp's lean frame. Both were beautiful in their own way, and the vampire was already looking a little better.

The urge to wake them with his mouth was strong. What would Briar taste like? What about the vampire? How heavenly would it be to taste both his mates as they made love? He'd have to make sure he was part of the next round, and maybe punish them both a little for leaving him out of the fun this first time.

The smell of food distracted him from his sleeping mates. There was a pile of stuff not too far away. Stretching out, he picked up a pizza box and settled it in his lap. There was only a slice missing and it had gone cold, but he wasn't a picky eater. He ate three slices, then dug through one of the bags before finding a pack of water and downing several bottles.

Feeling better, he looked around until he saw his phone. Checking the time, he realized it was going to be a little longer before they could leave the basement. There was no way he was going anywhere without the vampire in tow, which meant they had some time to kill until sunset. He couldn't wait to get both of them out of here. Not only had this place been a prison for the vampire, but it also wasn't a fit place to spend time for all three of them. He might be a chimera shifter, but he wanted a bed.

The sound of footsteps at the top of the stairs caught Memphis's attention.

"Briar? How's it going down there?" a voice called out. Memphis got to his feet and crossed the room, meaning to ask the guy who he was. Before he could open his mouth, the scent of gargoyle hit him.

Gargoyles were one of the few magical creatures as tough as chimeras. The sound of footsteps coming down the stairs triggered the protective instincts of Memphis's inner beast. His Briar and the vampire were laying on the floor behind him, asleep and vulnerable. He couldn't let this stranger get close.

He shifted between one breath and another. His changing form ripped out of his clothes as his beast emerged. The ancient Greeks had described chimeras as having the body of a goat, the head of a lion, and the tail of a serpent. They'd also claimed there was a goat's head growing out of their back.

That wasn't quite accurate.

His head did resemble a lion, with a full reddish-brown mane. But his body was closer to that of a moose than a goat, with a thick muscled torso, a muddy brown coat, and massive cloven hooves. His tail was long, scaled, and articulated with a stinger on the end, easily mistaken for a snake in dim light. But his back was nothing like a goat's head. A massive, muscled hump formed between his shoulders with several wicked spikes curving out of it. Ancient people must have thought the spikes looked like goat horns and decided chimeras had a goat head growing from their backs.

All those parts together might sound mismatched and awkward, but anyone who went up against a chimera knew they were deadly. Their bodies were tough, fast, and agile with teeth similar to an alligator but longer and a venomous tail that was lethal to many preternatural creatures.

He'd just finished shifting as the stranger stepped into the room. His chimera side was in charge now and the big beast opened his mouth to show off massive teeth at the perceived threat.

The gargoyle's eyes went wide as he hissed out a breath.

"Oh shit! You're awake," he said, freezing in place. "I'm a friendly! Tobias needs to feed again. I brought blood!"

The chimera didn't know this male and wasn't inclined to trust anyone near his sleeping mates, especially one as strong as a gargoyle.

Deep inside the chimera, Memphis the man saw the cooler and knew this gargoyle was probably telling the truth. He at least warranted some questions instead of an immediate attack. But unlike other shifters, the human side wasn't in charge when in animal form. A chimera's animal and human half could end up in a battle of dominance to see who got to be in control.

Because Memphis had been a little sleepy and distracted, the chimera took full control and wasn't interested in giving it back anytime soon.

With a threatening snarl, the beast lowered his head and raised his tail, striking impossibly fast. At its full length, his tail was twice his body length, putting this stranger well within striking range. The man didn't have time to duck out of the way, but in the blink of an eye, his skin turned a dark gray. He grunted as the stinger hit, but it didn't penetrate the gargoyle's stone-like shifted skin.

"What the fuck is that?" Briar's panicked voice made the chimera shift his head around. Briar's eyes were wide, and she was clutching a broken chair leg like a weapon. "Stay back! Oh god, did you eat Memphis?"

Trapped in the back of the beast's mind, Memphis screamed not to scare their mate. She was human and might not understand. The beast doesn't believe him. The chimera was sure she'd love every part of them. But first, he needed to deal with the intruder.

By the time he swung his big head around, the gargoyle had already disappeared up the stairs, leaving the cooler on the floor. He ignored Memphis's mental sigh of relief when he didn't chase after the gargoyle. Of course he wasn't going to chase the gargoyle after he ran away. He'd won and besides, gargoyles can't be eaten.

He stepped up to the cooler, thinking he'd gained some kind of prize. With care, the chimera hooked one of his massive teeth in the handle of the cooler so he could present it to the human and vampire. He was excited to give them something of value.

No sooner did he turn than the little human made distressed sounds. He froze, unhappy to notice that his female's eyes were wide and she smelled of fear. Had the stranger done that to her? Maybe he shouldn't have let the gargoyle run off. The human might be worried the threat could return.

If the gargoyle thought to tempt fate a second time, the beast would make sure he died. His human would never be in doubt of his fighting prowess.

She's afraid of us, dumbass! His human side hissed in his head.

No, his human side had to be mistaken.

But the smell of her fear was overwhelming now, and the little human wouldn't stop staring at him. Could Memphis be right? Could she really be afraid of him?

That thought broke his heart and made him sink to his belly. Setting the cooler down, he nudged it forward with his snout. One of his long tusks scraped the concrete floor and made sparks, causing the female to jerk.

The vampire put an arm around her shoulder to soothe her. Thankfully, the vampire didn't look or smell scared. If anything, he looked amused as he comforted the female.

"Friend," the vampire murmured. "Man. Big man. Friend." He stammered to get the words out, but his tone was confident.

His female turned wide eyes to the vampire. "You're talking!"

The vampire smiled and nuzzled her neck. "Love you."

"That's sweet, but what the fuck happened to Memphis and what the hell is that thing?" she asked.

Did she just call him a thing? The chimera's heart hurt at the female's disregard. Did he need to do more to prove himself? There was food down there with them, but he hadn't provided it. Looking around, he noticed the den was dirty with no soft comforts for his mates. No wonder she was dismissive.

"It's him," the vampire told her. "He ours. He . . . he friendly."

"Friendly, right," she stated, but her tone was anything but convinced.

Giving up on talking, the vampire stood up and pulled her to her feet. His female let the vampire do this, but the chimera watched cautiously. He wasn't sure how he'd handle it if his mates got into an argument.

"Hold up. I'm naked, damn it," she groused as she found her pants and pulled them on, covering all that luscious brown flesh. Then she wiggled fully back into her shirt.

Deep inside of him, Memphis was demanding control back. But the beast wasn't ready yet. He wanted their mate to accept all of them, not only the human half.

"Meet," the vampire insisted. "Meet mate."

The woman didn't step forward, but her eyes flew to the chimera. With his head resting on the floor, he rolled his eyes up, trying to look harmless.

"Oh shit, are you trying to tell me that's Memphis?" She took a half step forward.

She must still be intimidated by him. He was a big, impressive beast. Even bigger than most of his brother's animal forms. He needed to show her that he was no threat to her.

In an effort to display vulnerability, he rolled on his back and exposed his belly. There were no spikes, scales, or thick coat there to protect his flesh from attack. Lolling his head to the side, he let his tongue roll out of his mouth to pant a little, prepared to wait in this uncomfortable position for as long as it took to gain her confidence.

His strategy got on unexpected reaction from his female.

"OMG he's so cute!" she cried out and hurried over to his side. Dropping to her knees, she rubbed her hands over the sensitive skin of his belly.

"Who's a pretty kitty?" she cooed to him as she gently raked her short, blunt nails through the sparse fur of his belly. "Such a handsome kitty!"

Surprised but also delighted by the touch, he couldn't help the way one of his hooved feet waved in the air. She grabbed one to get a closer look. "I would've thought you would have had paws. But I guess hooves work. I mean, you're super mish-mashie with a lion head, snake tail, and scorpion stinger, so I guess hooves fit right in."

He thought her tone was a happy one. She must still be interested in him even though he hadn't provided her with much. He'd change that. He knew his human half had access to all kinds of comforts the female would like. And the motorcycle they owned. Females approached Memphis all the time asking for a ride. They'd offer their mate all the rides she wanted.

Of course I will, now let me have our body back, Memphis insisted. As usual, the beast ignored his human half.

As she petted him, the vampire knelt behind her and placed his hand next to hers to feel his chimera belly. He liked having both of them touching him at the same time. It felt good. Someday, he wanted to sleep in a big soft bed with his massive, shifted body curled around his two mates.

But right now, he needed to hand control over to his human side. The little female had met and approved of him, so now it was time for his other half to care for her gentler needs.

Giving in to Memphis, his body reshaped under their hands. Hair receded, hooves turned to hands and feet, and snout morphed to mouth.

"Motherfucker," Memphis cursed the moment his body finished shifting. He took a few breaths before opening his eyes to meet Briar's gaze.

"I'm sorry, Baby Doll," he breathed. "I'm sorry my beast got out. Please tell me you're not scared of us now."

To his delight, she giggled. "Dude, your beast is fucking adorable! Does he purr?"

"For you I'm sure he'll figure out how," Memphis grumbled with a smile as he sat up. Both Briar's and Tobias's hands fell away from where they'd been resting on his chest.

He spied the cooler and snatched it up to shove it at Tobias. "Drink up, fang-face."

Tobias accepted the cooler with a lift of an eyebrow. Yeah, he didn't like that nickname.

Memphis grinned as he tried a different one. "Blood-sucker?"

The eyebrow didn't lower.

"Leech?"

Now both eyebrows lowered, and his forehead crinkled, his distaste obvious.

Briar laughed and joined the banter. "I'd be careful with the name calling," she said and nudged him with her elbow. "Considering what your shifted form looks like, I could come up with all kinds of great handles for you."

"Oh yeah?" Memphis challenged. "Like what?"

"Snake-Tail. Horny-backed Boy. I saw you sleeping, so I think the best one would be Sabre-toothed Snorez-all." Her grin was daring. "Try me. I could come up with dozens."

Memphis held up a hand to stop her. "You win." He looked back to the vampire. "How about I call you sweetheart?"

The vampire's expression turned indulgent, and he leaned forward to give Memphis a kiss while Briar made a muted exclamation that sounded both happy and sad.

"Oh man, you two are perfect together," she whispered. She tried to move away, probably to give them space, but Memphis snaked an arm around her and drew her close.

"You mean all three of us are perfect together," he argued. "It's all three of us, Briar. We're a triad, meant to be together. We're your family, Baby Doll. There's no getting rid of us."

And then he kissed her at the same time that he urged the vampire's face closer. Soon they were engaged in a sloppy but heated three-way kiss that left no one in question about how hot they were going to be when they all got to make love together.

They might need to keep a fire extinguisher near the bed.

"Everything okay down there?" Jody's voice pulled Briar out of the moment and doused her libido. She might absolutely want to jump into bed with these two, but the key word was bed. Not a disgusting basement floor.

There was getting nasty, and then there was downright filthy. She liked her sex nasty, but this level of filthy wasn't for her.

"We're good," she called up.

"We've got a place for you guys to stay until Tobias is feeling better," he called down. "Soren arranged it and said the three of you could stay there for as long as you liked."

"This is going to come back to haunt me," Memphis muttered. "Now I'll owe him."

"And he told me to tell Memphis that he's repaying the debt he owed Briar for helping him with the Volk pack," Jody continued. Then he coughed out a laugh and added, "And he said to tell Memphis not to bitch about it."

Memphis's expression turned relieved, then guilty before he called up the stairs. "Sorry about chasing you earlier."

"Don't worry about it, man," Jody said, his tone light. "If I ever find my mate, I'd be the same way."

"I figured a gargoyle would understand. You motherfuckers are some of the most protective guys ever born," Memphis shot back with a huffed laugh of his own.

"I've arranged for your driver to be a mated female named Jaynie. I thought that would be the safest," Jody explained. "Sun will be down in twenty minutes, and we'd like to get you guys out of here."

Briar eyed Memphis's naked, muscled body then glanced over to the clothing he'd been wearing before he shifted. It was all in shreds. "We need some clothes for Memphis."

Memphis followed her gaze and groaned. "My vest. Fuck, I loved that vest."

The vampire made a soothing sound and rubbed Memphis's back. It was sweet the way Tobias wanted to be comforting even though he couldn't talk yet.

A dark bundle bumped down the stairs to land at the bottom.

"There you go," Jody said. "I'll yell when it's safe to come up. Jaynie will be the one escorting you. The rest of us will be guarding you, but we'll be keeping our distance."

Grumbling, Memphis retrieved the bundle and shook it out so Briar could see. It was the same kind of black cargo pants and polo shirt with the company logo that Jody and Blake wore.

Briar laughed at Memphis's sour expression. "You could go naked." She made a show of raking her eyes up and down his form. The term built like a brick house applied to this man; nothing about him was slight, slim, or small.

Tree-trunk like legs led up to a thick ass that she wanted to take a bite of. Then a slight tapering at his waist only to flare back out to accommodate his massive chest and broad shoulders. It was hard to distinguish where the shoulders ended, and his bull-neck began. His jaw and chin were hidden under a russet beard she had the strongest urge to stroke.

Would he let her braid it? It looked long enough to get a few short braids in. And maybe some silver beads. He'd look good with a Viking style beard!

"Why are you looking at me like that?" Memphis asked. She refocused and realized he'd pulled on the pants and was holding the shirt out as if ready to pull it over his head.

"What do you mean?"

"You look like you're measuring me for a suit," he answered, then donned the shirt. It was a little tight around his neck but other than that, it looked like it fit okay.

Memphis grimaced as he looked down at himself. "I look like an asshole."

"You don't look like an asshole," she countered with a laugh. The man's identity was way too tied up in his leather and jeans.

"I look like a middle-class asshole," he countered, his lipped curled up. "You might as well call me Chad."

She couldn't help it; she laughed. Part of her sympathized. She'd hate it if she was forced to wear someone else's crop top and skinny jeans. But she'd also suck it up because it'd be better than running around naked.

"At least it's all black. You look a little like an ex-military asshole instead of a Chad. And that beard is still biker."

That made him grin and run a hand over his beard. "Yeah, that's true." Then Memphis looked down and his grin turned into a concerned frown. "Let me help you with that."

Briar turned to look and found Tobias sitting on the floor, unable to get the cooler open. He looked frustrated and ready to try to rip it apart. Memphis knelt next to him and took the cooler from the vampire's shaky grip.

His tone was gentle as he opened the latch on the cooler and handed Tobias a bag. "You're still recovering. Don't stress."

Feeling bad that they'd been ignoring him, Briar dropped into a crouch on the other side of Tobias. The vampire eyed both of them, then looked at the bag in his hand.

What was he waiting for?

"Drink up, sweetheart," Memphis urged.

"You need this," Briar said, wanting to make up for not noticing Tobias's distress earlier.

With both of them pressing him, Tobias raised the bag to his lips and opened his mouth. Long fangs descended from his upper gums, but he hesitated.

"You loved me even in my shifted form," Memphis said. "I'll love you even if I see you eat. I know you're not a monster."

Now Briar understood what was going on. She'd heard enough horror stories from Mikey to know that vampires were considered a malevolent group as a whole, lacking any morals or decency.

But Memphis had opened her to the knowledge that there were some vampires out there who rose above their bloodthirsty state to be decent people.

Tobias was obviously one of those few if he was scared that watching him consume blood might disgust them.

"I've seen you eat, and I'm still here," she reminded him. "And I bet Memphis has seen a whole lot worse than you sucking your meal out of a bag."

Memphis nodded his head as he cupped one massive hand around the one Tobias was holding the blood with and pressed the bag against his descended fangs. "I've seen things that are truly evil, and you're not one of them. You could never be that."

Closing his eyes, Tobias gave in and sunk his long teeth in and sealed his mouth around the puncture. Memphis kept his hold on Tobias, and Briar rubbed a soothing hand in a circle on his back.

"That's my handsome vampire," Memphis murmured. The moment the bag was empty, he let go of Tobias's hand and snatched up another bag. The vampire had barely discarded the empty before Memphis was pressing a second full one to his mouth. He cradled the back of Tobias' head with his other hand, as if afraid the vampire would try to pull away.

Tobias didn't fight Memphis's hold. He relaxed into the chimera's grip and drained the second bag. Memphis talked to him the whole time and then held the third and final bag to Tobias's face in the same manner.

Briar's eyes got hot as she watched Memphis care for Tobias. He might act rough and tough, but he was nothing but soft and squishy inside.

Leaning over, she rested her forehead on Tobias's shoulder and kept petting his back. Memphis's words were soothing her as much as the vampire. His clothes felt gritty, so she pressed her face against the side of his neck. He made a content sound and wrapped an arm around her.

"That was good," Memphis praised. She raised her head in time to see him discard the last bag and wipe the corner of Tobias's mouth with his thumb. It was such a casually intimate act that it felt like they'd been together for years instead of hours.

That perfect moment was shattered when Jody called down. "Time to go."

Because the sun had only recently set and there was still a lot of light, Memphis insisted on draping a shirt over Tobias's head and carrying him to the waiting car. Tobias was like a doll, letting Memphis do anything to him he wanted.

"Would the light burn his skin?" Briar asked as she carried their cell phones and the remnants of his vest in a bag Jody provided. He'd be damned if he was leaving that behind, even if it was ruined.

"It would be like getting a sunburn," Memphis explained as he followed Jaynie to a non-descript black van. "Not lethal, but not pleasant either. Vampires might be apex predators, but the sun is their one true weakness."

Jaynie opened the sliding side door to the van and Briar cocked an eyebrow at her. "What's with the kidnapper van?"

Jaynie grinned. "Want some candy, pretty lady?" Jaynie waited until Briar finished laughing before explaining. "We weren't sure if everyone was going to be able to walk or sit up. The seats can all be pulled out if someone needed to ride lying down."

"Clever," Briar commented as she climbed in and scooted over on the first bench seat.

"Necessary," Jayne responded and helped Memphis maneuver through the door without accidently smacking Tobias on anything.

As he sat, Briar lifted Tobias's legs into her lap and scooted closer to his side. Resting her hands on Tobias's legs and snuggling in close against Memphis, she sighed in relief.

"Even the short walk from the basement to the car had made me feel weird," she admitted. "Like my skin was itchy, but now that we're all touching, I feel fine."

Her words filled Memphis with happiness. "That's how it's supposed to be for new mates. They need to be touching each other constantly at first. Mom said that the first few days they were together was the longest she ever went without having the urge to shoot my dad."

Briar chuckled. "Are both your parents chimera shifters?"

That question reminded Memphis how little Briar knew about his world. "There's no such thing as a female chimera. They don't exist. We're all male and find mates outside of our own species."

"What, really?" she asked.

Jaynie spoke up from the front seat. "That's not uncommon. I'm a harpy and we're all female. I don't know of any harpies who ended up mated to another harpy, even if they're like me and have another female for a mate. My wife is human, and she didn't know there was anything out there that wasn't human when we first met."

"That had to have been an awkward conversation," Briar said.

Jaynie nodded her head. "You have no idea. When harpies find their mates, we go into this really protective mode and get aggressive with anything that tries to get close. My mate has a lot of pets. I almost ate one of her cats because my harpy side saw it as a threat."

"No shit?" Briar said then turned her gaze to Memphis. "Now I understand why you got so aggressive with Jody. I guess you couldn't help it. We'll be careful, and I'll stick close until you've got a handle on it."

Although she'd reacted so fondly to his beast earlier, it was still a relief to hear Briar accepted that part of him. "If Jody had been mated, my chimera might not have reacted so violently."

"Duly noted," Briar said with a grin. "I'll keep the flirting with other guys to a minimum."

Memphis knew she was joking, but that didn't stop his inner beast from rising up. Clenching his jaw, he focused on keeping that part of him under control.

Briar was staring at his face. "Your irises just changed color."

"You can't say shit like that," Jaynie said from the front. "Memphis's beast won't understand you're kidding."

Closing his eyes, Memphis worked on controlling his emotions. He knew from their conversations that Briar didn't do boyfriends. She had lovers, and her found family, but she never wanted a boyfriend. Now she had not one, but two mates.

He was sure that when the emergency part of their meeting was all over and the three of them needed to settle into a daily life together; she was going to freak out.

The only question was how bad it was going to be.

"It's fine," Memphis growled out without opening his eyes. On his lap, Tobias made a discontented sound and started wiggling, trying to get the shirt off. Briar was quick to comfort him.

"Hey, don't do that," she said as she reached over and grasped his hands in her own while Memphis tugged the shirt so it wasn't in danger of sliding off.

Tobias's free hand scrambled around until he found Memphis's hand, then clutched it and tugged a little. Memphis let him and soon the vampire was wrapping Memphis's hand around Briar's, then he held the two of them together with both his hands.

Looked like Memphis wasn't the only one who was scared the human might leave them. Out of all the creatures that you could pick as a mate, humans were the most dangerous because they often didn't feel the same pull as those with magic.

"I'm sorry if I upset you," Briar murmured. Then she raised her eyes to meet Memphis's gaze. "Both of you."

It wasn't a declaration of love, but it would have to do for now.

While his flock talked, Tobias held all their hands together and worked on making his brain cooperate.

My name is Tobias Becker.

That was good. But he needed more.

I was born in 1681 in an English colony. My mother was . . .

Who was his mother? She'd had black hair. She was . . . she was . . . *from the Wampanoag nation!* Triumph filled him from remembering that detail.

What else could he remember? He searched his memories. It was hard to remember either parent since they'd lived and died so long ago. Another memory filtered through his mind. His father swaying, drunk on the homemade alcohol he'd insisted his wife learn to make. He'd married a Wampanoag woman in order to form trading relationships with the tribes, but it had backfired when the other English colonists snubbed him and his "half-breed" child. He'd made money, but at the cost of social prestige.

It had made him a mean, spiteful man. And when Tobias's mother died of smallpox, his father had gone from screaming to hitting.

He could feel memories returning as he focused on his past. He remembered the vampire who turned him. Remembered his many years and travels. He'd seen many parts of the world only to find that San Diego was the place he wanted to stay.

And now he understood that he'd been drawn to settle here because of his flock. The Mother of Darkness had guided him and his flock.

He wasn't naïve; he knew this transition from individuals to flock wouldn't be smooth. Nothing ever was. But he was confident that he could make it work. He simply had to.

The vehicle around him moved at a gentle pace as his flock and the driver spoke among themselves. He focused on their words, thinking in his head how he'd respond if they were speaking to him.

"We've stocked the kitchen," the driver said.

That's good. I wouldn't want my flock to go hungry.

Yes, that would be the response a speaking person would give. How would his lips move to speak those words out loud?

He practiced by opening and closing his mouth, shaping the words without adding sound. It was difficult, but the last meal of blood was thrumming through his system, making him feel rejuvenated.

He could sense that there was no more sunlight, but he didn't try to remove the shirt. The privacy allowed him to keep practicing. Holding the hands of his flock tightly in his own helped keep him from getting frustrated.

"How long until Tobias is back to his old self?" Briar asked.

Soon, he thought. *Very soon!*

"Not too long," Memphis replied. "Vampires are resilient, and he's already come a long way from the almost-corpse you discovered."

Briar laughed. "Ewww, don't say that."

He liked the way they bantered; it made him feel like they were already a familiar flock.

"We've stocked the place with blood too," the driver added. "Keep feeding him those three bags at a time every few hours. And don't skip, even if he tries to refuse. You need to keep this up for the next day or two."

Humiliation hit him at the driver's words. He'd never liked consuming blood in front of others, not even vampires.

Having to feed with Memphis and Briar watching had filled him with shame and fear.

But then the chimera had been so gentle, and both his flock were so accepting of his need for blood. Lilith, the Mother of Darkness must be blessing him to have his flock find him when he needed them the most. He would prove to them he was worthy. He'd keep them protected and provide anything they needed. He'd—

A hard push of magic rolled over him. He felt Briar jerk and the air in the vehicle warmed considerably.

"What the hell was that?" Briar's voice was pitched high with startlement.

"Memphis?" the driver called back. "How close are you?"

"I'll make it to the house," Memphis's answer sounded like he was speaking through a clenched jaw. Although he'd never experienced this firsthand, Tobias instinctively knew what was happening.

Letting go of his flock's hands, he pulled the shirt away from his head so he could look at Memphis. The chimera's eyes were closed, and his face flushed. He needed to see Memphis's eyes to judge how badly the chimera was being affected.

"Don't take that off," Briar said aggravatedly and tried to put the shirt back over his head.

He batted the shirt away then pointed out the window. Briar followed his finger. "Oh, yeah, no more sunlight. I guess you're safe now."

Another wave of heavy magic washed over them, making Briar suck in a sharp breath. Tobias felt like he'd been hit by an ocean wave.

"Jody, we need to pick up the pace," the driver said. When Tobias looked over, he saw the harpy was talking into a cell phone. "Memphis is about to go into rut."

"Rut?" Briar echoed; her voice sharp. Tobias realized the littlest member of his flock didn't know what that meant. He didn't have time to comfort her, he needed to help Memphis maintain control.

Framing Memphis's face with his hands, he worked on speaking one word. "Open."

The chimera's lids flew up and their gazes met. Memphis's eyes were bright gold and swirling with magic.

"Can you help me?"

"Try," Tobias agreed. He pulled at his still-weak powers and focused on Memphis. "Settle," he commanded, trying to use thrall on the chimera.

Although he wasn't as powerful as he could be, Tobias felt Memphis slide under his command.

Vampires used thrall to control others. When he was at full strength, his thrall was so complete that he could force someone to do things that might even cause them injury or death. He'd only ever used thrall to feed or hide his existence.

Normally, a vampire never wanted to use thrall on a member of his flock, but it was the only way to help Memphis.

Memphis shuddered out a breath and relaxed back in his seat a little. The temperature in the car lowered slightly, but Tobias could still feel Memphis's pressing need. His weak thrall would help delay, but it wouldn't stop it. Hopefully, he could help Memphis hold it off long enough to get to where they were going.

Otherwise, well, Jaynie had said the van seats did fold down to make a flat surface.

What was going on? Why were Tobias and Memphis staring unblinkingly at each other.

"Memphis?" Briar whispered, mostly ignoring the raging lust going through her body.

"Don't distract them," Jaynie barked out. "Tobias is keeping Memphis in control, but it's tenuous."

Briar curled her hands into fists to keep from reaching out to touch either of them. She felt both horny and pissed.

"What the fuck is going on?" she hissed. "What is rut? Why did I feel like I need dick inside me more than I need to breathe?"

Jaynie made a soft choking sound. "Damn, you don't mince words."

Briar almost laughed. She'd never been one to dance around a topic, but with her clit throbbing between her legs and her panties soaked, she wasn't interested in being polite.

"Explain," she demanded as Jaynie took a corner fast enough to press Briar into the side of the van. Memphis and Tobias swayed together; their eyes still locked.

"Every couple of years, adult chimeras will go into rut," Jaynie said, her hands tight on the wheel. "The rut can also be triggered by finding a mate. Or mates in this case."

"So he needs to get laid?" she asked.

"He needs to get laid a lot. Over and over again for the next twenty-four to seventy-two hours. Before he met you two, he would use his own hand, but now he'll need the two of you."

A shot of fear hit her. "No!"

Jaynie jerked a little at Briar's loud shout. "Keep it down! Do you want Memphis to come out of thrall and cause us to wreck the car?"

Briar wasn't repentant in the least. "You're basically telling me I have to spread my legs for a guy I only met a little while ago. That I'm not allowed to say no. That's bullshit. I won't be put in a corner like that."

Jaynie glanced over her shoulder at Briar. "You already messed around with the vampire, right?"

"That's different," she argued. "Jody told me Tobias wouldn't hurt me. Wouldn't do anything I didn't want to do."

Jaynie's expression turned relieved. "Oh, if that's what you're worried about, I can fix that. Memphis will be the same."

"But rut sounds like he'll need to stick his dick in me," Briar said. "And the way I'm feeling right now, I'd let him even though I'm not sure I want it."

"Not sure? Not sure," Jaynie chewed on those words for a moment. "Are you thinking what you're feeling isn't real?"

"It's not, right?" Briar insisted. "Memphis and his weird rut-magic is causing it."

"Humans," Jaynie muttered with disgust.

Briar saw red. "Harpy bitch!"

Her curse brought Tobias's attention on her. He didn't break eye contact with Memphis, but he did blindly reach out a hand to her. She took it in one of hers, anger evaporating as the vampire sought to soothe her.

"I'm not mad at you," she said quickly, giving his hand a squeeze. "We're good."

"Look, human," Jaynie said, spitting the word out like a curse. "What you're feeling is because you're already attracted to Memphis. Your soul has recognized his soul. It's a fate thing."

Briar scoffed. "Stop with the romantic shit. He's filling the car with fuck-me magic. That's not the same thing."

Jaynie's tone matched hers. "What he's sending only builds up what's already there. If you didn't want him, you'd be sitting there unaffected."

Briar's anger was overtaken by confusion. "Wait, are you telling me you can't feel this?"

"I can feel the powerful magic Memphis is bleeding, and I can tell all three of you are aroused," Jaynie said, her tone softening. "But I have a mate and she's my everything. That makes me impervious to Memphis."

She wanted Memphis because she wanted him, not because of magic. Clenching Tobias's hand tighter, Briar finally realized that her life had irrevocably changed.

"Nothing's going to be the same, is it?"

Jaynie's voice was kind when she answered. "No, it won't."

When Jaynie drove them to the elite area of Santa Fe Spring, Briar thought she was taking a back road to circumnavigate San Diego traffic. But then she pulled into the long driveway of one of the swanky properties.

"You've got to be shitting me," Briar said as Jaynie stopped in front of one of the fanciest houses Briar had ever seen. "This can't be right."

Jaynie turned in her seat to make it easier to look at Briar. "The guy that hired us, Soren, he's got some serious money to throw around. I'm not sure if he rented this place or owns it, but either way, it's where you guys are going to stay until everyone feels better."

"I didn't even do that much," Briar muttered. "I traced something and got into a server, that was it. I can't believe Soren is dropping this much cash on us."

"From what I heard, you helped rescue his flock," Jaynie said, and gave Briar a meaningful look. "Vampires will stop at nothing to keep their flocks safe. You helped, so he wants to reward you."

Briar knew Jaynie was making a bigger statement about vampires and flocks as a whole, but she didn't want to think about it. She didn't do boyfriends. They stuck around and if you were unlucky, they turned into husbands. Having some fun in the sack was great, but commitment like that was a hard limit for her.

And she was going to have to eventually tell this vampire she wasn't his flock. And what about Memphis? He'd been hinting at wanting to date her during their phone conversations, but never mentioned the chimera fated mate thing. She couldn't be anyone's mate. She just couldn't.

"This is all bullshit," she muttered, then felt Memphis shudder next to her. Looking over, she noticed the vampire's eyes were starting to turn a brighter red color.

"I don't care what you think," Jaynie said as she got out of the driver seat. "You need to help me get these guys inside. You can whine later."

"I wasn't whining," she whined as Jaynie jogged around the vehicle to open the large sliding door. Jaynie gave her an annoyed look the moment the door was open.

"Right, big girl panties," she muttered as she regarded Memphis and Tobias. Their eyes were still locked, but she could tell Tobias was struggling to hold the thrall. "How are we going to do this?"

"I can't touch any of you or Memphis might lose it," Jaynie said as she stepped back. "Here's what I'm going to suggest. You crawl out first and run. Front doors open. Go up the stairs and find the room with the biggest bed."

Briar cast her a confused look. "How's that going to help?"

"The moment you disappear from sight, Memphis will break through that thin layer of thrall Tobias is holding. He's going to chase after you, probably with Tobias over his shoulder."

Briar eyed the door, gauging the distance. "What happens when he catches up with me?"

Jaynie's expression was mocking. "I think you know."

"Right," she said as she started wiggling her way out. "Let the fuck-fest begin."

Jaynie laughed as she tucked herself around the back of the van. "I'll make sure the front door closes behind you. One guard will be stationed at the front gate and another at the back of the property. No one's going to come near the house unless you call us. Numbers are on the kitchen counter."

Briar almost fell flat on her face as she finally extricated herself from the van. She heard Memphis growl, but he didn't move.

"Run!" Jaynie reminded her. Feeling like the cheerleader in a horror movie, Briar stumbled toward the wide-open front door, gaining her balance and speed within a few strides. Flying through it, she heard Memphis roar outside as she sprinted up the stairs right in front of her.

All the doors were open, and she dismissed the first few rooms because the beds were all twins or queens. Then she found the master bedroom with a massive bed that looked like two king size beds put together.

"Damn," she said as she stood there and blinked. "I guess this one was meant for us."

The sound of thundering feet made her turn to see Memphis cresting the stairs. Jaynie had been right; Memphis was carrying Tobias over his shoulder and the added weight wasn't slowing him at all. His eyes were a bright, glowing amber and some of his teeth looked unnaturally long and shined silver as he snarled.

He didn't run at her, but his long legs ate up the distance with little effort, his eyes never wavering from her.

Briar backed up until the back of her legs hit the foot of the bed. "Hey, Memphis, it's me," she said as he stalked into the room, kicking the door shut behind him. "Baby Doll, remember?"

Memphis's face was downright feral as he stepped closer to her. When he was almost touching her, he leaned over and put his face next to hers.

He growled out one word, "Mine."

Normally, she'd be annoyed at his possessive attitude and neanderthal delivery, but so much magic bled off him that even she was able to feel it. Pure lust hit her hard enough to make her knees go weak.

"Well shit," she whispered. "Let's do this."

Memphis was dimly aware that he was acting like an asshole.

Very dimly.

Lust was riding him hard, pushing all the civilized parts of his mind to the back. He remembered when he was a teenager and his father had sat him down and warned him about what going into rut was like. He'd brushed it off as only a teenager could. Then he'd experienced his first rut and spent three days locked in his room, taking himself in hand until both his palm and cock were rubbed raw.

After that, he'd taken his father's advice, but the ruts hadn't gotten any easier. In fact, they'd gotten worse and worse over the years until he'd been forced to ask Soren to put him in thrall so he didn't start molesting innocent bystanders.

And now, for the first time, he had a mate. No, he had two mates. Both of them beautiful but frighteningly frail. Tobias was still weak from so many years without blood, and Briar was human.

But he couldn't stop. He needed them as much as his next breath.

Pulling Tobias off his shoulder, he gently tossed the vampire onto the bed. Tobias bounced once and grinned up at him with blood-red eyes.

The vampire was just as eager as he was.

Briar turned slightly to watch them but didn't move to get on the bed. Her eyes were wide and body stiff. He could smell her interest, but also her hesitation. That was fine, he could work over Tobias first and see if Briar wanted to join in.

With clumsy fingers, Memphis pulled the borrowed clothing off his overheated body, ripping both the shirt and pants in several places. As soon as he was naked, he stepped to the bed and knee walked to Tobias. The vampire watched with anticipation in his face and Briar pivoted in place to keep them in sight, but she didn't follow onto the bed.

"Memphis?"

Her soft voice made him look over his shoulder at her. Her pupils were blown, and he could smell the lust coming from her now. It made him lick his lips. "Join."

Turning his attention back to Tobias, he focused on shredding the vampire's clothes and tossing the rags aside. Soon Briar was the only one still dressed. Memphis straddled Tobias, both their cocks engorged and straining.

"Kiss," he demanded from the vampire.

Tobias eagerly leaned forward so their lips could meet. As they kissed, Memphis fisted their cocks in his hand, holding them together side by side. Tobias moaned against his lips as Memphis pumped his fist, keeping his movements slow and pressure light because they were both dry. They'd need lube if they were going to do anything more.

"Damn, that's hot!" Briar said in a breathy voice. He didn't stop kissing and touching Tobias as he listened to her walk around the bed.

When he felt the mattress depress as she crawled onto it to join them, he was glad his seduction plan worked.

Breaking the kiss, he looked over at her. She was still dressed but was holding up a bottle of lube. "Can I help?" She wiggled the bottle a little. "And it's edible. These guys thought of everything."

Memphis wordlessly nodded, and a grin broke out on her face. Her tan skin was flushed, and he could hear her heartbeat picking up. He hoped that meant their mate was growing comfortable with her arousal.

It took her a moment to get the bottle open, but soon she was slathering their dicks with lube. As she did it, she massaged first the head of his cock, and then Tobias's, making both of them groan. When she let go, Memphis took over.

"Nice," she whispered as Memphis started pumping again, the motion smooth and making Tobias shudder.

When the vampire reached out to her, Briar flowed over to him. The two kissed as Memphis worked their dicks. He wished Briar was naked so he could finger her sweet pussy with his free hand. His chimera pushed against his skin, screaming that both his mates needed to come. His beast wouldn't be happy until they were both writhing with pleasure.

Memphis worked hard to gain some control. He wasn't going to tear off Briar's clothes. He wasn't going to force her to do anything. His Baby Doll deserved so much more than that.

Tobias placed a hand on Memphis's forearm while he was still lip-locked with Briar. Memphis didn't let go, but he did stop holding and caressing the two of them and loosened his grip. The last thing he wanted to do was hurt Tobias, but he couldn't bring himself to release the hold he had on their engorged shafts.

When Tobias broke off the kiss and pulled back, Briar looked a little dazed.

Tobias smiled at her, showing a hint of fang. "Clothes," he said simply.

Briar's brow wrinkled with confusion for a second before she nodded her head eagerly. Flopping back, she fumbled with the button and zipper to her black pants, toeing her untied boots off at the same time. The boots thumped onto the floor next to the bed and her pants followed right after. Memphis was happy to note she wasn't wearing any underwear.

Sitting up, she reached for the hem of her shirt and pulled it off with a flourish. The moment she was naked, she scooted back over.

Memphis was struck dumb at how beautiful his human was. Her body was thick with curves that would overfill his hands. He wanted to lick, kiss, and bite every inch of her tan flesh, paying special attention to those glorious breasts.

And, of course, he wanted to dive between her legs and feast on her. That reminded him that Tobias had already gotten a taste of her, but he hadn't. That wasn't fair.

Suddenly he had an idea he was eager to try.

Picking Tobias up with ease, he settled the vampire at the head of the bed with his back resting on the cushioned headboard. "Stay," he ordered.

"Wha—"

Briar didn't get a chance to finish her sentence because he plucked her up and set her on Tobias. With confidence, he positioned her on Tobias's lap so her legs were on either side of his and bent at the knee, exposing her dark-skinned pussy for him to feast on. A bonus of this reverse-cowgirl position was that Tobias's erection stood proud right in front of her pretty pussy, making it easy for Memphis to play with both his mates at the same time.

"I'm too heavy for this," Briar protested and tried to get off the vampire.

Tobias brought his arms around her and cupped a breast in each hand. "No. Perfect."

Briar's arms came up, hooking over Tobias's neck as he leaned over to nip at the shell of her ear. Kneeling between their splayed legs, Memphis admired the beautiful sight the two of them made, spread out before him like a feast.

Need to taste!

Uggh, his chimera half was impatient now that both mates were naked and touching. Not that he could blame his beast, they were both tempting beyond reason.

"I need to taste both of you," he whispered as he lowered himself to his belly.

"Memphis, I should probably shower before—"

Whatever excuse Briar was about to give to try and move away from him was cut off when he nudged Tobias's beautiful, uncut cock out of the way with his face and nuzzled her dark curls.

"Are you really going to—no, you shouldn't—I haven't—oh Tobias!" her jumbled words ended in a moan. He looked up to find Tobias sucking and biting at the flesh of her neck without breaking skin. His hands were also busy alternating between plucking at her beaded nipples and kneading the whole breast.

The erotic sight of the vampire's lightly tanned hands on Briar's darker flesh would never get old for him.

A slight shift of her hips drew his attention back to the section of her body he got to enjoy. Running a finger through her curls, he revealed glistening flesh and that little nub of nerves he was eager to play with. Despite his eagerness, he took his time, licking and nibbling at her sensitive flesh until he finally closed his mouth over her clit and sucked.

She jerked as if he'd touched her with a live wire and then moaned again. "Memphis, oh God that feels good."

As he sucked, he sank a finger into her hot, tight pussy. Tobias's erection rested against his cheek, and he felt bad for neglecting one mate over the other, not that the vampire was upset at all. But the way Tobias's cock moved and jumped from need gave Memphis an idea.

Rearing up slightly, he pressed Tobias's dick back, so it was nestled along the length of Briar's sex. With the two situated against each other, he could lavish both of them with attention. Using his tongue and hands, he worked them both over until he could hear Tobias panting and Briar couldn't remain still any longer.

"I need more," Briar begged.

The need in her voice made his chimera crazy to satisfy her. He couldn't deny either of them any longer.

He wrapped a hand, slick from Briar's dripping pussy, around Tobias's cock and slowly stroked while he focused his mouth on sucking that nub and working it over. It didn't take long until she was shuddering and crying out.

"Right there, *oh fuck!*"

Obeying her demands, he maintained what he was doing. His mate moaned and convulsed. He felt the orgasm roll through her, tightening her muscles and stiffening her spine. He kept going until her body went lax and she dropped one of her hands to his head.

"Easy," she murmured. He lifting his head and found her eyes were closed and her head was resting on Tobias's shoulder. The vampire's hungry gaze met his.

"Do you need relief too, sweetheart?" he asked. Tobias nodded his head eagerly. Without hesitation, Memphis drew back a little and fitted his mouth around Tobias's cock. He'd never given a guy head before. He'd doled out a few hand jobs and reamed one eager individual, but he'd never wanted to taste a man on his tongue. Not until now.

Tobias wasn't as big as he was, but that didn't mean the man was small. Memphis tried to swallow him down and ended up gagging as the head of Tobias's dick nudged the back of this throat.

Eyes watering and coughing, he drew back.

Tobias put a hand under Memphis's chin, urging him to look up. "Easy," he said. Then he reached for Memphis's hand to put that back around him instead of using his mouth.

"I'm fine, sweetheart," Memphis assured him, tangling his fingers with Tobias. "I can figure this out."

This time, he attacked Tobias's cock slowly, taking the time to lick and suck at the tip before letting it slide further into his mouth. He brought his free hand up and grasped the base of Tobias's dick, pumping in time with his mouth.

Tobias groaned. "Good."

"Fuck, that's hot," Briar said. "I want to help." Sitting up a little, she reached down to push Memphis's hand away so she could grasp Tobias instead. Memphis let go and dropped his hand lower to cup Tobias's balls. They were pulled up tight, telling him the man was close.

"One of these days, I want to touch both of you at the same time," Briar said. "A hard dick in each hand. See if I can get you both to come at once."

Memphis could easily see the picture she was painting. Her kneeling in front of him and Tobias. Her hands stroking their cocks. Her face would be flushed from a recent orgasm and her hands might even be a little shaky. She wouldn't even have to work that hard because he and Tobias would be concentrating on not coming the moment that she lowered herself to the floor. They would cover her breasts with their cum, both of them marking her at the same time.

He didn't realize he'd started sucking harder and faster on Tobias until the vampire's hips jerked forward and he cried out with pleasure. Memphis's mouth was suddenly flooded, and he swallowed down every drop.

He kept working Tobias until he began to soften. Briar let go as Memphis let Tobias's dick slide out of his mouth. Pulling his legs under him, he sat up and surveyed his mates.

Both were flushed and sweaty and looking back at him with heavy-lidded gazes.

He wished he could take a picture of them like this.

The chimera pushed hard under his skin, reminding him that he was still in rut and hadn't gotten to come yet. His inner beast was pleased that their mates had been satisfied, but now it was his turn.

Grabbing Briar's thighs, he shifted her a little, so she was back in the position with her legs wide apart, exposing her glistening sex. The move caused her to slide down until her ass was on the bed instead of Tobias. The vampire wrapped his arms around her to help keep her in this new position for Memphis, his eyes sparking with renewed lust.

Holding her thighs steady, he placed the head of his shaft at the entrance of her hot pussy. He wanted to thrust hard into her, but he was big and didn't want to hurt her. He started to ease in, then froze.

Wait, he hadn't gotten consent for this, and he wasn't wearing a condom. He could get her pregnant!

It took every ounce of willpower he possessed to stop himself. "Tell me to stop," he ground out. "If you don't want this, order me to get off you."

If Briar demanded something of him, his beast would do it. Everyone thought chimeras were controlling bastards, but the truth was that they were powerless when it came to their mates.

Briar moved her hips up, urging Memphis deeper. Because Tobias's arms were around her, she didn't go far, but her intent was clear.

"I want you inside me. Please!"

"You never need to beg," Memphis said. "Demand anything from me Baby Doll. I want to give you everything. But I'm bareback."

"You have an STD I need to know about?" she asked, panting out the words.

"No, we shifters don't, I mean we aren't susceptible to human—"

"Good enough," she barked out. "Now start moving!"

"Anything you want." As he spoke, he eased himself into her. It was torture to go so slow, but he worried about hurting her.

"Yeah, that's the spot," she moaned as he slid home.

"Fuck, you feel good," he groaned out. She was so hot and tight; he didn't think he would last long.

He pulled almost all the way out and then shifted his hips slightly to change the angle. As he pushed back in, he rubbed against her clit, making her jerk under him. Yeah, that's what he wanted!

Now that he'd found the ideal slant, he increased his pace with every thrust. Watching his cock slide in and out of Briar's heat was spectacular, and he could feel his orgasm getting close.

"Wait," he ordered himself. He could tell Briar had another climax in her, and he wanted to ride her through that.

"I can't," Briar wailed as she jerked under him. He looked up in time see Tobias capture her mouth with his. She came as they kissed, and the vampire drank in her scream of pleasure.

In that moment, his mate's velvety channel started convulsing around him, her second orgasm crashing through her. She squeezed his cock like a fist, he couldn't hold back any longer. He pounded into her with a roar, his balls slapping against her ass. She whimpered under him, her orgasm stretching out as he kept stimulating her.

His vision whited out as the most powerful climax he'd ever experienced hit him. He stuttered to a stop, pleasure and magic ricocheting through his body.

For a breathless moment he could feel both Briar's and Tobias's heartbeats sync with his. He could feel their startlement, joy, and pleasure.

This one moment, they were all perfectly connected.

Then he opened his eyes and the connection vanished. Sweat trickled down his face as he leaned forward to claim Briar's mouth for a kiss, then Tobias's. The three of them ended up in a position where their faces were all huddled close together, breathing hard and dazed by the pleasure.

It was Briar who broke the silence.

"That was one hell of a ride. You guys were definitely worth the extra money for the Express Ticket."

Briar woke up overheated. Why had Maddy cranked up the furnace? And why were her covers so heavy?

When she opened her eyes, her vision was filled with russet-colored beard hair and recent events came flooding back.

She wasn't covered in a duvet; she was tucked into Memphis's massive body with Tobias curled up against her back. Tobias was pleasantly warm, but Memphis's body was like a furnace. She'd even sweated enough to dampen the sheet under her.

Not only was she sweltering, but her bladder was full, her throat was dry, and her stomach was empty. She needed to go take care of all those things while she could before Memphis woke up and needed to *bunk like funnies* again.

She cracked herself up.

Not that she was complaining about all the *bunking*. She'd never had so much sex and so many orgasms in such a short period of time. Damn, these guys had rocked her world. Repeatedly.

It took some wiggling and grunting, but she got out from between the two men. Crawling over Tobias, she finally made if off the bed. Memphis grumbled in his sleep and blindly groped around until he found the unnaturally still vampire. He pulled the smaller man to him, snuggling him into a similar position that Briar had been in.

Despite the urgent signals her bladder was sending her, she stood there and admired the men for a moment. They were so adorable cuddled up like that.

Was that the sound of her ovaries exploding from cuteness overload? Yup.

Smiling to herself, she used the bathroom, pulled on one of the robes she found in there, and made her way downstairs. Neither man stirred the entire time.

She understood why Tobias hadn't moved the minute she entered the kitchen. Unlike upstairs and the living room, the kitchen's curtains were drawn and bright early morning sunlight was streaming through. The vampire must be sleeping heavily because of the light.

Would she be able to wake him up enough to get him to feed? Jaynie said the kitchen was stocked, and he'd need three bags of blood every couple of hours until he was back to normal. She'd get some food, check her phone, then take some blood upstairs for him.

She guzzled down two bottles of water as she unpacked the massive amount of food left in bags on the kitchen counter. Her eyes lit up when she came across a box of Danishes from a bakery in Northpark. Oh man, these were the good stuff!

She stopped unpacking in favor of ripping open the bakery box and snatching a flaky pastry. Sweet, buttery flavor exploded across her tongue as she bit into the breakfast food.

Holding the pastry with her mouth, she picked up another one and a third bottle of water then made her way to the kitchen table. She noticed that the bag with Memphis's vest and their phones was there, but also chargers for both her and Memphis's phones. Perfect! She wasn't sure who had been heroic enough to enter the house to drop them there but bless them for their bravery.

She plugged in Memphis's phone, but her phone still had a charge, so she started to check in while she ate. She contacted a few clients to warn them she would be late with their projects.

One pinged her back almost immediately to say that being late was unacceptable and he wouldn't pay. If he'd left it at that she'd probably have let it go. But then he cussed and called her incompetent.

She sent him a link titled *Click Me to Get a Refund*. If he was dumb enough to click on it, he was toast.

She might be a hacker, but she wasn't an asshole, so she was careful to vet her clients. She never did a job without knowing who she was working for and building at least a rudimentary file on them. She didn't mind helping people play it fast and loose with tax evasion, getting some dirt on the competition, or even a little corporate espionage. But there was no way she was going to be party to something really evil like human trafficking.

And because she'd had a feeling about this guy, she'd done more digging than normal on this client, Mr. Joe Nielson. If he clicked on the link, it would set off an automated system that would contact his employer, family, and friends with information about his nefarious wheeling and dealing.

Like that mistress he was keeping in Boca Raton.

And that government official he was bribing to get permits through.

And the CEO he was blackmailing.

She really hoped he clicked that link. The money he paid for projects had been good, but she was tired of his shitty attitude.

While she was bringing up her missed calls list, her phone dinged a notification to tell her that dumb Joe had clicked the link. She wished she could see his face when a single notification popped up on his computer before giving him the blue screen of death:

Ain't karma a bitch?

Grinning, she polished of the second Danish. Licking her fingers clean she scrolled through her missed calls with her other hand. Almost all of them were from her mother. What fresh hell was this?

Ignoring all the missed calls, text messages, and voicemails from her mother, she tapped Lily's number instead.

"Hey Baby Briar," Lily said in her usually cheerful tone. Briar didn't know how Lily managed it. You'd think after having to basically raise her five younger sisters, Lily would be bitter and reluctant to have anything to do with them. But no, Briar's eldest sister was always excited to talk to her, more like a mother than a sibling.

After the last twenty-four hours, it felt good to hear her voice. It sounded so normal that Briar teared up a bit.

"Briar?" Lily's voice turned worried. "Honey?"

"I'm fine," Briar answered and tried to cover up a sniff.

"Are you crying? Why are . . . wait, did mom get ahold of you? I thought for sure you wouldn't answer the phone. I'll talk to her again! I promise—"

"I'm fine," Briar hurried to tell her before Lily could get a good rant going.

Unlike Briar who mostly ignored their mother Tiffany, the rest of the sisters tried to continue to have a relationship with her.

Forever thinking of herself as the seventeen-year-old debutante who got pregnant the night of her sophomore prom, Tiffany never truly transitioned to adulthood. She spent her life focused on her looks and waiting for a prince charming to sweep her off her feet.

But, of course, there were no prince charmings. Only a series of men, some worse than others. Except for the twins, Jasmin and Violet, all the sisters had different fathers. Tiffany was sure that each one was going to be her true love but some didn't even make it an entire year.

Thankfully, Tiffany had been so busy looking for the perfect man that she left the raising of her children to her "first mistake," as she liked to refer to Lily.

She called Briar her "biggest disappointment."

"If it wasn't Mom, then what's got you crying?" Lily demanded. Briar knew that tone. It was Lily's *I will beat anyone who's hurt you* voice. It made Briar smile through her watery eyes.

"Some stuff happened recently," she said slowly, trying to figure out how to explain things to someone who didn't know there were vampires or shifters in the world. "I met a guy. Well, two guys. And it got, um, complicated."

"Hmmm," Lily murmured. "Two guys that you need to pick between or two guys who are together and want to add you to the mix?"

Briar grinned; her sister wasn't a prude. "More like we all three sort of found each other at the same time."

"That sounds like fun," Lily said with a chuckle.

"It was. I think there's more fun on the schedule," Briar quipped, making Lily laugh.

"Then why the sniffles and watery voice?" she asked.

"I think they're going to want more from me than sex," Briar admitted.

"Relationship isn't a dirty word," she said. "Being open to having a boyfriend, or boyfriends in this case, doesn't mean you're going to turn into Mom."

It's the same thing Lily said to her before, but this time, Briar almost wanted to believe her. Almost.

In typical fashion, she changed the subject before Lily could delve any deeper into messy emotional stuff. "Speaking of Mom, what does she want to talk to me about?"

She could hear the mild frustration in Lily's voice when she spoke. "Fine, we can talk about the number one reason all of us are fucked up. She's eager to set one of us up with her new chiropractor. Apparently, he's AH-mazing."

Tiffany was desperate to see all her daughters married to "successful" men. She refused to believe Lily was gay, even though she'd been in a committed relationship with a wonderful woman named Shandra for the last twelve years. And she despaired that any man would ever find Briar and her punk style attractive. According to Tiffany, *Briar was hiding her beauty by trying to be manly.* Whatever that meant.

"I thought she'd given up on me," Briar groused. "Why isn't she trying to set Chrissy up with this guy?"

"Oh, you didn't hear? Chrysanthemum is dating an electrician," Lily told her. "Mark Sampson, or Simpson."

"Sawyerson," Briar corrected. "She's still seeing that guy? I thought for sure she'd break up after Mom met him. Is Chrissy finally standing up to Mom?"

"Stop calling her that, you know she hates it," Lily reminded her. "And I guess Mark cleans up really well and makes good money. He told Mom all about the car he wants to buy Chrysanthemum, so he's got her stamp of approval."

"Well damn, good for him," Briar said. "I met him last week. He's got good taste in beer."

Lily snorted out a laugh. "Your approval criteria is almost as bad as Mom's, but in the opposite direction."

They talked for a little longer before Lily got called away. As usual, Briar felt better after talking to her oldest sister. She checked on a few more things, making sure nothing was going into meltdown.

There was nothing going on that needed her attention, so she was free to finish up in the kitchen and then take some blood up to Tobias.

A sound made her look up to find Memphis standing in the doorway, unabashedly naked and looking worried.

"You okay there, motorcycle man?" she asked as she set down the phone and stood up. Once she rounded the counter, she could fully see him. His beautiful, thick cock was at half-mast with his balls hanging heavy below. All that was surrounded by a lovely nest of dark, russet hair. When she got a little closer, she felt magic bleeding off him, rubbing along her skin and making her hyperaware of his nakedness.

He was gripping the door jamb with one hand. His other arm was across his chest with his hand gripping his shoulder. It was a posture that screamed anxiety.

"Do you hate me now?" he whispered, his eyes dropping to the floor between them.

Briar was shocked that he'd think that. "No, of course not."

She tried to reach out to embrace him, but he took a step back. He was still staring holes in the floor and his eyes were blinking rapidly.

"If you touch me, the rut will start again. It isn't over yet, this is only a break," he said grimly.

She stopped trying to touch him, but wished he'd at least look at her. "I promise I'm not mad or anything like that. You're a chimera, right? So ruts happen. It's all normal."

Her words didn't have the desired effect. He shook his head and crossed his other arm over his chest to grab the opposite shoulder, hugging himself. "But I wasn't gentle. I wasn't like a good human boyfriend would be. I was going to find you and take you on dates. I wanted you to see that I could be a good mate."

She ignored the term "mate" and focused on the fear and insecurity in his words. This wasn't the wise cracking, blunt, and confident Memphis she was used to. Or the boldly sexual male she'd experienced last night. This version of Memphis, who shied away from her touch was uncertain and afraid.

"We're good," she rushed to assure him. "You didn't hurt me and when this is all over, we can go back to the way things were. No harm, no foul, right?"

"Sure," he mumbled. "I'm going to shower and go back to bed. If you leave, my chimera will need to hunt you down and bring you back. But after the rut's over, I'll have more control of him. I don't have to touch you, but please don't leave the house until it's all over."

She belatedly realized she was doing a shit job of comforting Memphis. She had to do better. He was in a vulnerable place and needed more from her. She barreled into him without giving him any warning, wrapping her arms around his neck. She hugged him tight, trapping his arms between their bodies. He froze in her embrace, his eyes flying to meet hers.

She gave him a peck on the nose. "Let me show instead of tell, because I suck at words."

"Show?" he croaked. Between them, she felt his cock come to full attention and press against her.

"Fuck me, motorcycle man," she demanded. "I want to see if that delicious cock of yours can reach all the right places."

She'd half expected him to act immediately. To take her to the floor and dive between her legs. So when he stayed there, with her arms wrapped around him, she was a little surprised. She was about to let go and drop when he moved.

Slowly, as if he was afraid he'd spook her, he pulled his arms out from between them and wrapped them around her. Holding her tight against his body, he started swaying a little, as if they were dancing to music only he could hear. She kept her arms around his neck and moved with him.

She'd been ready to get pounded but ended up doing a senior prom slow dance. It was romantic enough to make her melt against him a little.

"My mind is all messed up right now," he told her as they moved. "One moment, it feels like everything is in hyperfocus, and I could conquer the world if I wanted to. Then my brain will get foggy and there's nothing but threats everywhere and if either you or Tobias leave my sight something bad will happen."

"Hey, I've got you," Briar said. "You don't need to worry. I'm not going to judge you or anything."

"But what if I can't bring the 'normal me' back?" Real fear crept into his voice. "What if I'm stuck like this? This doesn't feel like the ruts I've gone through before. This one is so much more intense. My head never felt as mixed up before. What if something's wrong with me?"

"Then we'll figure it out," she said with confidence. "And it's only been a day. These things last for a few days, right?"

"Usually," Memphis agreed.

"Well then, we wait a few more days before we start worrying. Until then, let's enjoy ourselves. Life's too short to waste on something as useless as regret."

He let out a long exhale and his body relaxed slightly as he stopped the swaying movements. "Yeah, okay."

Pulling her arms from around his neck, she framed his face with her hands and waited patiently for him to open his eyes. When he finally lifted his lids and met her gaze, she smiled at him.

"I've got you," she promised. "I won't let anything happen to you. Both you and Tobias are safe."

His eyes bored into hers. "But are you going to leave me when this is all over?"

She refused to lie, even to spare him, but she hoped to soften the blow. "I don't know how this will end. But I'll promise this; I won't ghost you. We'll talk. We'll hang out. I won't disappear on you."

She expected gloom or dejection from Memphis, but instead, his expression turned gentle. "As long as you don't vanish, we can make this work. The three of us together."

It was good to see his expression hopeful again. Going up on her toes, she meant to place a quick kiss on his lips, but his broad hand captured the back of her head and the kiss turned heated.

His cock had softened as they danced and talked, but now it hardened, a baseball bat pushing against her stomach. It was both a relief to be back on familiar ground and also exciting to think that Memphis was going to sink that beast inside her again.

It was a good thing she was on birth control because all three of them were displaying the sexual common sense of horny teenagers fumbling in the back of the family minivan.

"I need you," he growled as his magic tingled along her skin.

"Yes," she agreed.

A shudder rolled through him. "I want to be rough. Tell me no if you don't want that. We can go upstairs."

"I like it rough sometimes," she whispered.

The hand holding the back of her head dropped to her waist. "I might not be able to stop after we start."

She smiled up at him, feeling all kinds of gentle emotions for the chimera. "I trust you, Memphis."

His hand on her waist tightened briefly before she felt another wave of magic roll over her. Memphis's eyes flashed with power. Then, without warning, he reached up and ripped the robe off her.

She jerked a little from the speed of his movements but didn't ask him to stop. His big body backed her up until her butt hit the kitchen countertop. His strong hands spun her around and a hand between her shoulder blades bent her over. The countertop felt cold against her breasts and cheek, a sharp contrast to Memphis's hot hands.

He gently kicked her feet apart and stepped between her spread legs. His fat cock nudged her opening, and she reached out to grab the edge of the counter over her head to help brace herself. That nudge was all the warning she got before Memphis thrust into her with barely controlled violence.

It should have hurt, but she was already so worked up that it felt good. Oh, so good!

"Memphis," she moaned out.

"I'm going to fuck you," he growled as he held himself still, his massive dick deep inside her. "I'm going to fill you with my cum until it's dripping down your legs. Then I'm going to make you stay like that all day. No cleaning up. No washing me off. I'm going to make sure every other creature on this earth can smell me on you. My female. My territory. Mine!"

Tension and desire built inside her with every word he spoke. She'd never experienced this level of sexual aggression and damned if it didn't turn her on. Not that it took much for Tobias or Memphis to get her hot, but this was a fun new facet to their dynamic.

"Please," she begged. "Move!"

He took his time pulling out, but when he thrust forward again, it was with the same amount of ferocity as before. He pushed her hard against the counter, pinning her with his erection.

Leaning over her body, he put his lips to her ear. "You're going to take everything I give you like a good girl."

"I've never been a good girl," she shot back, annoyed that he wasn't moving more.

"You will be for me," he answered and stood back up, pulling himself free of her body.

She tried to stand up straight. "What the hell—"

One of his hands on her back kept her bent over while the other cracked against her ass. The blow was so fast it didn't even start to register until he'd shoved his thick cock back inside her. He started moving with purpose, pushing in deep and pulling out in a rhythm that promised a big payoff.

She wanted to complain, to tell him to fuck off with the idea he could spank her. But the problem was that it hadn't hurt as much as heightened everything. The flesh where the slap had landed throbbed slightly, but it only made everything else she was feeling all that much better.

Was she a damn masochist and didn't even realize it?

Whatever, it didn't matter. What was important was how close she was to an orgasm.

Leaning his bigger body over hers, he worked one arm underneath her while he pushed his other hand between her legs. The arm beneath her held her tight against his chest as his hips increased in tempo. The hand between her legs slid along her sex until he found her clit.

She expected him to start rubbing but he pinched it instead. Unprepared for the sensation, she cried out and bucked under him. "That's it," he said, voice heavy with lust. "Struggle."

Oh, he wanted her to fight back a little? She grinned; she could give him that.

Grunting with the effort, she got a hand free and went for his face. He tucked his head against her back and moved to trap both her arms with his one. It took some effort, but eventually he managed to get both her wrists in one hand. Stretching her arms up over her head, he held her immobile.

At the beginning of the struggle, the fingers between her legs had started stroking. They never stopped and now she was panting, sweating, and unbelievably turned on.

"You are mine!" he roared, his hips pistoning faster.

He had her so well secured that she couldn't even raise her head, not that she wanted to. There was no more fight in her as the pleasure built in her belly. She tilted her hips a little, trying to get his fingers to press harder.

"Come for me," he demanded, his voice a deep animal growl. She felt sharp teeth run along her back and then a bite on her shoulder. He didn't break skin, but it was enough pressure to know he was leaving some marks.

Why did that feel so good?

Gasping for breath, she tried to hold back her orgasm. She wanted him to come first. Wanted him to lose control. He must have guessed what she was doing because he bit her again and kept pounding into her.

The pleasure hit her like an electrical charge, zapping through her body and making her eyes water. She opened her mouth in a silent scream as a powerful climax made her vision blur.

He made a triumphant sound against her shoulder as he bit down a last time. After releasing her flesh, he whispered, "I win."

She wanted to clap back, but she was too busy pulling air into her lungs. Letting go of her hand, Memphis straightened up and grabbed her hips. His pace got faster, and she was dimly aware of the sound of flesh slapping against flesh.

His grip tightened, his hips lost rhythm and warmth flooded her pussy.

As he came, she climaxed again. Or maybe it was the tail end of one long climax. She couldn't be sure. All she knew was that she didn't even need his fingers on her clit at the moment.

"Mine!" be bellowed, his voice so loud the guards outside could probably hear him.

"Yes," she whispered and closed her eyes, too content to think about anything beyond this moment. "Yours."

Panting, Memphis came back to himself. Briar was limp, her entire body supported by the kitchen counter. Gently, he pulled himself free and leaned over to check in with his littlest mate.

"Baby Doll, are you okay?" he asked. She blinked open her eyes, expression dazed.

"Fuuuuuck," she breathed out. "Bring me a blanket and pillow, I'm going to bed down right here. After that wild ride, walking isn't an option." She closed her eyes before she continued talking. "But come get me for the next round, I don't want to miss out. Especially if it's all three of us."

Relief made Memphis chuckle. "No sleeping in the kitchen."

With the same care he used to carry Tobias when they'd left the bar, he picked Briar up and cradled her to his chest. He left the bathrobe puddled on the floor and easily carried her back up into the bedroom. She petted his beard and mumbled something about how soft it was as he walked to the bedroom.

When he moved to lay her on the bed, she wrinkled her nose. "Do you want to be on the other side?" he asked. "Tobias can be the meat in the sandwich instead of you."

"That's not it," she admitted, rolling her head against his chest to look up at him. "I feel grungy. I want to get clean, but I'm too relaxed to stand."

Enthusiasm filled him and he set her on the bed. "I can fix that. Stay here, I'll be right back."

She mumbled something as he hurried into the master bath and turned on the tub taps. The thing was large with jets, perfect for bathing his tired female. When the tub was half full, he went back to fetch her. She was still awake, but barely. He worried that he should have left her to sleep until he slid her into the water.

A low, long moan came out of her that made his cock twitch as her body settled in the water.

Sinking down so the rapidly rising water covered most of her, she rested her head on the lip of the tub, her hands floating on either side of her. "Oh man, this feels good."

On one end of the long vanity was a stack of white towels. Grabbing one he rolled it, then lifted her head and put it between her and the hard tile of the tub.

"Thanks," she mumbled, never once opening her eyes.

The water was high enough now that he turned off the taps. He soaped up a washcloth and diligently cleaned his mate. He didn't neglect an inch of her. When he cleaned between her legs and she shuddered, his rut tried to rise up. But both the human and animal part of him could see that Briar was exhausted and needed rest. That was enough to quell the desire.

"You could make a fortune doing this," she said when he started massaging her feet. "You're really good."

Pleasure washed through him at her words as he replied, "Only for you Baby Doll. You'll always get the best I have to offer, including rub downs. Now and forever."

He felt her tense. "There's no such thing as forever, Memphis." She didn't open her eyes as she mumbled those words out.

He understood her struggle and didn't take those words to heart. Instead, he kept his tone light. "That's true. In about eight billion years, our sun will turn into a white dwarf and all life on earth will die."

She relaxed back into his grip as she snorted out a laugh, finally opening her eyes and lifting her head to look at him. "So you're giving us eight billion years?"

"Eight billion years in this lifetime," he countered. "Who knows where our souls will go from there. But wherever you float off to, Tobias and I will be right behind you."

She grinned and let her head flop back down on the rolled-up towel. "You're such a romantic bastard. I bet you read those romance books and everything."

"Don't knock 'em until you try 'em," he said, setting one foot back in the water and picking up the other one to start rubbing. "There are preternatural authors out there that write all this sexy shit about us shifters and everyone thinks they're making it all up. The stories are good and the sex is hot. I'll lend you a few, and you'll be addicted in no time."

"Learn something new every day," she said as her head lolled to the side. "Memphis has a collection of smutty novels. Who would've guessed?"

Her words were starting to slur a little. He needed to finish up and get her into bed. Letting go of her foot, he opened up the drain and then stood up. He leaned over and grasped her under the arms.

"Up you go," he said as he gently lifted her to her feet.

"Nooooo," she whined. "Wanna sleep here."

Huffing out a laugh, he set her on her feet on the bathmat. "Trust me, that won't end well."

"Whatever," she mumbled. She didn't open her eyes as he dried her off, then rubbed lotion over every inch of her delectable dark skin. Damn he loved the contrast between his pale, freckled self, and her flawless tan flesh.

When he was done, he lifted her into his arms to carry her back to the bed, and his chimera practically purred when she rubbed her cheek on his chest.

"Love the smell of you," she murmured.

It wasn't a declaration of undying love or a promise of commitment, but he'd take what he could get. "I love everything about you, Baby Doll."

"You shouldn't," she mumbled, her head lolling to the side. "Not lovable."

Those few words made his heart break. He knew the words were a direct result of her childhood. And that was the biggest hurdle he and Tobias had to overcome to convince her that this relationship was real and could work.

"Not true," he whispered as he settled in the center of the bed next to Tobias. She curled up on her side, snuggling close to him. Memphis eased himself down next to her and framed her smaller body with his massive one. Reaching across her, he rested a hand on Tobias's chest so he could be touching both his mates.

She was asleep before he even finished getting settled, but maybe his words would register in her subconscious.

"You're worthy of all our love and so much more. Maddy and the rest of your found family love you without reservations. Tobias literally wants to share his soul with you, and I'd die to protect both of you. You're loved, Baby Doll. Deeply and irrevocably. I plan to spend the rest of my life showing you that you can trust me enough to love me back."

The moment the sun dropped below the horizon Tobias's body urged him to wake. Sitting up, he found his flock sound asleep in the bed with him. Briar was curled against his side with Memphis behind her, his long arm draped over her hip and his hand resting on Tobias's belly. Ignoring his hunger, he gave himself a moment to gaze at his flock.

They were both different but so perfect. Where Memphis was big with the bulging muscles that came with being a chimera shifter, Briar was soft and round. The fine hairs that covered her body were almost invisible, making her look smooth and flawless. That juxtaposed nicely with Memphis, who had a lovely thick pelt covering his chest and abdomen, not to mention the beard taking up half his face.

His flock couldn't be more different or fit together better. Unlike their physical appearance, Briar and Memphis's auras looked similar. They were strong with hints of vulnerability in the soft yellow interspersed with the powerfully glowing purples and blues. Both his flock would need to be watched over and cared for so those ribbons of yellow weren't allowed to grow.

He traced Briar's many tattoos with his eyes, recognizing most of the various plants that covered her shoulders, arms, and torso. He grinned. They were all poisonous and depicted with bright clarity on her tan skin. The colorful tattoos went well with her brightly dyed hair and fierce personality.

Unable to help himself, he reached out to rub a hank of Briar's hair with his thumb and fingers. When he'd first seen her, it had been gelled into stiff spikes, but now it lay around her head in short, fat curls. The vibrant turquoise color made him smile even as the soft silky strands made him want to bury his face and nuzzle her hair.

Letting go of her hair, he looked over to Memphis. Like Briar, he was covered in colorful tattoos. He recognized some of them as images from chimera lore. One arm was entirely taken up with depicting the first chimera being born from an underwater volcano and emerging from the sea, steam coming off his body as he roared at the world.

His flock was a colorful one, and he looked forward to finding all kinds of ways to spoil them. But right now he needed sustenance. He had vague memories of Memphis and Briar waking him periodically and holding bags of blood to his lips.

He'd be at full strength soon and caring for his flock as a vampire should.

Although Memphis made a grumpy sound when he eased the chimera's hand off and scooted away, he didn't fully wake up. Wrapping that muscled limb around Briar, he hugged her closer and settled right back down.

The whole scene made Tobias's heart speed up a little. A vampire was lucky when he found one member of his flock, but it was rare to find two at the same time. He was going to make sure he didn't squander this gift.

Unconcerned with his nude state, Tobias made his way downstairs. The kitchen was a mess and the faint scent of sex hung in the air. His flock had had some fun while he'd been asleep. Grinning, he opened the fridge and pulled out four bags of blood. He consumed them quickly, enjoying the way it felt to feed. He'd never take the act for granted again.

The sound of a body hitting the floor upstairs made him drop the last empty bag to the floor and practically fly back to the second floor as he took the stairs in three long jumping strides.

He entered the bedroom ready to do battle only to find no enemy. Looking grumpy, Memphis was on his butt on the floor next to the bed, his feet tangled in the sheets. Briar was leaning over the edge, blinking sleepily at him. Her body was oddly positioned crossways on the bed and Tobias surmised that when Memphis fell and took some of the sheets with him, he shifted Briar's body over at the same time.

"Are you hurt?" Tobias asked as he knelt at the chimera's feet and untangled his legs.

"Only my pride," Memphis grumped, making Briar laugh.

"What were you trying to do?" she asked and started tugging off the sheets wrapped around her body so she could re-position herself in the bed.

"I needed to take a piss, and I didn't want to wake you up." He gestured to the edge of the bed. "I thought I'd work myself over to the edge of the bed and put a foot down to roll out without having to sit up and jostle you."

Tobias chuckled as he knelt down and pulled the sheet away, freeing Memphis. "My poor male, tossed to the floor by a humble set of sheets."

Memphis didn't respond to his teasing, and when he looked up, he found both Briar and the shifter staring at him with wide yes. "What?"

"You're talking," Briar stated as a wide, happy smile uncurled across her face. "You're talk-talking. Full sentences and shit."

Reaching out, Memphis dragged Tobias into a hug. "This is great."

Nodding, Tobias hugged him back. He felt the chimera let go with one arm and shift a little. There was a little gasp of surprise and then Briar was part of the hug.

"Warn a girl," she said even as she wrapped her arms around them as best as she could. It was awkward but also perfect.

Without any effort, Memphis got his feet under him and stood. He took the half step to the bed and sat, still holding the two of them.

Now securely back on the bed, Briar pulled back a little to grin at the chimera. "Show off." Then she focused her gaze on him. "Can you remember what happened? At the bar, I mean. How you ended up in the basement."

Tobias thought about it for a moment. He let his mind ease into the memories. After the first few stuttered into place, they flowed smoothly.

"Hal Sheridan was a man I thought of as a friend. I'd known him for years and we owned several businesses together, including the restaurant you found me in," Tobias explained as the memories shaped into a clear series of events. "What year is it?"

Memphis looked sad but Briar told him, making Tobias realize how much time had passed while he'd been held captive in that basement.

"Right, so ten years ago, Hal asked me to visit Il Crepuscule while it was closed getting ready for the dinner crowd. When I arrived, there was no staff cleaning or prepping, but I thought perhaps I'd hit the exact moment when the day staff and evening staff were changing over. He offered me some blood, and I didn't think anything of it. He kept a supply for me in a small, locked fridge in his office."

"It was laced with something, wasn't it?" Briar asked, her expression grim.

"How could you know that?" Tobias asked, startled.

Briar's face turned hard. "When me and my girlfriends go out, I'm the one who makes sure no one gets roofied."

"Roofied?" Tobias asked but even as the question came out of his mouth, the information about date-rape drugs and Rohypnol filtered into his brain. "Yes, I was roofied. With microscopic silver shards suspended in the blood. I only took one swallow, but that was enough."

Memphis hissed out a breath. "You drank silver? If you'd been a younger or less powerful vampire, you wouldn't have survived that."

Tobias nodded. "He would have done less damage if he'd stabbed me with a silver blade. I fell to the floor and my body started seizing. I didn't even have time to throw it up before it incapacitated me."

"Don't vamps normally take a sample with a fang before drinking?" Memphis asked.

"Yes, usually," Tobias admitted. "I made the mistake of thinking I could trust the source. And I love the first rush of blood when a large swallow slides down your throat, so I didn't hesitate."

"And the chains?" Briar pressed. "Why didn't he kill you and get it over with? Why chain you in the basement? Was he a sick bastard or something?"

"No doubt he was, but the chains and basement cage have an alternate explanation: greed. He wanted me gone so he could gain controlling shares of the businesses we owned and thought he'd make even more money by selling me to a tooth-puller."

Memphis looked disgusted, but Briar's face was pure confusion. "Tooth-puller? Like a dentist?"

That made both of them laugh. "No, my sweet one, tooth-puller is a term for a vampire hunter."

"Vampire hunter, like religious zealots who think you're evil or something?"

"They started out as secret order in early medieval Europe," Memphis explained. "They focused on finding the Children of Lilith."

"Hold up, Children of Lilith?" Briar asked.

Tobias grinned. "Our lore says we started with Lilith, the first wife of Adam."

Briar looked even more confused. "I'm not religious or anything, but wasn't that Eve?"

"There were two women before Eve, one of them being Lilith," Tobias explained. "She took one look at Adam and said no way and went off on her own. In our legends, she's believed to have founded our kind."

"If she was a woman with power, then of course she was demonized by the church," Briar muttered. "Anyway, enough about that. Why call a tooth-puller person? Why not just off you himself? Was he super religious or something?"

Memphis explained before he could. "Tooth-pullers aren't religious zealots anymore. At first, they were about hunting down evil, but later they figured out they could make money off vampires. That's when the order went from religious to a business. They look for young vampires mostly, ones who can't really defend themselves. Then they incapacitate them and sell their parts off to the highest bidder. There's a lot of powerful magic you can perform with a vampire heart, or blood, or other parts."

"Why do you call them Tooth-pullers?"

"Because they like to pull out the vampire's fangs as trophies," Memphis said with disgust. "Sick bastards."

"I'm impressed you know that," Tobias commented. "Most people don't know the roots of the tooth-pullers, only what they do."

Memphis gave him a small, pleased grin. "I'm best friends with a fang-face. We've spent some time talking over drinks, and he's told me some about vampire history."

He wasn't back to his full self, which meant his control was shaky. Knowing Memphis was friends with another vampire made his body heat with a sudden and intense rage.

Between one breath and the next he'd grabbed Memphis by the back of the head and wrenched it to the side, exposing his muscled neck.

"You're mine!" he hissed and bared his fangs.

On the other side of Memphis, Briar made a startled sound and grabbed his wrist, trying to free Memphis. "Tobias!"

"You're both mine!" His fangs had fully descended and made speaking hard. It was only long practice that kept him from cutting his tongue on one of the sharp fangs.

Instead of letting go of his wrist, Briar pulled back her other fist, as if to punch him. He waited, prepared to grab her hand before it reached his face. He would use that hold to drag her across Memphis. When she was off balance, he'd subdue her and—

"Let him go!" Briar let her hand fly, but it was Memphis who stopped her blow from connecting with Tobias's face.

Briar tried to pull her hand free. "What the hell Memphis? I was trying to help."

"He's not going to hurt me," Memphis said, his voice calm and soothing. He kept still under Tobias's grip and tugged Briar a little closer, so she half ended up on his lap. The move caused him to let go of the hand he was using to hold Memphis's head at a severe angle.

"Not going to hurt you? He went all aggro and was going to bite you!"

"He might be talking like he's back to normal, but he's not. It's going to be a few weeks before he's really recovered. And he's found his flock; that's a strain on any vampire's control. You have to know he'd never hurt me."

"I don't know," Briar snapped. "You can see his eyes, they're bright red."

"And he hasn't bitten me, has he?" Memphis pointed out. "Let me talk to him. Calm him down before you go looking for a knife down in the kitchen to gut him with."

"Fuck it, fine," she cursed, and Tobias saw her stop struggling against Memphis.

The chimera let go of her hand and started rubbing his hand down her arm in a long petting motion. "It's going to be okay," he said to her.

"Whatever." Despite her dismissive tone, her gaze stayed focused on his fangs.

She was frowning, and her body language was still bordering on aggressive, but he could tell she was scared of him.

No vampire wanted his flock to be afraid of him. He needed to stop. Needed to pull away to show Briar that he was a reasonable man.

But he couldn't.

Another vampire had been near his chimera. Potentially even touched a member of his flock. He had to claim Memphis. Had to make sure everyone knew who Memphis belonged to. And Memphis must understand because he wasn't fighting Tobias's hold and didn't look fearful or upset.

"Tobias, you don't need to worry," Memphis murmured as he relaxed into Tobias's hold. "Soren has his own flock. He's only ever been a friend. And now I think fate made him and me friends so he could teach me about vampires. So he could teach me how to take care of you."

His calm, soothing words helped pull Tobias back from his rage. He shuddered, the gums around his fangs throbbing. His instinct was to bite. To put his mark on Memphis. Make it so anyone who saw him would clearly see who he belonged to.

But that was something a monster would do.

Panting, he dropped his head until he could rest his forehead on Memphis's neck. He could feel the chimera's blood pumping through his veins. Feel the shifter's powerful magic snapping between them as it came into contact with his own.

It worried him that even though he'd taken his lips away from Memphis's neck, the fangs hadn't receded.

He tried to reassure Memphis that he was in control again even if his body wasn't entirely obeying him. "Mine."

Fear rose up in him when Tobias realized his words were escaping him again. No! He needed his words. His flock needed his words. He didn't want to go back to that mindless thing from before.

"You can bite me," Memphis said, continuing to talk in a quiet, deep voice that sunk into Tobias, grounding him. "It will make you feel better and help cement our bond until you're ready to share souls. Taste my blood, sweetheart. I promise you won't hurt me."

Memphis's permission was all it took for him to lose his tenuous control. Closing his eyes, his fangs unerringly found Memphis's vein and pierced the chimera's thick skin. Memphis moaned, his solid body shaking with pleasure.

This was the way it was between a vampire and his flock. Biting wasn't about feeding; it was about passion. The chimera was feeling the natural result of vampire magic let loose on someone they cared about.

Raw, passionate power built between them, so strong that it bordered on painful. The moment Memphis's blood entered his system, stars exploded behind his eyelids. He'd never tasted blood so powerful or so sweet.

"Memphis? Tobias?" Briar's worried voice helped bring Tobias back.

Content after only taking a sip from Memphis's body, Tobias pulled away and licked the wounds closed. The small amount of blood he'd swallowed from the shifter was rocketing through his body, making him pulse with the strength of it.

"I'm okay, Baby Doll," Memphis told her in a husky voice. Although Tobias drew away from Memphis's neck, the chimera didn't move to straighten up. "I'm better than okay, I'm fucking fantastic."

Tobias stroked Memphis with the hand he'd used to wrench his neck to the side, silently telling him that he could move now. It was with a sigh of regret that Memphis straightened up. His face was flushed and his eyelids heavy.

"Anytime you want another little snack," he said in a lazy drawl. "Help yourself."

Tobias was scared to look over at Briar, but when he finally forced his gaze to move, he found her looking at him with curiosity but no fear.

"That wasn't a hunger thing?" she asked.

"That was a territorial reaction thing," Memphis said before Tobias could even open his mouth. "Vampires are really protective of their flock, which makes sense if you think of us being his biggest weakness. It was instinctual that he wouldn't want me to be around anyone who might hurt me as a way to get to him. That kind of biting isn't about feeding, it's about claiming."

Briar moved until she could see where he'd bitten Memphis. She even touched the chimera's neck. "There aren't any marks though. I can't even tell where he bit you."

Memphis moved his hand to rub at the spot Tobias had bitten. "That's not where he left a mark. You can't tell, but my aura is saturated with his now. Any other preternatural creature that comes near me will be able to see me covered in vampire power." Memphis flashed a bright smile. "Between the sex and biting, I'm so covered in vampire that someone might mistake me for one."

Briar let out a loud sigh, her shoulders slumping a little. "There's lot going on here that I don't understand, isn't there?"

"Probably," Memphis agreed. "But no one's going to force you to do anything you don't want to do, Baby Doll."

"I'm starting to think that's not my biggest worry," she muttered mysteriously under her breath.

After watching Memphis's eyes flutter closed and hearing his moan as Tobias bit him, Briar was tempted to ask for a turn. The fact that she was equal parts turned on and terrified meant she kept her mouth shut.

She'd hung out with shifters, pixies, witches, and a bunch of other preternatural creatures, but this was the first time she felt overwhelmed. She'd always known there was a big power gap between herself and the preternaturals she interacted with. When one of the shifters picked up a dumpster and carried it because three of the four wheels had stopped working, she didn't even bat an eye. When Izzy levitated so she could reach something on a top shelf, Briar had jokingly asked for a ride.

But now, faced with a man she was both attracted to and afraid of, she finally realized she hadn't truly understood their world.

Before now, everything had been black and white. Easily divided between friend or foe. Family and not-family. Then Tobias had threatened to hurt Memphis, and everything went sideways.

He'd gone from mild mannered and talkative to a red-eyed monster in .0001 seconds flat. How was she supposed to correlate the two different versions of Tobias? How was she supposed to relax around a vampire who could hurt Memphis? Worse yet, the chimera wouldn't even try to stop him!

It was all too much.

"Baby Doll," Memphis whispered to her, drawing her focus to his golden-brown eyes. "I need to know what you're thinkin' right now."

"I can't do this." She hadn't meant to say that out loud, but the words popped out of her mouth before she could think them through.

Tobias made a pained sound and dropped off the bed. At first, she thought he'd suddenly become ill. Was he having a weird reaction to drinking chimera blood?

Then he prostrated himself in front of her, his forehead touching one of her feet that was hanging off the bed.

"Not leave me," he begged, his words coming out in bursts between sobs. "Be better. Be more controlled."

Fuck, now she felt like the monster!

Her guilt escalated when Memphis cast her a disappointed look before he pushed her off his lap onto the bed next to him. When her foot shifted, Tobias followed it, continuing his sobs and begging.

"He wouldn't have hurt me. He'd never hurt either of us," Memphis said before sliding off the bed. He pulled the distraught vampire between his legs and murmured soothing words. Tobias didn't fight him as Memphis drew the vampire to his chest. He stopped sobbing but she could see dark trails and black, pearlescent tears dripping off his face.

"He's not recovered yet," Memphis reminded her, his voice soft but his expression upset. "Try to put yourself in his place. Yesterday he couldn't talk. The day before that, he was waiting to die. And now he's been rescued and found his flock all at the same time."

When he put it like that, Briar realized how narrow-minded she was being. Tobias had PTSD, and she was acting like he needed to just get over it.

Damn, when did she become her mother?

Shifting to the floor, she moved to sit in front of where Memphis and Tobias were cuddling on the floor.

"I'm sorry," she whispered. Tobias didn't talk, but his wary expression said it all. She'd managed to traumatize someone struggling with mental health issues. She rubbed a hand over her face, trying to figure out how to undo the damage she'd done.

"Look, I didn't have the best example of healthy relationships growing up," she started. Maybe if she explained a little about her past, Tobias might understand. Even if he didn't comprehend all her words, she hoped he'd hear the sincerity in her voice.

"Tell us about it," Memphis requested. It was a relief to meet his eyes and find kindness there instead of accusation.

"Um, this might take a minute," she warned him. "It's a little complicated."

That made Memphis snort out a laugh. "You think that's going to scare us, Baby Doll?" he asked. "You're going to have to do a hell of a lot better than having a complicated history to make us want to leave."

Although she shrugged off his words, she felt warmed by them inside. "So I'm the youngest of six girls. Lily's the oldest, there's Rose next, then the twins Jasmin and Violet, Chrysanthemum, and finally me."

"I see a theme in the names," Memphis commented. "Except for your name, Briar Thorn isn't a flower. I have a feeling that the reason for that isn't a good one."

"And you'd be right," she agreed, deciding to lay herself open to these two men. They might as well know all the shitty details. "But let me tell you about Mom first. She grew up in South Carolina and was very much the southern belle. She had only one goal, marry some rich, well-connected guy and be a socialite. She talked her parents into sending her to this expensive, elite high school so she could meet the sons of rich, powerful families. Her plan half worked when she met the perfect guy, but when she got pregnant, the guy's parents weren't interested in their son marrying some lower, middle-class girl from a no name family. They pushed her to have an abortion."

"But she didn't?" Memphis asked.

"She refused. The few times I've heard Mom talk about it; I think she was convinced that once she gave birth, the family would change their minds. Spoiler alert, they didn't. Not only did they not want anything to do with Lily after she was born, but they were so pissed they got Mom ostracized from the community. They had to pay child support; there was no way to get around that, but they made it so that she wasn't welcome anywhere. Mom's parents lost their jobs and their house ended up getting foreclosed on."

Memphis blew out a long breath. "Damn, that's vindictive. What did she do?"

"She did what would become the pattern for the rest of her life, she found another guy," Briar explained. "I think his name was Ted. He lasted the longest. Lily was almost five when he left, but she only remembers him as the guy who smelled like butterscotch. When Mom got pregnant, he vanished. But the child support for Lily and welfare kept them housed and fed until she recovered from Rose's birth and found another guy. He moved her, Lily, and Rose out here. After about a year, he kicked her out and she had to find another man. That became the pattern."

"Did these men . . . were any of them . . ." Memphis gave her a helpless, pained look as he struggled to ask her the same question a lot of people had asked her over the years.

"None of us were ever sexually assaulted," Briar told him, watching twin expressions of relief form on their faces. She didn't add that the only reason that never happened was because Tiffany was so jealous and possessive of the men that she dated that if any of them paid the kids too much attention she'd get upset. In a weird way, her possessiveness inadvertently kept her daughters safe.

"She ended up marrying one guy, the twins' father. But he was almost forty years older than her and retired. He didn't have much and when he died of a heart attack, we found out they hadn't been married long enough for her to get much of his retirement. Mom went a little crazy and spent all her spare time at bars or places where she could meet men. The twins weren't even two and she was never home. Lily was the one taking care of everybody. She was about seven or eight years old at that point, but she did everything."

"Everything?" Memphis asked.

"Yeah, you know. Changed the twins' diapers, fixed their bottles, did laundry, cleaned the house, and took care of Rose. Lily learned early to hide money away if she could because Mom would spend it on dresses and make-up."

Memphis gave her a sad smile. "Smart girl, your sister."

"The smartest," Briar agreed. "She's a CPA, even has a super fancy office over in La Jolla."

"I'm pretty sure you're just as smart, Baby Doll," Memphis insisted. "Don't forget, you've helped me find people a couple of times. I've seen what you can do."

Briar felt her face get hot. "I've got some tricks, but I'm not like Lily. She's got a degree and everything."

Memphis looked like he wanted to disagree, so she rushed to change the subject. "Chrissy, Chrysanthemum, was born next. Lily thinks her dad was a drug dealer or something because he was all about buying mom bling but didn't want to be around her kids. She lived the highlife with him for a while. And he even gave her a bunch of cash when Chrissy was born, but then he disappeared. The police laughed when she tried to file a missing person's report on him." Briar shook her head in disgust. "How a twenty-eight-year-old woman who'd had five kids by that point could think that Ajax Strongman was someone's real name is beyond me."

Both Tobias and Memphis grinned briefly when she said that, making it easier to tell the next part.

"Then she met my dad. She'd only dated white guys up 'til then, but Alejandro said he was a member of a really wealthy family back in Argentina. His father was making him live on his own for a few years before he let Alejandro take over the family business." She rolled her eyes. "Mom believed every word. He moved in with us and never contributed because it was only a matter of time before he went home and lived the life of luxury."

"Sounds like a scam," Memphis commented.

"It was one hundred precent a scam. One of the things that led to my current occupation was tracking that guy down when I was a teenager. It took some time, but I found his family. His parents are dirt poor and living in the slums of Buenos Aires. During the course of my tracking, I found a clear line of women that he'd pulled this scam with. Most of them were way more well-off than Tiffany, but I guess he was a little desperate at the time. So Mom gets pregnant, and he pretends to be all happy and excited. He even tells her that when she gives him a son, he'll take us south and present the boy to his parents. They'll get married and Tiffany will get to live like a princess in Argentina."

"Why make a big deal about wanting a son?" Memphis asked.

"No idea," Briar said. "It wasn't like he was going to stick around even if I'd been male instead of female. He ended up taking off right after Mom found out I was a girl. It wasn't hard to piece together that he'd found a better sugar mama. But Mom was sure he left because of me. Added bonus was that she started hemorrhaging after I was born, and they had to perform a hysterectomy. To her, I was the reason she lost her best chance at a happy ending, and I took away her ability to have children."

"How could she be so dumb as to blame you for any of that?" Memphis asked and Tobias made a sound of agreement

Briar gave him a bitter smile. "It's how her brain works. For her, the only way to succeed in life was to have a rich man. Part of getting a rich man was having his kid, and I took that away from her."

Understanding dawned on Memphis's face. "So instead of naming you after a flower, she named you Briar Thorn."

"Because I was a thorn in her side. The weed that ruined her garden," Briar said. "Use any analogy you want; it all means the same thing. I'm the one she blames for messing up her life."

"That's fucked up," Memphis said, and Tobias made a pained sound, as a stray black tear rolled down his face.

"Don't get all weepy on my behalf. Lily was the one who raised me while Mom kept chasing after the next Prince Charming, so it's not like I was getting a daily dose of verbal beatdowns with breakfast or anything. A lot of kids had it way worse than me."

"Doesn't mean it didn't leave you with scars," Memphis argued. "You know that not all males are like your dad, right? Or any of the men Tiffany dated. We aren't all selfish assholes. And your mom was an idiot for how she viewed you."

Briar blinked. "I know that."

Memphis's eyes narrowed. "I don't think you do, Baby Doll. Deep down, I think you're scared that you're not worthy. But you are. You're perfect. From the tips of your bright hair to the ends of your cute toes, you're flawless."

His compliments made her feel uncomfortable and vulnerable, mostly because she wanted him to say it again. Ignoring how much she craved more of the same words, she forced a smirk on her face.

"You wouldn't be saying those things if you had to live with me. I don't cook or clean. I cuss, a lot. I don't like most people, and I have a nasty temper with a short fuse."

"Where are the negatives?" Memphis asked, then grinned when she snorted out a laugh. "Hi, I'm Memphis and you recently saw me completely lose my shit because my chimera side took over and I couldn't stop him. Then I went into rut. All the shirts I own are black, that vest was my favorite piece of clothing, and I think drinking beer out of a glass bottle instead of a can makes it fancy."

Then Memphis dropped a soft kiss on Tobias's head. "This is Tobias. He doesn't eat food anyway, so he couldn't care less that neither of us knows how to cook."

Tobias nodded his head quickly and gave Briar an imploring look. She crawled closer, feeling strangely unburdened by telling her story and receiving unwavering acceptance from her two lovers.

"I guess we're all a hot mess," she murmured as she curled up against Tobias.

Memphis wrapped his long, thick arms around the two of them. "I prefer to think of us as a spicy trio."

"A piquant triangle?" she asked with a soft chuckle.

Tobias huffed out a laugh and joined the banter. "Zesty Triad."

Memphis squeezed them all tight as he chuckled. When he spoke, it was in an exaggerated announcer voice. "Ladies and gentlemen, he's back. And better than ever!"

Closing her eyes, Briar let herself relax into the men's embrace. She wasn't sure if she was ready for what was happening between the three of them, but she owed it to herself to give it a try.

Freshly showered and dressed, Tobias descended the stairs. The sounds of Briar and Memphis talking to someone else drew him to the kitchen. He recognized the voice of the harpy that drove them to this location several days ago, but he wasn't sure about the other person there.

The instinct to demand these people move away from his flock was strong enough to make him stumble to a stop as he entered the kitchen. He closed his eyes to concentrate. He needed to maintain control. He couldn't risk scaring Briar again.

A light touch to his arm made him open his eyes to find Briar was at his side. "Hey there, you're not looking too steady. Do you need to eat?"

Then Memphis was on his other side, wrapping a massive hand around his arm to help support him. "Let's get you a seat and then some blood."

Having his flock next to him and touching him had an immediate calming effect. He was able to rein in his instincts and focus on using his words instead.

"I'm fine," he said even as he let the two of them lead him to a nearby counter and settle him on a stool.

The male that smelled like gargoyle strode to the fridge and pulled out a bag of blood, then tossed it to Memphis.

Memphis caught it easily and gently held it to Tobias's mouth. "Here you are, sweetheart. Drink up and when you're feeling better, we can talk about the next step."

He loved the way Memphis used endearments with him. He slid a hand under the shifter's shirt even as he opened his mouth to sink a fang into the bag. Resting his palm on the hot flesh of the chimera's belly, he sucked the cold blood and let it slide down his throat.

Briar petted his head, as if encouraging him to drink his fill as she talked to the room. "I told you what the next step is. We go over there and confront the bastard living in Tobias's house."

"We can't be sure—" the gargoyle started to say only to have Briar cut him off.

"Do I need to show you everything I found again?" Her words were confrontational, but her hand touching him remained gentle. "We need to get Tobias's life back, and this is the first step."

His house? His life?

Those words reminded him that he might not have any wealth after being missing for so long. The thought filled him with despair. One of a vampire's main responsibilities toward his flock was to care for them. How would he provide for Memphis and Briar if he no longer had any wealth? He knew he could rebuild, but it would take time, maybe even decades. Would he be able to convince these two to stay with him even though he had so little to offer?

He was so lost in his thoughts that he must have stopped drinking because Memphis leaned over and put his lips to Tobias's ear.

"Don't stop," he whispered, still holding the bag to Tobias's mouth. "Please, sweetheart, you need to feed. Just a little more, for me."

Eager to finish this meal, Tobias started sucking down the blood in long swallows. Memphis made an approving sound before straightening back up to re-join the argument.

"I agree with Briar," Memphis said. "We can at least go over to the place and talk to the guy living there. Figure out if he's renting the property from the trust or works for the trust. He might be able to give us more information."

Tobias finished the bag as Memphis talked and a gentle tug at the chimera's hand pulled the empty bag away. He looked at Briar. "What have you found?

A wide smile unfurled across her face. "You're talking again!"

Tobias nodded and gave her a shaky smile. "I'm in control. Mostly."

"We'll take 'mostly,'" she was quick to say, still petting him. "I did a little searching and found out that the house you lived in is owned by the Midnight Hour Trust. There's a guy living there, but I couldn't find his name. Everything circled back to the trust."

Tobias felt hope at the mention of the familiar name. "That's my trust."

"That would explain why the trust is so damn old," Briar said with a laugh. "Looks like you still own a bunch of shit, but we have no idea what state anything's in. Your house could be a crack den at this point."

"How about we stay positive?" Memphis said with a frown at Briar. "No need to jump to the worst conclusions."

Briar was unrepentant. "He needs to be prepared in case it's bad. I don't want him to think he's going to be able to do a slow roll back into his old life only to find out the place is ghetto now."

"Even if the house is whole, my life will never be as it was," Tobias was quick to say.

Briar's expression turned pained. "I know, but you'll be back to normal soon, and I promise that all the shit you went through will fade. It might take a while, but it will."

Tobias was confused for a moment, then realized that Briar thought he was speaking about the trauma of being caged for ten years. While it was true that he might never be able to stand a closed door again, he'd spent most of his time in a vampire coma. He remembered little of the last decade, only the hunger.

"I was referring to having you and Memphis in my life," he explained and then watched as her expression shut down.

"Sure." She stopped petting him and stepped to the side, looking at everyone but him. "Then we all agree. We head over there and yeet this rando out of Tobias's place."

He glanced over at Memphis to see the chimera cast Briar a disappointed look before clearing his expression and nodding his head. "I agree with Briar."

The gargoyle rubbed a hand over his bare head, then looked over to the harpy. She pointed at Briar. "I agree with the human. She says the house is owned by the trust and Tobias owns the trust, so then it's his."

"And when he shows up after a ten-year absence, how do we explain that to the authorities?" the gargoyle asked with a frown.

"Not our problem," the harpy answered. "Not our job."

"Fine!" the gargoyle growled, then looked at Tobias. "If any of this comes back on me or my people, I'll personally take you out."

Tobias wasn't concerned with the threat, but Memphis reacted strongly. "Try to hurt Tobias and I'll rip your stone dick off and sell it on eBay as a dildo."

Everyone blinked at his sudden violent threat, then the harpy started laughing.

"Sell it on eBay!" she chortled, making everyone chuckle and breaking the tension. Wiping a tear of mirth from her eyes, she spoke. "Everyone in the van, we're going on a road trip."

The property and house off the windy Del Dios Road overlooking Lake Hodges was the same as he remembered. He noted the long drive was still lined with native plants and ended in a circle at the front of the house.

Contentment hit him as the three-story majestic Queen Anne came into view. It was still the same house he'd fallen in love with fifty years ago when he'd first moved to the area. Nothing about the house spoke of disrepair or neglect. Except for the addition of dozens of large pots filled with non-native flowering bushes, everything was as he'd left it.

He should have felt some sense of coming home or relief, but instead, he focused on his flock's faces as they took in the impressive dwelling.

Both remained silent as Jaynie came to a halt in front of the house. Memphis's lips were pursed as his eyes rapidly surveyed the building. "There's a metric shit-ton of windows there. That can't be safe."

Briar's expression was pure delight. "Holy shit, is that a turret? Please tell me there's a library up there with one of those rolling ladders. This looks like a place where Poe would have written tortured poetry. This is so goth! I might need to change styles. I mean I'll always love punk, but for this house I could go goth."

"There are too many windows," Memphis argued. "We need to get a house that's safer for Tobias to live in during the day."

Briar frowned. "I hadn't thought of that. What about, like, blackout curtains?"

Memphis snorted. "No go, Baby Doll. If we're gone, someone could troop in and kill him by pulling the drapes."

Tobias listened to the two argue over him as Jaynie tapped at her phone on the driver seat. Soon a black, nondescript sedan pulled in behind them. Looking over his shoulder, he could see Jody in the driver seat and someone wearing a matching shirt in the passenger seat. When he returned his gaze to Jaynie, she met his eyes in the rearview mirror.

"Back up," Jaynie explained. "Jody picked up Blake on his way over. We can all get out now."

Memphis and Briar didn't hear her, they were still too busy discussing his safety. He felt bemused and loved by their concern. They both quieted when he took one of their hands in each of his.

"Why don't I show you the house?" he offered. "Then we can discuss things. Even if I own the house, I might not be able to move in until we evict the people who live here. That could take some time."

He was proud of his steady, unhesitating speech. It felt good to be able to speak again. But his words didn't have the calming effect he expected.

Briar scowled. "I'll evict their freeloading asses with my boot!" she announced as she fumbled with the van's sliding door. Then Jody was there, opening it for her and stepping back quickly when she came tumbling out.

Tobias wasn't at peak ability yet, but he was fast enough to jump from the van and catch Briar before she nose-planted on the pavement. Memphis was close behind him. The moment he set her back on her feet, Memphis moved in close, squishing her between the two of them.

Tobias didn't mind at all.

"How about you look before you leap, Baby Doll?" Memphis teased, but he could hear the real worry in the chimera's voice. "Between the two of you, you're going to turn me gray before my time."

Briar grinned up at the two of them. "I was testing your reflexes," she claimed. "Tobias gets an 85%. If you want that A, I expect to be swept off my feet next time. Memphis gets a 45%. You know why you didn't pass."

Memphis shook his head, then leaned over to give her a quick kiss. "I'll do better next time and sweep you and Tobias up in my arms."

When he pulled away, Tobias moved in. "My turn."

The door to the house swung open before their lips could meet. Distracted, Tobias looked up to see a familiar, pale, thin figure standing in the open doorway, hands clasped over a wide open mouth.

"Master Tobias!" he screamed, then he fell over in a dead faint.

Memphis winced as the guy's eyes rolled back and he went down like a felled tree. His skinny body hit the floor with a loud thump as all of them stood perfectly still, stunned.

It was Tobias who moved first. Rushing up the few steps to the front door, he knelt next the man. "Greg?"

The rest of them moved to follow as Greg groaned. They were all crowded around and staring down at the human when he opened his eyes and let out a startled cry and curled into a ball.

"Don't let them hurt me, Master Tobias," he begged.

"No one here is going to hurt you," Tobias assured Greg. Pulling his arms away from his head, Greg looked to Tobias. He tried to grab the vampire's hand, but Tobias was quick to move out of reach.

It was Jody who reached down to help the man to his feet as he talked in a calm, soothing voice. "My name's Jody and this is my brother Blake and one of my colleagues, Jaynie. We were hired to protect Tobias and get him home safely."

"Yes! Yes this is Master Tobias's home!" Greg announced, his expression one of sheer joy. Again he tried to touch Tobias, but the vampire managed to stay out of reach.

It was good that Tobias didn't let Greg touch him. His chimera half wouldn't have been able to handle that.

Greg swayed a little and Jody steadied him. "You don't look very good, maybe you should sit down."

He wasn't exaggerating. Greg looked pale, sweaty, and ready to cry. Although he was in obvious distress, Memphis didn't like him. Something about this human felt wrong. His impulse was to tell Jody, Blake, and Jaynie to drag this guy out of the house and drive him somewhere far away. But logically that wasn't an option. Greg hadn't even done anything.

Yet.

And then Greg started crying. "I don't have any blood!" Frantically, the man pulled the starched collar of his shirt and stretched his head to the side, offering up his neck. "Please master, take from me if you need it."

"I'm getting a serious Renfield vibe here," Briar muttered with a frown. It looked like she didn't like Greg either.

"Agreed," Memphis murmured back. "This guy is several cans short of a sixpack."

She grinned. "Are there even any cans or is it just the empty holder?"

Tobias ignored their banter as he focused on Greg. "Be at ease. I'm well fed at the moment. But thank you for the kind offer."

"Welcome home. So nice to see you. May I offer you my neck?" Briar commented under her breath. This time, her sarcastic remark caught Greg's attention and made him realize he wasn't alone with Tobias.

Looking at everyone surrounding him in the foyer, he gave them a shaky smile. "Thank you for returning Master Tobias safely. Please submit your invoices, and I'll see that all of you are paid in full with large tips included."

There was a beat of silence as everyone, including Tobias, stared at Greg in surprise. It was Tobias who recovered first.

"This is Memphis and Briar," he said, stepping back. Both he and Briar shifted a little so Tobias could stand between them. Greg's expression turned confused as he took in first Memphis's large, bearded frame and then Briar's bright hair and many piercings.

A distinct expression of distaste formed on his face. "Master?"

"They are my flock," Tobias explained as he turned to nuzzle his face in Briar's hair. Memphis didn't take his eyes off Greg, so he saw the flash of anger before a very large and fake smile stretched his lips.

"Congratulations!" he cried out with enthusiasm that wasn't fooling Memphis. "I'll make sure the guest rooms are prepared."

"No need. They'll be sharing my room and bed," Tobias told him.

There was no missing the look of disgust on Greg's face. "Them? These two? But Master, you deserve better."

Briar made a hissing, angry sound and looked ready to put a fist in Greg's face, but Tobias's arm around her kept her at his side. Standing on Tobias's other side, Memphis felt the vampire's magic spark and his aura spread out in a powerful wave.

Jody, Blake, and Jaynie quickly stepped out the front door to get away from it. The magic slipped around Memphis and Briar, not affecting them at all. But Greg wasn't so lucky. As the focus of Tobias's gaze, he bore the brunt of the vampire's displeasure.

"They're my flock. The most precious thing in my world. They are the souls I've been waiting to find for over three hundred years. You will treat them as well as you've treated me or walk out my door."

Greg dropped to his knees, clasping his hands in front of him. He looked up at Tobias with tears pouring out of his eyes. "Master, no! I've been a good and loyal servant. I've kept the house as you left it. I looked after the trust and your finances. You're wealthier now than you ever have been. I've done all this for you. Don't cast me aside."

Switching his gaze to Tobias, Memphis watched the vampire's expression turn cold. The old and powerful ones could do that. If he and Briar weren't protected from his magic because their auras were so saturated, Memphis was sure they'd both feel the weight of his gaze like pressure on the skin. It would feel cold and menacing.

To his credit, Greg didn't turn and run. He did choke and started shivering violently. "I w-w-w-will love them as y-y-y-you do," he stuttered out.

As quickly as he unleashed his power, Tobias drew it back. Panting, Greg sat back on his heels, shoulders slumped.

"Your loyalty does deserve a reward," Tobias said as he stepped forward and lifted Greg to his feet. Memphis felt Briar jerk and he knew why. Neither of them wanted Tobias touching this man. He blindly groped for her hand. She tangled her fingers with his the moment they connected.

Unaware of his and Briar's struggles, Tobias kept a hand on Greg until the man was steady, then let go. Only then did he feel Briar relax her tight hold on his hand. His chimera half didn't like Greg and wanted to shift and eat him.

He pulled in a deep breath and told his shifter half to chill. If they ate Greg, it might upset Tobias and that would be bad.

As threats went, it was a surprisingly effective one. His beast huffed and calmed. It looked like his chimera wouldn't want to do anything to upset either Tobias or Briar. He'd need to keep that in mind for the future.

It also helped that Tobias put a little distance between himself and Greg as he spoke. "Pick any house I own, except for this one, and it's yours. You might like the villa in Italy, I seem to remember you asked if we could spend winter there once. I'll continue to pay you the same salary for as long as you live. You can retire in comfort, Greg."

"Don't make me leave you, sir," Greg begged. "I don't want to retire. I don't want to move. If you want to reward me, let me stay here."

He eagerly stepped to Tobias's side, his gaze bouncing back and forth between himself and Briar. His eyes strayed down to their linked hands, but then rose to meet their eyes.

"Are you hungry? I could make you a lovely three course meal. I've been taking cooking lessons for the last few years, and I've gotten quite good. Do you like lamb?" Getting excited now, his eyes unfocused a little as he talked. "And wine!

We have a lovely wine cellar now. Would you like a red or white? I have a nice pinot noir."

Memphis was feeling a little stunned by both Greg's quick change of attitude and his rapid-fire questions. Briar's expression didn't change.

"We're beer drinkers," Briar stated flatly, and Memphis knew she was hoping that would upset Greg. But the man took it in stride.

"Beer!" Greg said with enthusiasm. "Of course, there are so many excellent craft breweries. I'll have to order the two of you a selection. And neither of you answered if you were hungry or not. It's a little late for a full dinner, but perhaps a charcuterie board?"

"That's a good idea," Tobias praised him.

Greg beamed at Tobias's words and nodded his head rapidly. "I'll see to it right away. Do you want it in the den, library, day room, or conservatory?"

"You pick," Tobias answered.

"And I'll put an order in for you, sir. I'll double your normal amount." He pulled a phone out of his pocket. He tapped the screen, then suddenly looked up, his hands freezing. "Will you tell me what happened? Where you've been for so long?"

"Later," Tobias agreed, and Memphis noticed he suddenly looked tired. Briar must have seen it too because she stepped forward and tugged at their joined hands. It didn't take any further urging for him to follow her lead.

Their linked hands ended up at the small of Tobias's back as they each took a side. A soft sigh escaped the vampire as he leaned slightly on Memphis and draped an arm over Briar's shoulders.

The sight made Greg stiffen slightly, but he maintained a pleasant expression. "I'll inform you when the blood has arrived and the food is ready. Is there anything else you require in the meantime?" Tobias shook his head. "Very good, sir." With that, he turned on his heels and strode off, mumbling something to himself about beer orders and what charcuterie board to use.

"I'm guessing you don't need us anymore," Jody said from behind them. The three of them swung around in unison to find the gargoyle standing in the open doorway with a half-smile on his face.

"Yes, I believe we're fine," Tobias agreed. "But your assistance has been invaluable. Everything you did couldn't have been cheap. I'd like to offer appropriate compensation over your normal rate."

Jody grinned broadly. "Don't worry. We've been well paid by Memphis's buddy Soren."

Memphis felt Tobias stiffen at the name of the other vampire, and if he wasn't mistaken, a little fang peaked past his upper lip. He'd never make Tobias jealous on purpose, but he did get a little thrill at the vampire's possessive attitude.

"Don't worry about Soren. You're the only fang-face for me," Memphis whispered. Tobias glanced up at him and relaxed slightly.

"Do you guys happen to know if my car is still parked in front of the bar?" Briar asked Jody, drawing their attention. "I'm not sure how many days it's been there, but San Diego is really shitty about parking."

Jody went into work mode. He pulled out his phone as he talked. "Color, make, model?"

"It's 2002 Honda Civic, 2-door. And as far as color goes, uh, rattle-can rainbow is the best way I can describe it."

"I'm sorry, what?" Memphis asked as Jody typed in the information.

Briar grinned up at him. "So, the car's paint job was already toast by the time I bought it from Maddy's cousin, Markus. I figured I would turn it into a positive, make sure I'd always be able to find it in a parking lot, you know? I bought a bunch of cans of spray paint and went to town. Maddy tried to help and make it artistic, but really it looks like a unicorn took acid and vomited on my car."

"How, uh, distinct," Jody said as he typed a few more things into his phone. "Should be easy to find. If it got towed, which is 90% likely, we'll see about collecting it and delivering it here. Will that work?"

"That'd be great, thanks," Briar said.

Memphis grinned when he noticed Tobias's appalled expression. He wasn't surprised at all when the vampire spoke up. "Perhaps I could purchase you something nicer. Something painted a single color?"

Briar snorted out a laugh. "Get rid of Squid? Never! Besides," she pointed her own hair, "I wouldn't think you'd judge something by color."

Tobias fought a grin as Memphis laughed. "She got you there."

It was only as the gargoyle was turning away that Memphis realized the implication of this conversation for himself. "My hog!"

Because he yelled, it made Briar jump. "Sorry, Baby Doll," he muttered before turning his attention back to Jody.

"I rode my Harley down here. She was parked near the bar too. Shit, you need to get her!"

Jody shook his head sadly. "I'll look, but it was probably already stolen by the time we got there."

Memphis wasn't ready to give up on his prized possession. "Maybe she got towed, like Briar's car."

"Was it an old, beat-up POS bike?" Briar asked.

Memphis felt as affronted as Greg had looked earlier. "Baby Doll, she is not a POS. She's a 2012 Road King. Loud-as-fuck aftermarket exhaust, sweet custom paint job, LED lights on the undercarriage, and shiny-ass chrome all over the place."

After a beat of silence, Briar declared gently, "Stolen."

Memphis looked to Jody who nodded. "Stolen."

Then he turned his gaze to Tobias. The vampire didn't hesitate. "I'll get you another one."

Tobias was jubilant to find out that he still owned his house and that it had been well maintained. He regretted being so hard on the faithful Greg. He'd diligently cared for the grounds and the house, and handled Tobias's businesses and finances with care. All that and the man had kept his original downstairs quarters, not even moving upstairs to one of the spacious guest rooms.

Then Tobias returned home after a ten-year absence with not one, but two strangers in tow. It would be enough to upset even the most mild-mannered human.

After Tobias bonded the three of them together, he'd need to take some time to find Greg a meaningful gift. Something that would reflect his deep appreciation of the man's exemplary loyalty and hard work.

"This place is amazing," Briar gushed as Tobias led them up the staircase to the second floor.

"It's nice," Memphis grumbled. Tobias felt bad for Memphis as it was obvious that he was devastated by the loss of his precious motorcycle. He'd meant it when he told Memphis he'd buy him another. It would be a good way to show Memphis that not only could Tobias take care of his flock, but that he was willing to indulge them.

He'd heard of vampires who were very strict with their flocks and limited their freedom out of fear for their safety. He couldn't think of a better symbol that would grant his flock autonomy than a motorcycle, as it was a rather dangerous mode of transportation. The road to his house, Del Dios, was a popular one for motorcycle enthusiasts and he'd seen his fair share of accidents over the years.

As Tobias remembered those wrecks, worry hit him.

Perhaps safety gear. He'd order Memphis every piece of safety gear he could find and have it delivered with the motorcycle.

"I feel a little like Alice in Wonderland," Briar admitted, drawing Tobias out of his thoughts.

"Welcome to the world of vampires," Memphis said. "There aren't many of them, but the ones who survive being turned usually end up being rich fuckers."

"What do you mean most don't survive being turned?' Briar asked.

"Being turned is an iffy process, only about 15% survive," Memphis explained.

"Less than that," Tobias said as he walked them into his bedroom. "I think the statistic is about 10% survive being turned. And out of that, only half survive past their second year. Young vampires suffer from constant hunger, and it often drives them to attack humans or other preternatural creatures. In the old days, you could slaughter a small, remote village and cover it up with ease. But now it's far more dangerous."

"Yeah, the last thing you guys want is someone catching a young vamp with a cell phone camera and posting that shit on social media," Memphis said as he crossed the room to sit on the bed. Stretching his arms out behind him, Memphis rested his weight on his hands and crossed his legs at the ankles. Tobias couldn't help admiring how good the chimera looked sitting on his bed.

Briar toured the room, touching every piece of furniture and decoration. "What happens if a vampire gets recorded doing a vampire-y thing?"

"He's executed," Tobias said. "And usually his maker is hunted down as well."

Briar swung around; her expression startled. "Damn, that's harsh. There's no prison, reform school, or anything?"

Memphis barked out a laugh. "Getting caught feeding by the general public is about the only thing all the vampires agree is a no-no. They're apex predators among preternaturals, Baby Doll, but they have one giant ball-of-light-in-the-sky weakness. If humans in general found out about them, you can be sure they'd start hunting them down in zero seconds flat."

Grinning, Briar swung her gaze over to Tobias. "So you don't sparkle in the sun?"

Tobias chuckled and shook his head. "No, but I char very well."

"Sparkling in the sun isn't the most unbelieve part of that series," Memphis muttered. "It's the idea that anyone would *want* to go to high school. High school sucks, why would you want to repeat it?"

"Excellent point," Briar responded as she opened Tobias's wardrobe then wandered away to look at something else. He missed whatever Memphis said next because he was too busy striding over to his wardrobe.

He missed these clothes!

He started pulling out suits, wondering which one he'd change into. The cargo pants and polo shirt he was wearing needed to go. Ah yes, there was his favorite charcoal gray suit. He could forgo the jacket and tie for a casual dinner at home with his flock, but where were his favorite pair of oxfords? They would go perfectly with this shade of gray.

All of these clothes must be out of fashion by now, but he could visit his tailor and order a new wardrobe soon. He could even take Briar and Memphis and have them measured. Would Briar like a suit also? He could picture her in a modified double breasted suit jacket in the British style. Of course the suit would need to be dark so a bright shirt and tie would really stand out. And he could—

"Whatever you're thinking, you can stop right there," Briar said, interrupting his thoughts.

Shaking his head a little, he blinked at her. "What?"

"You went from staring at those suits to looking at me with a lot of intensity." Striding up, she placed a gentle hand on his crotch. "By the feel of it, you're not interested in partying, so

I can only assume you're fitting me for some kind of clothing."
Stepping back, she crossed her arms over her chest and lifted her
chin up. "I can tell you right now, you're not getting me into a
dress or anything like it."

Blood rushed to his cock the moment Briar had touched
him through the thick cotton. He blamed that for how slow his
brain was at processing her words.

"I'd never want you to wear anything you didn't like,"
he said quickly. "I was actually considering how good you'd
look in a suit."

Her shoulders relaxed and she gestured to the clothing in
his hands. "A suit? Like one of those?"

"Similar," he said, unsure how much she knew about
men's fashion.

She reached out and rubbed the legs of a pair of pants
between her finger and thumb. "Sure, maybe. But with flashier
buttons and maybe some rips."

"Anything you want," Tobias said. "Until we can find a
tailor, both of you are welcome to order anything you might need
online."

"I wouldn't need to if I had my hog. Everything I packed
was in saddle bags," Memphis said, his tone morose.

"There used to be a custom leather shop that made
chaps, vests, and jackets," Tobias offered, remembering the
specialty coat he'd had made for an acquaintance's hundredth
birthday. "If they're still open, I'm sure they could produce some
quality garments for you."

"Yeah?" Memphis said with more enthusiasm. "I'd like
that."

"I'll make the arrangements," Tobias promised,
happiness expanding in his chest. He was going to enjoy spoiling
his flock.

Briar was being deliberately gross, and she knew it, but the urge was too strong to resist.

Greg had come looking for them in Tobias's bedroom and found them all cuddling on the bed, talking and laughing. Wrinkling his nose like he'd smelled something disgusting; he'd told them dinner was ready. Then he'd turned on his heels and strode out.

He didn't look any more pleased as Tobias took a seat at the table and insisted that she and Memphis sit on either side of him. Greg sat across from Tobias, trying to hide his disappointment.

Even though Greg tried to keep his expression pleasant as he told Tobias about his businesses, she got a distinct impression of disapproval every time his gaze swung over to her or Memphis.

He didn't like how she sat at a table, ate, and drank? Fine, she'd be even worse.

Instead of delicately picking up items from the fancy charcuterie board, she grabbed big handfuls and dumped them on her plate. She drank the fancy water directly from the bottle instead of pouring it into a glass.

She even managed to get a good belch in despite the lack of beer. All in all she was quite proud of this level of uncouth behavior. Her mother would be appalled, and Greg looked a little red in the face. Probably because he had to work hard to hold back snide comments.

"As I was saying," Greg continued after her belch had interrupted him. Memphis flashed her a grin and Tobias didn't seem to notice. He was sipping a wine glass full of the last of the blood Jody had left for them before leaving. Greg assured him the order he put in would be arriving in only a few hours.

"I'm not concerned with your decision to sell TriSurg," Tobias said before Greg could launch into another monologue. "I want to know the state of Third Street."

"I'm afraid we had to shut down Third Street," Greg said. "About six months after you disappeared, all the backers pulled out."

Briar sensed Tobias's sadness. Memphis must have felt it to because as she reached out to tangle her fingers with the vampire, the chimera wrapped a beefy arm around his shoulders.

"I'm sad to hear it," Tobias murmured. "I had great hopes for that program."

"What was it?" Memphis asked before Briar could.

"San Diego, and really all of southern California, has a large homeless population. Third Street was a non-profit set up as somewhere they could go for help. It was a safe place for them to store items, shower, eat, receive mail, sign up for classes, counseling, or get basic medical care. I wanted to add a second location that offered apartments."

"No reason you can't start it up again," Briar offered.

"I've started over many times in my life," Tobias agreed, squeezing her hand. "I'm simply upset that Third Street hasn't been there for people for the last ten years."

Distraught on Tobias's behalf, Briar pinned Greg with an angry stare. "Tobias is rich as fuck, right? Why didn't you put more of his money into the place when the other guys pulled out?"

Greg stiffened and scowled at her. "It wasn't my decision to make. If you remember, the Third Street building was rented by the Third Street Trust Board of Directors. They decided to dissolve it, and I wasn't even on the board."

Briar didn't think Greg was lying outright, but she was sure he wasn't telling them everything. This guy was so slimy he should be leaving a snail trail everywhere he walked. She was going to need to have a heart-to-heart with Tobias about Greg living in the house with them and . . .

No, wait, what was she thinking? Why would she care who lived in Tobias's house! That was a girlfriend or wife type thing. She, Memphis, and Tobias were . . .

Lovers?

Partners?

What did it matter? It wasn't like they were a forever thing, no matter what everyone kept saying. If her childhood taught her one thing, it was that relationships don't last. End of story.

There were no happy endings. There were no prince charmings. Especially not for someone like her.

"Briar?" She looked up to find Memphis and Tobias looking at her with twin expressions of concern.

Shaking herself out of her dark thoughts, she tried for a smirk. "What? Do I need to change for a fish course?"

"You don't change clothing between courses," Greg said. "But dressing nicely, for even a casual meal, is considered appropriate."

Man, she really didn't like this guy. "I'll make sure to pack my ball gown the next time I find a starving vampire in a hidden room," she answered.

Greg ignored her comment. "A nice set of clothing can make up for many shortcomings."

Memphis let out a growl and swung his gaze over to glare at Greg. "What did you mean by that?"

Tobias put a restraining hand on Memphis's forearm. "I'm sure Greg was trying to be helpful." He sighed as he looked at Greg. "Perhaps now would be a good time for you to retire for the evening."

"But there are deliveries coming," Greg protested.

"We'll see to that," Tobias assured him, his tone firm. "You've worked so hard that you deserve some time to yourself. We'll finish this fine meal in the den where we'll be able to hear the front door."

It was with obvious reluctance that Greg got up from the table. "Very well," he said stiffly and left.

Briar was almost sad he was gone; it had been a fun distraction to antagonize him. But she managed to keep from meeting the guys' eyes as she and Memphis gathered the food and followed Tobias through the house.

As he passed a window, Memphis paused to look at it closely, frowning in concentration.

"Interesting," he grunted as he straightened up.

"What?" she asked, trying to figure out what Memphis was seeing.

"This glass is weirdly thick with some kind of coating on the outside. Probably helps to keep Tobias safe, but I still don't like him living in a house with so many windows."

Memphis's comment made her glance around. He wasn't kidding, there were a ton of windows in this place, all of them potentially deadly to Tobias. Maybe they should talk to him about moving or . . .

No, she reminded herself forcefully. *It's not your business. Not your place.*

"This house is secure," Tobias said. He was standing in the doorway of a room a little further down the hall, waiting for them to finish examining the window.

"I don't know," Memphis said, glancing around. Briar counted ten windows she could see from where she was standing next to Memphis in the foyer. That was a lot of potential for Tobias to get hurt or killed.

"Every window is polycarbonate layered glass that can withstand small arms fire up to rounds from a .357. On top of that, all the windows have metal shutters that come down at daybreak and retract as sunset."

"Fancy," Memphis said as he and Briar joined Tobias.

"Necessary if I'm going to live in a place as sunny as San Diego," Tobias countered with a grin as he gestured for them to keep following and walked into the den. "And I refused to be confined to a basement or single room during the day, so I made sure I could access my entire house." His lips quirked. "It's not the dark ages anymore, I don't have to live in a crypt."

She and Memphis chuckled as they followed. Tobias set his wine glass full of blood on the coffee table and flopped down onto a couch. Reclining back, he shut his eyes and sighed.

"It almost doesn't feel real," he admitted as Briar set the food down and Memphis followed suit with their drinks. The vampire looked the way someone living in a country where they don't speak the language might: overwhelmed and fatigued.

Settling in next to him, she snuggled close and started running her hand through his hair. "What do you mean?"

"That feels nice," he murmured before answering. "I worry that this is a dream, and I'm going to wake up back in the basement."

"This is real," Memphis said, his deep voice a little grumbly.

"I can prove this is real." She leaned over and licked her tongue up the side of Tobias's face in one long, messy swipe.

Tobias jerked away and cast her an incredulous look. "Why would you do that?"

"Bet you never dreamed a girl would do that to you, huh?" she asked, and it took a moment for Tobias to understand. Wiping his face off with the sleeve of his shirt, he smiled ruefully.

"I stand, or rather, sit corrected. This is not a dream," he agreed.

"I dare you to do that to me," Memphis challenged her, turning his face and tapping his cheek.

Without hesitation, Briar got to her knees and leaned over Tobias to try and lick Memphis's face. Just before her tongue would have met Memphis's cheek, he turned his head and opened his mouth. His timing was perfect, and she found herself engaged in a very sloppy and hot kiss.

"This is fun," Tobias said as he moved his hands under her shirt and palmed one of her breasts through her bra.

Heat flared through her. She tried to move her mouth away, but Memphis fisted her hair and kept her still. That move made her pussy throb.

Normally, a guy grabbing her hair would have her throwing fists instead of moaning. But there were a lot of things that were different about being with Memphis and Tobias, including getting two dicks to play with.

Finally, Memphis let her pull away. Panting, she met his eyes at the same time she reached back to palm Tobias's thickening cock through his pants.

"I want both of you," she demanded. "I want Tobias in my mouth and Memphis in my cunt. Now!"

"Yes ma'am!" Memphis replied. "Sign me the fuck up!"

Tobias would never ever regret having a strong female in his flock. He'd heard the best flocks weren't made up of subservient followers, but those ready to take action and act independently. Briar's demands made him a believer. Tobias couldn't be happier that she had such a formidable personality.

If he was going to have a human in his flock, he couldn't think of a better one than this female.

After Memphis's exuberant reply, Briar scrambled off the couch, scooted the coffee table out of the way, and practically ripped her shirt off over her head.

Then his beautiful human stalled, standing with her shirt bunched in one hand. She pulled her lower lip between her teeth and chewed, her eyes sweeping the two of them still on the couch.

"Um," she said, her eyes dropping to the straining fabric of Memphis's crotch, then his. "How are we going to do this?" She waved the hand still holding the shirt as she pointed at the ceiling. "Should we go upstairs?"

Tobias didn't understand what caused Briar to go from bold to self-conscious, but as he was about suggest they retire to his bedroom, Memphis spoke up.

"I'm thinkin' we need to christen every room of this house," he declared. "That means no bedroom this time. Come over here, Baby Doll, and I'll show you what to do next."

Sitting up, he spread his knees wide and invited her to step close. Tobias watched with interest as the most intuitive one of their threesome moved with the same caution one might use with a wary animal.

"First we need to get you all naked and ready," he explained as he undid the top button of her pants. The pants were one of the pairs Jody had given her and much too big, so they sagged low on her hips. She wasn't wearing underwear, so the small V created by the open button revealed her dark curls and before he even lowered the zipper, Memphis leaned forward and nuzzled them.

Tobias watched her shoulders relax and her mouth open slightly as she sucked in a breath. "If you're sure," she whispered.

He hated her uncertainty, so he stood and moved to stand behind her. Wrapping his arm around her shoulders, he put his mouth to her ear. "You made a demand, and it's our pleasure to fulfill it."

Memphis moved his head up a little, and he gently bit the generous swell of her belly. "I'm never going to get enough of you, Baby Doll. Either of you. There will never be a time when I won't want you. In the bed, on the floor, or bent over the couch. Freshly showered or stepping through the door after a long hard day. Doesn't matter."

"That's sweet," she said, her voice a little breathy. "But I won't hold you to that after I've spent a night gaming with my buddies, shirt stained with Mountain Dew and my hair all greasy."

"Even then," Memphis promised.

Letting the chimera charm her with words, Tobias focused on helping to get her naked. He found the fastening that secured her bra, but the garment was stubborn and resisted his effort to unhook it. Annoyed, he grasped the strap across her back in two hands and pulled until the metal hooks gave up holding her lovely breasts hostage.

"You didn't just ruin this bra, did you?" Briar asked as he slid the offending garment off of her. "Jaynie found it for me and she's got good taste in underwear."

"I'll buy you all the ones you want, or none if I can convince you to go without," Tobias answered without remorse.

"Unlikely." She started to laugh but it ended in a soft exhalation when he wrapped his arms around her to cup her breasts. Kneading the flesh gently, he kissed her neck as he watched Memphis carefully drag Briar's pants down. He tugged at her ankles to get her to lift each foot so he could pull her pants all the way off.

Still sitting on the couch, Memphis pulled her forward, nudging her legs apart with his. Tobias followed her, eager to see what the chimera would do to their human mate. While he continued to tease Briar's breasts, Memphis ran his hands up the insides of her legs until his fingers could brush the dark curls hiding her sex.

Briar made a little distressed sound when Memphis didn't go any further.

"Memphis," she whined, wiggling her hips.

Tobias leaned over and brushed his lips against her neck. "Is the big, mean man tormenting you?"

"Whatever, I can do it myself," she snarked and moved to slip a hand between her legs.

"Bad human!" Memphis said with a chuckle, grabbing her wrist. "That pretty kitty belongs to me."

Briar blinked down at him before bursting out laughing. "Did you just call my pussy a pretty kitty?"

Memphis shrugged. "I did. Now let's see if we can make her purr."

When the chimera held Briar's wrist up, Tobias understood what he wanted. Taking a wrist in each hand, he pulled them behind her back and wrapped one hand around them to secure her. Then he reached back around and started plucking at her nipple.

Between his movements and whatever Memphis was doing, Briar's laughter abruptly stopped. Moaning, she arched back against him, trying to press harder against Memphis's hand.

Because they were both familiar with Briar's body by now, they slowly increased the pressure. Tobias got rougher with her nipples, alternating between them until she was sucking in her breath every time he let go. Memphis was kissing, nibbling, and licking her stomach as his hand worked between her legs.

The sweet smell of her arousal filled his nose, and he was desperate to bury himself inside her. He wanted to feel her heat clenching around him as she came.

"I think we need to change positions a bit," Memphis said, his voice low and thick.

"I couldn't agree more," Tobias said readily. He let go of Briar's wrists, thinking he'd lay her down on the couch, but Memphis had other ideas. Grabbing Briar's thighs, he pulled her down, so she was straddling his lap, then stood up, cradling her ass in his hands. A quick pivot had him facing the couch and he dropped both of them on it.

Briar gasped in surprise as Memphis roughly parted her legs and maneuvered his broad shoulders between them. With her legs splayed like that, Tobias could see Briar's glistening sex. For a moment, he almost pushed Memphis out of the way so he could put his mouth on her.

Then Memphis looked over at him, eyes glowing gold. "What are you waiting for? Get naked and get to work." Then Memphis pointed at Briar's chest. "I want your mouth on her sucking those gorgeous titties."

He loved it when Memphis ordered him around. Eagerness made him a little clumsy as he hastily undressed, leaving his clothes in a pile on the floor. Dropping to his knees next to the couch, he took a moment to admire Briar.

"You're perfect," he whispered.

He could tell she was about to open her mouth to argue so he kissed her. As they kissed, she jerked, then moaned. When he broke the kiss, her eyes remained shut, her expression tense. Turning his head, he looked down the length of her body to see Memphis feasting on her.

The sight made his cock throb and start weeping pre-cum. Desperate to get her in his mouth, he dropped his head to her breast. Sucking a nipple into his mouth, he worked it with his tongue and teeth.

"Oh!" she moaned and brought a hand up to rest on the back of his head. Her fingers tangled in his hair, and she pushed him down harder. His little human liked it rough.

Enjoying himself, he switched between breasts. Occasionally he'd blow air over a wet nipple, grinning as she shivered. Every time she moved; her many earrings made a soft windchime sound as they clinked together. As she got nearer to orgasm and her entire body started to shudder, the soft clinking sound became erratic.

After tonight, he might develop a Pavlovian reaction to the sound of windchimes!

Crying out, she tangled her fingers in Tobias's hair and tugged. For a brief moment, he worried he'd caused her pain, but then realized she was orgasming. Without pausing as he lavished her nipple with attention, he tugged her hand free from his hair and grasped it in his own.

When she went limp under him, he sat back to see her looking at him with dazed eyes. "You guys are really good at that," she whispered.

"Not done yet, Baby Doll," Memphis said. With the easy strength of a shifter, Memphis grabbed her hips and turned her over. Tobias saw her eyes go wide before her hand let go of his hand to flail as she found herself unceremoniously flipped face down on the couch.

The chimera grabbed her hips and pulled her up on all fours as he pinned Tobias with his gaze. "Get on the couch in front of her," he ordered. "Feed her that pretty cock of yours."

"With pleasure," Tobias said. He moved to the opposite end of the couch. He knelt in front of Briar, cupping his hand under her jaw. "Hello love," he whispered.

"Hey," she said back. Then she sucked in a breath, her eyes fluttering closed. Tobias looked up to see Memphis working his thick erection into Briar.

"Fuck, Baby Doll," he groaned. "You're so fucking tight!"

Briar moaned as she rocked back a little. "You feel so good."

Looking over her back, Tobias could see Memphis sinking into her. She nuzzled his cock, pulling his attention away from Memphis.

With one hand still under her jaw, he used the other hand to guide his shaft between her lips. "Suck on it, my heart," he demanded. "Swallow me down."

She opened her mouth and worked her tongue over his crown, taking her time to run the tip of her tongue over his slit. Tobias hissed as electric pleasure jolted up his cock.

"Is our little human teasing you?" Memphis asked.

Tobias met the chimera's gaze with a half grin. "I might be too big for her."

"I don't think that's true, is it Baby Doll? I think we both fit in you perfectly." He squeezed her ass as he talked.

Briar moaned around his shaft, the vibrations feeling amazing. Then she opened wide and sucked him in. He felt the back of her throat as the warm suction of her mouth worked him.

"Sweet Mother of Darkness!" Tobias shouted.

Memphis made a satisfied sound. "Fuck that's hot. That's it, Baby Doll, work him with your mouth. Look at you not even gagging. You'll have to show me how to do that."

The chimera increased his pace, and every time he pushed forward, it sank Tobias deeper into Briar's mouth. He knew he wouldn't last much longer. Maybe in another hundred years he'd be able to hold back his orgasms in this situation, but today he was overwhelmed by the pleasure of Briar's mouth and the sight of his gorgeous flock.

"I can't wait . . . I'm going to," he stuttered out, not even sure what he was saying.

"Come in her mouth," Memphis ordered. "I'm going to fill this sweet pussy."

The chimera increased his pace and Briar started shuddering between them. By the way her body shook, Tobias could tell she was close as well.

When she moaned around him again, he couldn't hold back. He cried out as he came in Briar's mouth. Even though he could feel her swallowing, some of his cum dripped from the corner of her mouth.

It was one of the most erotic sights he'd ever witnessed.

Memphis gave a hoarse cry as he came. As he orgasmed, magic burst around them. It rushed against their skin and washed through their bodies. Tobias felt himself come again, something he didn't think was possible. Briar shivered violently, her warm mouth tightening and loosening around his throbbing erection as she swallowed. Tobias's vision grayed out for a moment as the magic swept through him making his second orgasm as powerful as the first.

The three of them froze, caught up in a breathless moment of pleasure.

Briar was the first to collapse, releasing Tobias cock as she went boneless. He opened his eyes in time to see Memphis gathering her to him. The big shifter was still buried inside her as he drew up his legs, lay back on the long couch, and snuggled her against him.

Tobias was struck again by the beauty of his flock. Briar and Memphis, so different in skin tone and body type, were a perfect match in personality. They had so much in common.

And then there was him.

A three-hundred-year-old vampire who'd been dumb enough to get himself caged for a decade. How did Briar and Memphis feel anything more for him than pity?

For a brief moment, he worried he didn't fit. Then Memphis held out a hand to him.

"Come here," he demanded. "Come cuddle. Don't make me get up and get you or I'll smack your ass a couple of times."

His concern evaporated. Carefully lying on the couch, wiggling himself between Memphis's legs and the back cushions, he laid his head on a part of the chimera's muscled abdomen. Briar reached down to run her fingers through his hair and Memphis rested his arm on Tobias's shoulder.

"That was a really great idea," Tobias murmured. "I'm glad you thought of it."

Briar sounded a mischievous chuckle. "Wait 'til you see what I come up with next."

Memphis woke feeling rested but lazy. He'd never slept so well before. Another surprise was that his chimera wasn't agitated or demanding control over their body like every other day of his life. His animal half hadn't even tried to take over while he'd been asleep since he'd found his mates. This last week with Briar and Tobias had been the best of his life so far.

His father was right; mates made the chimera and man pieces all fit together.

It would be the best feeling in the world if he wasn't sure that Briar was waiting for it all to fall apart.

It wasn't that he thought she'd walk out on them, but that she didn't really expect this to last. Part of it was because she was human and didn't understand how flocks or mates worked. But the other part was her fucked up childhood. He had been raised by a loving family and couldn't truly understand what it was like to grow up with an unreliable mother and no father. But he hoped that she'd realize that both of them were committed to her.

They had no intention of leaving her or letting her leave them.

"Memphis, are you awake?"

The chimera opened his eyes to find Tobias propped up on an elbow and looking down at him. The sun must have set to have the vampire so wide awake. He'd gotten enough meals in him, so he could wake up during the day and interact, but he was sluggish and uncoordinated. But the moment the sun dipped below the horizon, Tobias was awake and ready to move. Memphis figured it was because the vampire had time to make up for.

"Good morning, uh, evening," Memphis said. Because Briar routinely stayed up so late and he was always trying to catch her online to talk, he'd slipped into a more vampire-style sleep pattern over the last few months.

Briar's preference for working at night match Tobias's sleep schedule and she'd been unwittingly preparing Memphis for life with a vampire. It was yet another sign they were always meant to be together.

He'd have to point that out to her in a few years after she stopped trying to doomsday their relationship.

Looking over, he found Briar curled up against his other side, eyes closed and breathing steadily. "Looks like our hacker is still asleep."

Reaching across Memphis's body, Tobias started petting Briar's head. Her eyes opened slowly, focusing first on him, then sliding over to look at the vampire.

"Is it time to get up already?" she asked without moving.

Her consistent reluctance to get up was a source of amusement for him. He'd never met anyone who fell asleep as easily, but on the flip side it was hard to wake her up.

"I have a surprise for both of you," Tobias said with a wide grin. He was so excited he was almost vibrating. "Up, up, up my darlings!"

Briar grumbled something Memphis didn't catch as Tobias bounced out of bed. He watched the vampire stride naked across the room. He would never get tired of seeing either of his mates' bare bodies. Tobias with his long, lean swimmers build or Briar with her statuesque, voluptuous curves.

Between these two, he felt like he won the fucking mate lottery.

Pulling some clothes out, Tobias turned and scowled to find them both still in the bed. "You two need to get moving or no surprises!"

"But what if I have surprise for you?" Memphis asked as he flipped the sheets off him and Briar. She snuggled closer to him but didn't try to pull the sheets back over them.

Tobias gazed at their naked bodies hungrily, but then shook his head. "You won't distract me, pretty beast. We're going out!"

That made Briar sit up. "Going out? Like leaving the house?"

Tobias's grin turned broad, his eyes dancing. "That's exactly what I mean. I finished making all the arrangements yesterday. Everything's planned out. I promise you'll both love it!"

Yawning, Briar got off the bed and reached for some clothes neatly stacked on a nearby table. "I really need to get a few more changes of clothes," she muttered as she dressed.

Memphis got out of bed next to her and thought the same thing as he dressed.

Thankfully, Jody had delivered Squid, Briar's rattle-can rainbow Civic, the day after they arrived at Tobias's house. Unfortunately, Memphis's hog was in the wind. And, of course, Memphis lost all his gear packed in the stolen bike's saddle bags, so all he had were the clothes Jody had provided back at the bar and then the safehouse.

Briar had been lucky to have a few items of clothing in her car. She grumbled about wearing the same two outfits but was afraid to run home for more. She didn't want to explain to Maddy what was going on yet.

The only silver lining was the expression on Greg's face when Jaynie pulled up in the Civic. Then the guy went almost apoplectic when Tobias told Jaynie to park the car in the six-bay garage between the Land Rover and Alfa Romeo Giulia.

Greg had done it, but it was obvious he hadn't been happy about it. When Tobas wasn't around to hear him, Greg would probably be full of snide remarks that he and Briar would need to ignore. They didn't want to upset Tobias who felt responsible for the loyal Greg.

As much as Greg's elitest attitude bothered Memphis, there was something else about Greg that troubled him much more.

Over the last few days, he'd caught Greg staring longingly at Tobias. It was obvious the guy was in love with the vampire, but it was going to be an unrequited love from here on out. Tobias belonged to him and Briar, no one else. And certainly not some pasty, smug dickhead.

Best thing would be to find out if there was something going on or if his suspicious about Greg were an overreaction because he didn't like the guy.

"Memphis?"

Briar's questioning voice brought him out of his thoughts. "Yes, Baby Doll?"

"You were, uh, growling?" she said tentatively.

Grimacing, Memphis gave himself a mental shake. "It was nothing. Just trying to wake up."

Briar offered him a relieved smile and sat on the edge of the bed to pull on and lace up her boots. "Coffee will make it all better."

"Yes, coffee and breakfast for both of you," Tobias agreed as he ducked into the bathroom with his clothes. "I'll be done in a moment. We leave in thirty minutes."

"We better get a move on," Memphis said as he held out his hand to Briar's. "He sounds like he means it."

Finished putting on her boots, she tangled her fingers with his and stood. Grinned as they walked hand-in-hand down to the kitchen.

"He better not try to take us to some fancy-ass restaurant or anything," she said. "I want pizza or a burger and fries. The best kind of foods are the ones you eat with your hands."

"No argument here," Memphis said as they entered the kitchen. Greg was there, fussing with items on the counter. Looking up, he graced them with a big smile and gestured to the table.

"Master Tobias has a big evening planned for the three of you," he said. "I've prepared a light repast to tide you over for now."

Briar let go of his hand as they took a seat at the kitchen table. Greg bustled around, bringing them both bowls full of yogurt with fruit topping, plates with toast, and cups of coffee. Memphis was so starved for coffee that he downed the entire delicate cup in one swallow and looked up to Greg.

Greg didn't lose his smile, but Memphis could see his jaw tighten. "I'll bring you the carafe, shall I?"

"And more toast," Memphis said, eyeing the paltry amount of food Greg had given him.

A frown finally appeared on Greg's face. "But you'll ruin your appetite and disappoint Master Tobias."

Memphis eyed the thin, pale man. "First of all, he keeps telling you to drop that master shit. Second, did you not notice my size? A couple pieces of toast and some fruit might be enough for Briar, but I'm going to need more, or my chimera might break through my control and eat anyone one he's not happy with. A hungry chimera isn't to be fucked with."

Amazingly enough, Greg managed to pale even more at Memphis's implied threat. "I can cook you up some sausage and eggs, would that suffice to keep your animal under control?"

"That should do," Memphis agreed, ignoring Greg's condescending attitude. "Over easy with the eggs."

Grumbling under his breath, Greg turned on his heels and got busy pulling items out of the fridge and banging skillets together.

Briar leaned over the table and pointed a spoon at him. "I hope you like spit in your food."

"I can see him cooking," Memphis pointed out.

"Not now, but later," she responded. "When we aren't in the kitchen with him."

He grinned at her. "Hopefully, he'll be gone soon. Tobias is working on putting together a retirement plan for Greg and talking him into leaving."

"Fingers crossed," she muttered and went back to eating her yogurt.

When Greg put a heaping plate of eggs, sausage, and rolls down in front of him, he forked some onto Briar's plate before she could even ask. His female might be smaller than him, but he knew what Greg had served hadn't been enough for her either.

They were both finished when Tobias stepped into the room, taking Memphis's breath away.

The vampire looked resplendent in a deep blue suit, his hair combed and styled, and his eyes sparkling. He appeared every inch the handsome, powerful, and elegant man he was.

"Damn, you look good," Briar said, voicing his own thoughts.

Tobias's smile lit up the room as he tugged at his cuffs. "You like?"

"Like is too mild. You look good enough to eat," Memphis said.

A faint blush appeared on the vampire's face. "Thank you. I wanted to look my best for both of you."

Memphis looked over to Briar to say something but stopped when he saw the look on her face. "Baby Doll, what's wrong?"

"We can't go out," she said firmly, making Tobias look upset and confusing Memphis.

"But why?" Tobias asked. "Have I done something wrong?"

"Nothing!" Briar was quick to say. "You didn't do anything. But you look so nice and you're gonna want to go to places that match how you look. I can't go to those places. I won't look right."

"And when have you ever cared what others think?" Memphis asked gently. He reached across the table and he took her hand in his.

She dropped her gaze to their joined hands. "I don't. Usually. But I . . ."

Memphis was ready to wait patiently for her to gather her thoughts, but Tobias acted. Striding forward, the vampire grabbed her free hand and tugged her out of her chair.

"What?" she asked as Tobias led her out of the kitchen and back upstairs. With his and Briar's hands still linked Memphis was quick to stand and follow his mates.

He was interested to see what the vampire was up to.

Tobias led her straight to the bathroom. Letting go of her hand, he turned her to face the mirror. It was tight in the room so Memphis dropped her hand and too a short step back to give Tobias room to work.

"You think because I dress this way that I want you to dress differently?" Tobias asked her reflection.

"Well, yeah," she answered. "Don't you?"

"My heart, I love your style," Tobias said fiercely. "And the only reason you should change is because you want to. Not because of anyone else."

With that, he grabbed the hem of her shirt and pulled it off over her head. "What—"

"Stay here," Tobias said as he strode out of the room with her shirt in his hand. He was back very quickly with a suit vest and a wooden box.

The vest was black and when he slipped it on Briar and buttoned it up; it showed off the beautiful curve of her breasts and then flowed nicely down her waist and over her hips. Then he opened the box and pulled out a gold chain with a pocketknife on one end and a pocket watch on the other.

He tucked the knife in one pocket of the vest and the watch in the other, leaving the gold chain hanging between them. But he wasn't finished. He opened a drawer and pulled out safety pins. Then he carefully ripped the vest near the top and safety pinned the rip closed. He did that in several other places until the garment started to resemble the punk style Briar favored.

But he wasn't done yet.

Rooting around in another drawer, he produced a bottle of gel. He applied a liberal amount to Briar's hair and then worked the chin-length strands until they were all stiff and pointing straight up in the mohawk they'd both first seen Briar sporting in the basement of Il Crepuscule.

The turquoise hair with dark roots looked perfect in that style, making Briar look tough, but elegant at the same time.

"There, now I can be seen with you in public," Tobias announced with a big smile. "You were looking a little shabby before, but I've got you all dressed up for a night out."

Briar blinked at her reflection then at Tobias. "You like this?"

"I love this," he corrected. "All three of us are going to dress in the way that makes us feel the most comfortable and confident. You look both sexy and beautiful."

"I don't usually show cleavage," Briar murmured as she looked at herself in the mirror.

Tobias frowned. "We can put your shirt on under the vest," he offered quickly. "I only did it this way because I thought the effect would be more dramatic."

Briar shook her head. "No, I like this. I like the way it makes me feel both feminine but tough, you know?"

"You're both those things all the time," Memphis insisted as he stepped close. "All Tobias did was help the outside reflect the inside."

Briar turned and put her arms around both of them, hugging them tight. Abruptly, she pulled away, rubbing her eyes and sniffling suspiciously.

"Let's get out of here," she insisted. "Before I start bawling like a baby. Can we take one of those fancy-ass sports cars?"

"Of course—" Tobias started to say but Memphis cut him off.

"Hell no!" he said with a mock scowl. "I'm not folding myself into a pretzel to get into one of those toy cars."

That made Briar giggle as Tobias took one of their hands in each of his. "Very well, no small cars. Now, let's begin tonight's adventure!"

"This is why I ride a bike or borrow a truck," Memphis grumbled from the back seat of the Range Rover. "At least the van Jaynie drove was big enough. We should get one of those for when we all want to go somewhere."

Over my dead body will you get something as ugly as one of those passenger vans, Tobias thought as he looked over his shoulder at Memphis while Briar maneuvered the vehicle onto the I-15 freeway going south.

"I'll look into getting something more comfortable," he promised the chimera out loud.

"I'm supposed to hear from my insurance company soon. After they pay out, I'll be able to get another bike," Memphis said, a smile forming on his face. "I could take either of you for a ride."

"Get one with a side car so we can all ride together," Briar suggested and chuckled at the grumpy sound Memphis made.

Memphis narrowed his eyes at Briar. "Do I look fucking Russian to you? I wouldn't be caught dead on one of those vodka-powered Urals."

Briar's wrinkled forehead told Tobias she was as confused as he was by Memphis's statement.

"I'm sorry, what now?" Briar said.

"You said I should get a Ural," Memphis said, also sounding perplexed.

"I said get a bike with a side car," Briar answered, and Tobias looked back at Memphis in time to see the chimera grin.

"I see where this all went wrong. The most common bike you can get with a side car is called a Ural and it's made in Russia," Memphis explained with a chuckle.

"Looks like we need to learn to speak motorcycle," Tobias said to Briar.

Her expression lit up. "I could get my motorcycle license and get a bike too. Memphis and I could go on rides together. Oh, I want something flashy and red, like that one." She nodded to a motorcycle that zoomed past them at what Tobias considered a very unsafe speed.

Both he and Memphis spoke at the same time.

"No!"

Briar scowled. "I can do what I like, fuck you very much."

"I mean not yet, Baby Doll," Memphis amended quickly. Tobias wanted to argue that the answer was *never,* but kept quiet. He might not be as intuitive as Memphis, but he could see that telling Briar not to do something was a strategic mistake.

"You're a hundred percent human right now," Memphis explained, his tone gentle. "One crash could be the end of you. After you bond with Tobias, you'll be tougher and stronger. Much harder to kill. Then we can talk about getting you a bike."

"And all the safety gear," Tobias hurried to add. If she was determined to do something so dangerous, he'd do his best to mitigate the risk.

Memphis nodded. "And all the safety gear and you wouldn't be getting no Ducati or crotch rocket. How about a nice Harley or one of those Honda Rebels? Those are nice bikes. My brother Nash has one, and I've ridden it a few times. I thought about getting one, but I loved my hog too much." His expression turned morose, and Tobias realized he was remembering he didn't have that motorcycle anymore. "I guess I could get one now."

"When you get another one, I'll go for a ride with you," Briar said, not commenting about the sharing of souls. He noticed she was always quick to change the subject or ignore any reference to that aspect of their relationship.

"I'd like that," Memphis agreed, perking up.

"Jose rides and he says that San Diego has great roads for motorcycles," she commented as she skillfully drove through the evening traffic. Her phone was clipped into a holder on the dash, displaying directions to the address he'd given her.

As the two talked about motorcycles and San Diego roads, Tobias worked on not forbidding Briar from even riding with Memphis.

He wasn't worried so much about Memphis getting hurt, chimeras are almost as tough as vampires without the added weakness of sunlight. But his sweet Briar was all too human and could die from the simplest of injuries.

That thought made him want to bind their souls together badly, but he fought the impulse. Once they shared souls, Briar would be stronger and harder to kill, and Memphis would be nearly unstoppable.

But he had to wait.

No matter how difficult it was, he had to give Briar time to accept him and Memphis. Knowing her background and her views on relationships, he understood she'd need time to accept them. But hopefully not too much time.

Twenty minutes later, they pulled up to an industrial area where only a few shops were still open. Briar parked in one of the many empty spots and tapped her phone. "I guess we're here?"

"We are!" Tobias agreed, and he wrenched the door open and jumped out of the Range Rover.

"Is this Fight Club?" Memphis asked, making Briar snicker as the two of them got out and followed him at a slower pace.

"Nobody talks about Fight Club," Briar quoted as Tobias opened the door and ushered them inside. The place was crowded with rolls of leather, tightly packed racks of leather clothing, and stacks of boxes marked in penmanship so sloppy it looked like hieroglyphics.

Tobias grinned. It was nice to see nothing had changed in the last ten years!

"Tobias?" a male voice called out from somewhere deeper in the crowded place.

"Yes, Frank. It's me," Tobias called back. "I'm here with the people I was telling you about."

"Be there in a minute," Frank answered, and they heard boxes being shuffled around.

"What are we doing here?" Memphis asked as he took a closer look at one of the clothing racks.

"Getting your first present," Tobias answered.

"What—"

Frank, a fifty-year-old naga shifter, emerged from the back of the shop carrying a box. Memphis's nostrils flared, and he grabbed Briar to put her behind him.

"Don't get any closer," he warned Frank. "Tobias, get behind me."

Frank froze and looked at Memphis then Tobias. "You didn't warn him?"

Tobias could kick himself. "Don't worry, Memphis. Frank's an old friend and his Slither is peaceful."

"Slither?" Briar asked, stepping out from behind Memphis. The chimera let her but then put a hand out so she didn't step past him.

"He's a naga, snake shifter," Memphis explained. "They have a reputation for eating weaker shifters, especially wolves."

"Some do, but most don't. My Slither has never done that," Frank said as he pointed at Tobias. "And no one, even a member of a big Slither, would want to piss off a vampire as powerful as this one."

"I'd never knowingly bring you any place that would be dangerous to you or Briar," Tobias said, disappointment filling him. "But we can leave if you want."

Memphis crossed his thick arms across his wide chest. "I want a scale," he demanded.

"Scale?" Briar asked.

Far from looking scandalized by the demand, Frank looked relieved.

"Of course!" He shifted his gaze to Briar as he set the box down and extended an arm out in front of him. "Watch."

He looked down at his arm and focused. A line of thumb-sized iridescent, red-orange scales appeared. Making a fist, he flexed, and the scales bristled. With his opposite hand, he plucked one of the scales off his arm and held it out to Memphis.

The chimera didn't move. "Give it to Briar," he grunted.

Understanding dawned on Frank's face. As a human, Briar was the only truly vulnerable one of the three. With a gentle expression, he formally offered the scale to Briar. "Accept my flesh as a Promise Token that no harm will come to you."

Briar stepped forward to take the scale, looking a little confused. "Um, thanks?"

Frank chuckled. "You might not have felt it, but a spell snapped into place when you took the token. I can't hurt you without doing myself damage now. It means you're safe from me. Not that you weren't before, but now the chimera won't be so worried."

"He does fuss," Briar agreed as she examined the scale. "This is beautiful. Would it be weird if I wore it as a necklace? I don't want to insult you or anything. Or do I need to give it back when we leave?"

Frank beamed. "It's yours to keep, and I'd be honored if you wanted to wear it like jewelry."

"Thanks, Frank," Briar said and tucked it into her pants pocket.

The moment Briar had the scale in hand, Memphis visibly relaxed. Tobias was relieved that they wouldn't need to leave before he could give his flock their first presents of the evening.

"Is that the vest?" he asked as he picked up the box Frank had carried out.

"It sure is," Frank agreed. "I did my best with what you gave me, but if anything is wrong, I can redo it."

"Vest?" Memphis asked, his eyes locked on the box.

Excited, Tobias flipped open the box and pulled out the item. It was the vest Memphis destroyed when he shifted in the basement of the bar.

The chimera's expression turned delighted as he took the garment from Tobias. "It looks almost the same."

"I used the old one Tobias sent me for measurements, so this one should fit. I was also able to salvage almost all the patches," Frank said as he stepped up and pointed to areas of the vest. "And I hope you don't mind, but I added some decorative stitching."

"Try it on," Tobias urged.

Memphis donned the garment, his eyes shining. There was one narrow mirror in the shop propped up against a stack of boxes. Tobias grabbed it and held it up so Memphis could see how the vest looked on him.

"It's perfect," Memphis said as he admired his reflection from all angles.

Briar stepped up behind Tobias as he held the mirror. She wrapped her arms around his middle as she peered around his side. "You're good at the gift giving game."

Before Tobias could answer her, Memphis pulled the mirror from his grip and set it aside. Then he grabbed Tobias and Briar in a bear hug. "This is amazing. Thank you."

After a few minutes, Tobias pulled away. "There's more."

"Yeah?" Memphis asked and rubbed a hand over his eyes. "It can't be as good as this."

"Probably not," Tobias agreed, and then looked over to the Naga. "Frank?"

"Sure thing," he said as he took a few short strides to a nearby rack. He pulled out two leather motorcycle jackets.

The smaller one was in a vintage style with a front zip and mandarin collar. It was black with teal accent stripes from collar to cuff. The much larger one was in the classic bad-boy style with a wide lapel collar and an offset zipper.

"I'm pretty confident about the fit of this one," Frank said as he handed Memphis the bigger jacket. Then he held the smaller one out to Briar. "But I had to do some guessing on this one, so don't be shy about telling me if doesn't fit right."

"Holy shit," Briar breathed and eagerly pulled on the jacket. Then she made a face. "The elbows feel weird."

"That's the armor," Frank explained. "Tobias said to make it with all the safety protocols so there's CE Level 2 armor in the elbows, shoulders, and back. That's the best you can get." He pulled another jacket off the rack and showed them the inside. "All the armor is in pockets so you can pull it out if you want to wear it around outside of riding."

"I don't need the armor," Memphis said as he zipped up the jacket over the vest.

"Then pull it out," Frank said with a shrug. "All Tobias said was to make the jackets as safe as possible. I did everything except install an air vest."

It was easy to see that Memphis wasn't that impressed with the jacket, but Briar was delighted. "Armor? I feel like such a badass!"

"I knew you'd want to ride with Memphis someday, so I wanted you to be well protected," Tobias explained.

"Ride with Memphis?" Briar said with a laugh. "Maybe at first. But now I totally need to get a bike of my own."

"We'll see," was all he said. He had every hope that he could talk Briar into only riding on the back of a motorcycle with Memphis. "But we need to go, or we'll be late for the next appointment."

"Another surprise?" Briar asked as Tobias herded them out of the shop. She tugged on the jacket's zipper. "I'm pretty happy with this."

"The vest and jackets are only the beginning," he promised.

Even though it was a temperate evening, Briar kept her jacket on to drive them to the next location. Memphis pulled his off and Tobias caught him examining the vest a few times during the drive. The chimera was so distracted that he didn't look up when Briar stopped and parked the Rover.

Briar started giggling the moment they pulled onto a street that had nothing but dealerships. Then she met Tobias's gaze. "You really went all out."

"Too much?"

"No way!" Briar said. "Memphis deserves this."

"I deserve what?" the chimera asked, finally looking up from where he'd been examining the stitching around one of his patches. Then he got a good look at their location. "Fuck me!"

"I plan to," Tobias said with a wicked grin. "But not until we get home."

"Tell me you didn't," Memphis said as he got out of the vehicle. Tobias got out to follow him, Briar right behind them.

The chimera walked up to a shiny blue brand new Road King parked in a spot at the front of the dealership. A man wearing a polo with the dealership's name on it hurried up to them.

"Mr. Becker?" he asked.

Tobias raised a hand. "That would be me." He pointed at Memphis. "And this is the gentleman who the motorcycle is for."

"Oh baby, you're so pretty," Memphis murmured as he knelt next to the Road King. "Look at your gleaming pipes. I bet you sound throaty as hell."

"Should I be jealous?" Briar asked with a grin.

Tobias shook his head. "I hope not."

The guy held a folder out to Tobias. "Here's all the paperwork. When he's ready, your friend can come inside and pick out his helmet. We also have a nice selection of chaps, boots, and jackets if you're interested."

"We've got the jackets covered," Briar said proudly, making Tobias beam until she added, "But do you have any helmets in my size?"

Briar had desperately wanted to join Memphis on the back of his new motorcycle, but when Tobias looked downright terrified, she relented. The guy hadn't driven a car in ten years and San Diego traffic had only gotten denser and more aggressive in that time. She didn't blame the vampire for being scared of driving by himself.

Besides, it felt right to take care of him. Especially considering he was still recovering. Memphis said it would be at least another week of steady feeding until Tobias was back to fighting strength. Until then, she and Memphis needed to keep him safe.

"That was the best gift you could've given Memphis," she commented as they drove. When they'd first gotten on the freeway, Memphis had roared past them, grinning from ear to ear. Then he'd slowed down until she'd passed and taken up a position behind her. The motorcycle had looked massive back at the dealership, but Memphis made it look normal sized until you got close.

"It's only the first of many gifts," Tobias promised, his face shining with delight. "I have more planned."

For a brief moment, Briar felt jealous. Not because Memphis got an expensive motorcycle, and she didn't. It was more that Tobias seemed to have planned this evening around Memphis alone. First the leather shop to get his vest, with jackets for both of them thrown in. Then the dealership.

It reminded her a little of the favoritism her mother showed the twins because their father had been the only one to marry her. Leave it to her to be the only girl in a menage and still end up dead last in the favorites game. It wasn't that she wanted Tobias to like her more than Memphis, but she wanted to be liked as much.

Life was never fair.

"Briar?" Tobias said gently, bringing her out of her thoughts. "You're frowning. Is something wrong?"

I'm upset because you like Memphis better, she thought. *I'm being a giant cunt because I told you guys that I don't do relationships so you're getting ready to be together without me.*

"Not really," she said out loud. "Nothing I didn't do to myself, anyway."

He placed a hand on her thigh and the warm weight felt grounding. "Tell me what you're thinking about, maybe I can help," he offered.

"I was thinking about the past," she admitted after a beat. "And how it affects me today."

"I hate the smell of apples," Tobias said.

Confused, she glanced over at him. "What?"

"I hate the smell of apples. Can't stand them." He paused for a beat, then continued. "I should give a little background. I was born sometime in the 1680s, one of many children. We had a small grove of crab apple trees, and my mother would brew apple cider with them."

Tobias abruptly stopped speaking. She gave him a minute to collect his thoughts. Briar could tell there was way more to this story. After a few miles had passed and he still hadn't spoken, she pressed him.

"Was your mom a bootlegger?" she asked, trying to keep her tone light.

"There wasn't such a thing back then," he explained with a shake of his head. "Many farmers brewed something and sold it to the local tavern or neighbors. Assuming they didn't drink it all themselves. John Adams was famous for drinking a glass of cider at every breakfast."

Briar cast him a quick grin. "Founding fathers were day drinkers, good to know."

"Yes, drinking during the day was common. At the time, coffee, tea, cider, and beer were considered safe to drink, unlike water, which could make you sick. My father was the one who consumed most of my mother's cider. We rarely had any to sell off for extra pennies."

That told her the direction this story was going. "Did he hurt you?"

"All the time," Tobias answered with a gusting breath. "I've never told anyone before, but he was a mean-spirited man. Drinking only made him worse. He didn't touch my mother; she would have taken a rolling pin to his head. But all the children were fair game, and because I was the oldest, he beat on me the most."

Driving with one hand, Briar reached down to find where Tobias's hand was resting on her thigh. She covered it with her own and squeezed. "I'm sorry that happened to you. If you know where his grave is, I'll piss on it for you."

Tobias barked out a laugh. "I have no idea what happened to him after I was taken by a vampire named Benoit Le Seuer."

That startled Briar. "You were turned as a kid?"

"No, I wasn't. I've never heard of a child being successfully turned," Tobias answered thoughtfully. "It's such a brutal process with a very low success rate, even for a healthy adult, I can't imagine a child surviving."

"So this Benoit guy wanted to adopt you or what?"

"I'd say the answer is 'or what.' Benoit found me after a particularly brutal beating. I'd limped off to collapse in a far field and stayed there until night fall. I was a boy of fourteen doing a man's labors, and I decided I was going to run away. When I was sure everyone was asleep, I was going to sneak back into the house, gather my few things, and set out on my own."

"But he found you there?" Briar asked, her heart hurting for the teenager treated so cruelly by the man who was supposed to protect him. She'd like to say it was the time period, but it still happened way too much even today to say society had outgrown men like Tobias's father.

Tobias shook his head at the memory. "A falcon swooped down out of the night sky and landed right next to me. At first, I thought the bird had found some prey to hunt, but then he shifted form."

"Wait, vampires can shift?" Briar asked.

"Some of us can. But because we don't share our bodies with an animal half, we have to learn how to use the body we shift into. It can take decades to learn first how to shift, then to fly. Not many vampires turned in the last hundred years bother to learn. Modern methods of travel are so efficient that being able to take flight isn't as necessary as it once was."

"That's interesting, but I need you to tell me what happened next. He shifts into a human and then . . .?"

"He crouched down next to me and told me in very blunt terms that he was a vampire and then he gave me a choice," Tobias said. "I could be his dinner, or I could come work for him. I picked the second option."

"Weren't you terrified?" Briar asked.

"I might have soiled myself," Tobias admitted with a chuckle. "He pointed east and told me how to find his property and to start walking. If I didn't make it by the next night, he said he'd hunt me down and my death wouldn't be an easy one."

"That sounds more like the vampires from the stories Mikey tells," Briar commented. "You must have been so scared."

"I was," Tobias said, his expression turning serious. "I didn't even go home first to get my things. I started running as best as I could in the direction he sent me. I only stopped to drink when I crossed a stream. I didn't have shoes at the time, which normally wasn't an issue on the farm, but my feet weren't tough enough to do twenty miles in a day. About midway through the day, I tore my shirt up and wrapped my feet, so then I got badly sunburned. I showed up to his house just as the sun was setting, exhausted and barely standing."

"Why would he do that?" Briar asked.

"Benoit liked to make his servants prove themselves before he took them on." His expression turned hard. "To this day, I don't know if he would have bothered hunting me down if I hadn't shown up. He was capricious, sometimes going through with his threats and sometimes forgetting about them. I learned quickly to take all his threats seriously because you never knew when he'd go through with one of his warnings."

Something wasn't adding up. "Why pick a barefoot, beaten-up farm boy to be a servant? Was it hard to find staff back then?"

"Quite the opposite," Tobias explained. "But I was told that I was a handsome child." He tugged a lock of his light brown hair. "My skin had always tanned easily, but before I hit puberty around sixteen, my hair was ash blond. Many of the village women said I was a beautiful child. I think that's why he collected me."

Briar's expression turned horrified. "Did he molest you?"

Tobias shook his head. "Nothing like that. All his servants were physically striking. He liked being surrounded by beautiful people."

"That's good," Briar said. "So you show up at his door worn out and looking like hell. What'd he do next? Send you to sleep in the stables? Did you spend your days cleaning floors on your hands and knees and begging for scraps of food?"

Those questions made Tobias chuckle. "I blame Disney for your wild imagination. Life with him was far from harsh. He had some of the other servants clean me up and get me nice clothes. My only job was to follow him around and do anything he asked. Mostly, I stood silently, waiting to fetch something. He never drank from me, but he did have a steady stream of donors that would visit. For an abused boy, his home was heaven. I started to learn all about the magic world hidden from the human one. Those years were eye opening. I think he might have enjoyed all my wide-eyed shock as I met shifters, mages, druids, and witches. The first time a demon teleported to the house, I begged him not to take me down to hell. Both the Demon and Benoit laughed."

"That's sadistic," Briar muttered.

"Probably, but I wasn't being beaten and I had all the food I could eat, a soft bed, and a room to myself. And when I talked one of the maids into helping me get rid of my virginity and we were found out, no one was punished. Benoit was amused and told me not to get anyone pregnant and then gave me a very shocking speech about human reproduction."

"So you didn't get the sex talk from your dad?" she teased.

"I grew up on a farm with copulating animals. We all shared a small cabin and the door to my parents room was a curtain. I was the oldest, so by fourteen, I'd seen plenty. The talk wasn't about sex so much as birth control."

"Wait, hold up. There was birth control back then?"

Tobias flashed her a grin. "Nothing very advanced, but there were condoms made of sheep's gut and of course the pulling-out method, none of which I knew about before. I'd some notion that if we had sex standing up, she couldn't get pregnant."

"I'd give you a hard time, but there are teenagers who still believe stupid shit like that," Briar said with a chuckle. "Matty's cousin told us if we had sex in a pool, you couldn't get pregnant."

"It's sad to note that some things haven't changed much," Tobias commented.

"Back to you getting turned," Briar said. "So you're living in a big house with a bunch of other staff and a vampire and everyone getting along. What changed? When did he decide to turn you?" Briar asked.

That's when her phone started telling her she needed to exit the freeway in a few miles. She let the silence stretch until she'd gotten them onto the off ramp and in the long queue to turn left at the stop light. Judging by how slowly traffic was moving, they were going to be there for three or four cycles before they'd be able to turn.

As they sat there, Memphis pulled up and knocked at her window. Smiling, she rolled it down. "You should go ahead of us since you can lane split," Briar said before he could talk.

His smile was infectious. "I was hoping you'd say that."

Plucking her phone out of the holder on the dash, she showed him the screen. "See, it's right there on that corner. Only another mile down after this light."

"Right, I'll see you guys there," he said. Then he leaned in through the window to give her a quick kiss before roaring off between the lines of stopped cars. He looked so damn sexy riding off like that she almost forgot what she and Tobias were talking about.

Almost.

"You don't have to tell me if it's painful," she said. "I'd never want you to share something that was traumatic before you're ready."

"It's not painful, it's embarrassing," he finally told her. He tried to withdraw the hand on her thigh, but she placed her hand back over his to stop him.

"Whatever happened, I'd never look down on you," she promised.

"I begged him," Tobias finally said in a rush. "I begged him to turn me. I was the only human in a house surrounded by preternatural creatures. You can't be turned into a shifter, druid, or witch, but you can become a vampire. I wanted it so bad that I made a nuisance of myself. Finally, he'd had enough. He said I had to wait until I was an adult and every year on my birthday I was allowed to ask again."

"You shouldn't be embarrassed," she insisted. "If I'd been in your same situation, I might have asked too, especially back in the old days when life expectancy was so much shorter. Because you're sitting here now, I guess he eventually said yes?"

"I asked every year on April 7th, my birthday. On my twenty-sixth birthday he agreed. I was so excited, and I couldn't understand why the staff was so horrified when we announced it. But I understood later."

"Because being turned was so painful?" Briar asked.

"The process of getting turned was painful, but only lasted a little over a day. I barely remember it. But I have very clear memories of the two years after being turned. I was endlessly hungry. If Benoit hadn't kept me under tight control, I would have murdered every human in a ten-mile radius in one night. No matter how much I drank, it was never enough. There were nights he had to put me under heavy thrall. I'd follow him around in a stupor, barely aware of anything but the all-consuming need to feed."

Briar was appalled. "That sounds like you were turned into a zombie, not a vampire."

"Vampires under two years old are very often like your movie zombies. Strong, but stumbling and clumsy creatures that are never full. But we want blood, not brains. After about two years, I started to gain some control. I was still hungry all the time, but I learned to ignore it. After another four more months, the hunger eased to an ache. The moment I could control myself, Benoit threw me out. Vampires don't like to be around each other, and I had long since worn out my welcome with him."

She whistled out a breath. "Damn, that seems harsh."

"I wasn't as bad as you think. He gave me a large sum of money and warned me to invest well because I had the potential to live a long life. One of the men who worked for him was a bear shifter. Unlike most shifters, bears don't live in groups. He struck a bargain with me; he'd stay by my side if we remained equals. I agreed, and we traveled and invested together. He kept me safe during the day, and I provided him with all the creature comforts I could afford. Joseph and I were good friends until he died of old age."

They were finally at the point where they were turning at the light. "I'm sorry you suffered so much after being turned, but I thought your story was going to be so much worse. Mikey told me about vampires kidnapping and torturing their victims. Or keeping them under thrall and making them do things they didn't want to do."

"Unlike many vampires, Benoit wasn't evil. I'm the only person he ever tried to turn. Because I survived, he claimed he'd never do it again because the odds were against a second successful attempt. I also got lucky that Joseph was at my side. I probably wouldn't have lasted a year on my own without him, even with the money Benoit gave me."

"Do you know what happened to Benoit?" Briar asked as she pulled into a busy parking lot. The restaurant looked fancy but not exclusive. Cloth napkins but no dinner jacket requirement.

"I believe he lives in New York," Tobias told her.

"I'm glad he's alive but also happy he's all the way on the East Coast." She spotted Memphis. "Looks like we don't have to fight to find a parking spot."

Memphis had grabbed two parking spaces near the front, the bike parked in one and him standing in the other. He had his arms crossed and was scowling at anyone who even looked at the spot. When he saw them, his scowl turned to a grin and he waved them over, moving only when she was pulling in.

"About time you got here," he grumbled, opening her door and pulling her out. She didn't get a chance to answer because he had her pressed against the side of the Rover and was kissing her senseless.

She felt the world melt away with Memphis's kiss. His hard body pressed her into the car, and she could clearly feel the outline of his thickening cock through their clothing.

Suddenly, she wasn't hungry anymore. Not hungry for food at least.

"Oh no you don't," Tobias said with a chuckle. She felt his hand grasp her, then she was sliding sideways against the car. Memphis made a surprised grunting sound and released her. Unprepared for that, she tumbled into Tobias's waiting arms. The vampire set her on the ground.

"Dinner first, then play time," Tobias insisted. When Memphis looked like he was about to protest, Tobias added, "I promise, all your appetites will be appeased by the end of the evening."

Memphis sighed. "Fine, but the food here better be good, and no lingering over coffee or dessert. We eat and we go home."

His eager expression made Briar laugh. "Whatever you say," she agreed.

Memphis looked delighted before putting himself between herself and Tobias, then taking their hands in his. "And that's the way it should always be."

"I figure in a week or two, I'll fly up to Bend and pack my stuff up to move down here," Memphis stated casually, all the while trying to keep a subtle eye on Briar.

He'd been dropping hints about the two of them moving in with Tobias over the last few days. Because Briar was the only one of them gun shy about relationships, he'd been tiptoeing around the subject. But sooner or later, they were going to need to discuss it like adults.

The only outward sign that she heard him was a slight tightening of her shoulders. At least she wasn't objecting. That might be a step forward. When he'd mentioned it before, she'd been quick to tell him not to bother moving so soon. This was progress.

"You don't need to travel there and back. I can hire movers," Tobias offered.

"No need," Memphis assured him. "I want to go up to tell my parents and brothers about us. And they're going to want to meet both of you." The minute those words were out of his mouth, he knew they'd been a mistake.

"Maybe we should give it some time before we go meeting each other's parents," Briar said without looking up from her empty dessert plate.

Memphis hurried to do damage control. "Don't feel special," he said, trying for humor. "My mom's been wanting to visit Southern California for a while. She's always wanted to go to Disneyland and the studio place with the mechanical Jaws shark. I think hanging out with us would be low on the list of attractions."

"Universal Studios," Briar said, her tone wooden. "That's the place where you see the shark from Jaws."

"That's the one." Memphis wished she'd look up, but her eyes remained stubbornly downcast. Looking over, he met Tobias's gaze. The vampire was finally realizing something was wrong.

"Briar, are you upset at the thought of meeting Memphis's parents?"

Memphis winced at Tobias's blunt question. The way Briar jerked told him that the question hadn't gone over well.

"Um, yeah, no. It's fine. I mean, your place has lots of room for them to stay," she said. She was clenching her fork so tightly her knuckles were white.

Memphis wasn't sure what to say so he went with honesty. "They'll like you; I promise. My family will adore anyone I pick as a mate."

"Until they see me," she said under her breath. "Who would want me to be part of their family?"

That comment surprised Memphis. He thought anyone who enjoyed their style of dress as much as Briar did would be more confident.

"They'll take one look at you and think I've found my match," he said, hoping that would get her to smile.

She finally looked up to meet his eyes. "No they won't." She set the fork down on her plate with a clatter. "They'll take one look at me and ask you why the fuck you'd want to be with someone who knows fuck-all about dresses or make-up or even the proper way to do anything."

"Why would any of that matter?" Memphis asked. Logically, he knew this was coming from Tiffany's influence. If he ever met the woman, he'd make sure she knew his opinion about her life choices, including being so cruel to her daughter.

But how could Briar think that he or his family would think like that?

"You're my mate, Baby Doll," he explained gently. "You, Tobias, and me are destined to be together. To make each other whole. I know that sounds scary because you don't believe in forever's. So give us a chance in this lifetime and if it doesn't work out, you can pick someone else in the next lifetime."

The smile he'd hoped for didn't appear and she dropped her gaze again. "Destiny means you didn't have a choice but to pick me. It's a polite way of saying you lost the mate lottery but you're making the best out of it. Your family will figure that out the moment they meet me."

With that, she got up and dashed out of the restaurant. Memphis was too stunned to follow. How had this pleasant evening gone bad so quickly?

"Why would she think that?" Tobias asked, his eyes wide with surprise. Then his eyes narrowed, and he frowned. "She's got the car keys."

By the time they both made it out the door, the Rover was already gone.

Briar sped through a yellow light, jaw clenched and fingers gripping the steering wheel so hard her knuckles ached. She'd never been one for emotional dramatics unless she was picking a fight. That was a whole different scenario.

Hmmm, getting into a good brawl sounded like a great idea. Getting to punch some asshole in a bar fight would feel so much better than thinking about how twisted up her guts felt.

Making a sharp left, she ignored the horns that blared at her and navigated to a familiar area. Mikey's bar, the Downward Dog, was only a few miles further down, but she didn't go there. No, she headed for Pounders, a dive bar normally full of East County rednecks. She'd only been there once, years ago, but the fight that broke out had made the evening news.

Body humming with emotional energy and a brain buzzing for a distraction, she screeched into a parking spot. She didn't even remember the walk from the Rover into the bar. She paused for a minute inside the door to take everything in. There were a few guys playing pool, but almost everyone was at the bar watching a UFC fight on the big screens hanging high on the walls behind the bar.

There were two bartenders, a crusty old guy and a beautiful young black woman with her hair in braids, the magenta extensions hanging to her waist. Briar made her way to the woman's end of the bar and watched her skillfully evade a guy trying to grab her wrist as she set down his beer. Then she plucked the guy's twenty from his other hand and held it out of reach.

"Change in the tip jar, right?" she asked.

The guy looked like he was about to protest when she raised an eyebrow at him. "Sure, whatever," he grumbled.

She made change and tossed a ten in the beer pitcher tip jar on the counter. Then she ambled over to Briar. "Nice hair," she commented. "What can I get you?"

That's when Briar realized she didn't have any money on her. Fuck, she'd been so distracted back at the house she'd forgotten to pack her wallet. "I don't suppose you guys take Samsung pay or Venmo?"

The woman made a face. "We don't even take credit cards." She nodded her head at the other bartender. "Phill is beyond old school."

Briar sighed. For some reason, seeing the beautiful bartender had calmed her raging emotions and now she wanted a drink more than she wanted a fight. Before she could explain her lack of funds, the bartender leaned close and took a deep breath through her nose.

Startled, Briar reared back. "What the fuck?"

Before she could step away, the woman's hand snaked out and grabbed the front of her vest, keeping her from retreating. Unbelievably strong, the woman pulled Briar close until they were nose to nose over the bar. Knowing preternatural strength when she felt it, Briar went still as the woman shut her eyes, her brows furrowing in concentration.

Hopefully, she was a shifter whose animal side had taken over their good sense for a moment. After a good sniff she'd let Briar go. If she didn't, there were two empty beer bottles nearby and Briar knew from experience that they made good weapons.

"Your aura reeks of vampire," the woman whispered, her eyes popping back open. "Is he close? Is he chasing you?" Abruptly, the woman let go of Briar and started digging through her pockets. "Shit, I've only got one charm on me; otherwise I'd give you my extra."

It finally occurred to Briar that this woman thought she came into the bar to hide from Tobias. "No one's chasing me."

The bartender cocked an eyebrow at her, and Briar realized how effective that was. No wonder the guy gave up his change without a fuss.

"Really, no one's chasing me," Briar hurried to assure her again. The bartender remained silent, and words started pouring out of Briar.

"My, uh, boyfriend is a vampire. Or one of them, I guess, because I kinda have two boyfriends. I think. But both of them are stuck with me because of this whole mate thing. And Memphis's family wants to visit, and he wants me to meet his mom. And Tobias wants us to move in with him. And they want this to be permanent but how long until they figure it out? Like, how long until they realize I'm a mess?" Briar put her elbows on the table and dropped her face into her hands. "Oh fuck, I need a drink."

"I'd say," the bartender drawled. Briar looked up in time to see her point to the empty stool. "Stay there. I'll be right back."

Briar wasn't one to obey strangers, but this woman had an air of authority and command that was hard to resist. She plopped her size fourteen butt on the stool and watched the elegant bartender stride up to the crusty old man behind the bar. She was wearing tight black jeans that showed off her round ass and hips. Her crop top showcased a flat belly and hugged her small breasts, displaying her assets to the best advantage. Short nails were painted to match her extensions, and a delicate gold nose ring completed her style. She looked sexy but also powerful, especially the way she walked with so much confidence.

This was not a woman to be fucked with. Briar could only hope that she displayed half that level of self-assurance when she walked around.

Her new friend had a quick conversation with the crusty guy who didn't look thrilled but waved her off and returned to watching the fight with everyone else. After snagging two bottles out of a fridge and popping them open, she grabbed something from under the counter. Then she flipped open the pass through and gestured for Briar to follow her.

"Spill the tea," she said as she held out a bottle. "It's my dinner break, and it sounds like you got a story to tell."

Briar accepted the bottle of beer and followed her out a back door into a typical bar alley with dumpsters, stacks of empty plastic crates, and litter gathered next to everything.

"I'm Imani," she told Briar as she took a seat on the low cinderblock wall on the opposite side of the alley. Beyond that was another alley with much newer buildings but just as much trash.

Sitting next to her, Briar pointed to herself. "Briar."

"Like Briar Rose?" Imani asked as she set her beer on the wall and opened up her hand to reveal what she'd grabbed before stepping out from behind the bar. A pack of cigarettes and a lighter.

"As in Briar Thorn," she answered.

"I like that better," Imani said with a grin before putting a cigarette in her mouth and lighting it up. Briar had started smoking when she was fifteen. That was the year she gave up on pleasing Tiffany and went to the far opposite end of doing anything and everything that would upset her mother.

But when Lily found out about the smoking, Briar quit. It was one thing to piss off Tiffany, but she couldn't handle Lily's disappointment.

The craving had stuck with her all these years later, and if any time called for a little indulgence, it was now. "Can I bum one of those off you?"

"Sure thing," Imani said and handed her the one she'd just lit. Briar accepted it and took a deep drag. It felt amazingly soothing to suck on that cancer stick, then down a swallow of cold beer.

Fuck, she'd needed this.

"Okay, you wanna tell me what all drove you into my bar looking like you were ready to pick a fight?"

"You saw that?" Briar asked, feeling sheepish.

"Honey, your eyes were blazing, and you looked downright disappointed we weren't wall-to-wall with assholes," Imani said with a grin. "Now tell Aunty Imani what happened. And what is smothered all over your aura besides vampire? It's some kind of shifter, but I've never seen it before."

"Chimera," Briar said. Then she spilled her guts. She told Imani everything, starting with finding Tobias and only stopping when she got to walking into Pounders.

By the time she was done, their beers were empty, and they'd smoked the pack between them. Her throat felt raw from the combination of talking and cigarettes, but all the emotions that had been banging around in her head like bumper cars piloted by rabid children had calmed down.

Imani picked up their empty beer bottles and chucked them into the recycling bin. "So now you're freaking out because you think they're forced to be with you?"

"Wouldn't you be?" Briar asked. "They didn't get to choose me. I was chosen for them, like some kind of old-fashioned bullshit arranged marriage. They're going to end up resenting me. I'm not good at this shit."

Imani tilted her head as she regarded Briar. "You mean you'd cheat on them?"

"No!" Briar protested loudly. "I'd never do that."

Imani didn't react to her outraged tone. "What about being mean? Like telling them they're not good enough for you."

"I'm not a bitch like that," Briar said, understanding the point Imani was making. "I meant I'm not good at being like, you know, a girlfriend."

"What do you think it means to be a girlfriend to a vampire and chimera? You've already seen Memphis shift and that didn't seem to bother you. You saw Tobias at his worst because nothing's as violent as a starved vampire, except maybe when their flock is under threat. So even though you're human, you're cool with all that. What else is there?"

Briar let out a long breath as she pointed to herself. "This is me. This is it. I'm not some white skinned, size 4, woman who cooks and cleans. I'm not going to wear a skirt or dress, and I think fancy is wearing boots without scuffs on them. I won't change, not even for them. That means they'll eventually figure out I'm shit at this relationship thing and want out. Or end up hating me."

Imani was quiet for a moment. When she did start talking, her husky voice was gentle and kind. "You're focused on the wrong things. If they'd wanted a girly-girl, the three of you wouldn't have ended up together."

Briar made a loud ah-ha sound. "See! That's the problem, they didn't get a choice. Fate did."

"No, she didn't," Imani argued. "Let me explain to you what the whole fated mates thing is. Everyone thinks it's a one-time thing. That it's about those two or three people that are meant to be together."

"Isn't it?"

"Nope," Imani said with a shake of her head that sent some of her long braids flying over her left shoulder. "Preternaturals have a sense when they find someone that's perfectly compatible with them. Vampires, shifters, harpies, druids, gargoyles, they all do it. Even humans have it to a much smaller degree. Have any of your human friends ever talked about just clicking with someone? That's their limited ability to sense compatibility. Those are the same humans that often find their partner young and have the storybook marriages."

"Yeah, I know what you're talking about. My friends Melody and Dave were like that. Met in high school, married in college, and have been happily together ever since."

"See, that's what I mean. Memphis and Tobias aren't 'stuck' with you. They want you because all three of you are super compatible. And brace yourself because sometimes a fourth and fifth person can show up in these matches. You should be dancing with joy because if Memphis had found someone else that he matched with first, he would have settled there and not looked further."

The sounds of a motorcycle roaring nearby and the angry honking of horns filled the air as Briar thought about Imani's words.

Far from feeling insulted that she was one of many who would've been a match for Memphis and Tobias, a heavy weight was lifted off Briar. It was easier to think of their relationship as being one of many permutations that could have happened by chance. Seeing it that way made it feel less mystical and momentous. Instead of them being fated to always be together and get along, they could be lovers who enjoyed spending time together.

No pressure. No expectations.

And now she felt ridiculous for having stormed out of the restaurant and leaving the guys behind. Dramatic much?

Pulling out her phone, she pulled up a chat with Memphis. "I should probably—"

Her words were cut off when the back door to Pounders crashed open with such violence that one of the hinges broke.

Memphis appeared with Tobias right behind him. Their expressions flashed with relief until they saw Imani. Memphis growled and Tobias's eyes turned blood red as he pulled back his lips to reveal fangs.

"What the hell?" Briar asked, jumping to her feet. Next to her Imani leapt backwards, clearing the low stone wall and landing across the second alley.

"I intend no harm to your flock!" she yelled out. "I was giving comfort only."

"Mine!" Tobias started stalking forward. Fearing for her new friend, Briar put herself in the vampire's path.

Grabbing the lapels of his jacket, she kept him from moving past her. "She was being nice to me. She gave me a beer and let me talk."

Her words seemed to have fallen on deaf ears because Memphis moved to walk past her, his posture menacing. Still holding on to Tobias's coat with one hand, she reached out to grab Memphis's thick wrist with her other hand. That made him stop and look at her.

"*Friend!*" she repeated loudly. "You hurt her, and I'll be pissed. Trust me, you don't want to see what I can do when I'm angry."

It took a great deal of control for Tobias to pull back the rage threatening to overwhelm him. He knew Briar was already upset with him and ripping her new friend in many small pieces wouldn't help him talk her into coming back to the house with him and Memphis.

Without trying to move away from Briar, Tobias raised his gaze to Imani. "Who's your maker?" he asked, his fangs receding back into his gums.

"Vincent," Imani said. "But I'm on my own now. I have been for months."

Tobias reared back, his eyes widening with surprise. "Vincent Petrov made you?"

Letting go of both his jacket and Memphis's wrist, Briar turned so she could be part of the conversation. "Made? What does he mean, Imani?"

The woman in question shrugged her elegant shoulder, her face impassive. "An asshole vampire named Vincent made a wager with one of his flock that he couldn't turn someone successfully. I'm the result."

Far from being alarmed, Briar only looked mildly surprised. "You're a vampire? I wouldn't have guessed." Then her expression turned horrified. "Some douche canoe turned you because of a bet?"

"Lucky me, right?" Imani said, her stance relaxing a little as she spoke to Briar. "I was having a fun night out with a few girlfriends. Some cute white guy with an accent comes up and starts dancing with me. I don't think anything of it because it's a crowded room." She shook her head sadly. "The next thing I know, I'm in a strange place and my body feels like it's on fire."

"Do you want me to fuck him up for you?" Briar offered without hesitation. "Not like physically, but I can totally make his life hell. Give me a last name and any other details like an address, and I can make sure his number is on every telemarketing list out there. I'll destroy his credit, cancel his credit cards, put stop payments on all his stuff, and maybe even get him reported as dead. I mean, I know he's already a vampire, but I could get his current identity identified as deceased. No charge for any of it."

Imani blinked slowly at her as she processed everything Briar had offered. After a few beats of silence, a slow grin unfurled across the young vampire's face. "We're definitely going to become friends."

"No!" Tobias spoke before he could think better of it. He caught Memphis's look of disapproval before he dropped his gaze to see Briar's narrow-eyed expression.

"Oh really?" she asked in much too quiet of a voice.

"I meant I'm not comfortable with you being alone with a vampire so young," he explained hastily.

"What does that have to do with anything?" Briar retorted. "We've been hanging out for the last hour, and she didn't try to do anything. If she was going to 'steal' me, she would've tried already."

"He's not worried that she'll try to make you into her flock. He's concerned because young vampires have a harder time controlling their appetite," Memphis explained for him. "I think Tobias is scared she'd succumb to blood lust around you."

Briar still looked skeptical and pointed at the back door they all came through to get to the alley. "Dude, she works at that bar. And it's not like the Downward Dog. Pounders is for humans, and not even very classy ones. If she was going to go all uncontrollably vampy, I'm sure she would've done it by now."

Imani snorted out a laugh. "Truth," she commented. "Not that I haven't been tempted to rip some throats out. Nothing so annoying as entitled, drunk white guys."

That simple statement brought Tobias up short. "You work around humans? How old are you? Five years?"

"Vincent turned me a year and a half ago," Imani told him. "And I hauled butt out of his place a year ago."

Tobias pulled in a startled breath. "That's impressive."

Imani doesn't look convinced. "So I've been told."

"What's impressive?" Briar asked.

Unable to keep from touching her, he cautiously stepped up behind her and loosely wrapped his arms around her shoulders. He moved slowly to give her plenty of time to move away or shrug him off. She didn't do either, and once he was embracing her, she relaxed into his arms.

"Young vampires suffer from blood lust so strong that they have no control over their actions. No matter how much they consume, they want more," he explained.

"That's right," Briar said. "I remember you telling me about what it was like when you were first turned. So being able to control yourself within six months is rare?"

"So rare that I've never heard of it," Tobias admitted. "Imani might become the most powerful vampire to ever live."

Far from looking flattered, Imani's expression was grim. "If I survive long enough."

"What do you mean, survive? I thought vampires were apex predators and shit," Briar protested.

"I will be, eventually," Imani said, her expression turning mournful. "But each day comes with a question mark. Most other preternaturals don't like us. The moment I left Vincent's house, I became prey to anyone who wants to brag they killed a vampire or a tooth-puller looking to make some money. But I'd rather die than spend even another day with Vincent and his flock. They're all sadistic bastards."

"Come home with us," Briar offered.

Tobias jerked and opened his mouth to talk Briar out of it, but Imani beat him to it.

"Vampires don't share homes. We're territorial." A kind smile curved her lips as she spoke. "But damn girl, you go around offering your crib to everyone?"

"Only to my friends," Briar answered with a matching grin. "After sharing beer, smokes, and my life story, you're one of my besties now. There's no getting rid of me."

"You drank beer?" Tobias asked Imani, interrupting their conversation.

"I can drink beer or water or whatever, doesn't bother me," Imani answered. "Why?"

"You should be sick!" Tobias answered, feeling intrigued by this young vampire in spite of himself. "At under two years old, you should be violently ill after the first swallow. I'm over three hundred, and I have to brace myself if I need to consume something besides blood." Everything about this woman's vampire nature was shocking. She was truly going to be an extremely powerful vampire, and because she'd been so kind to Briar, he felt compelled to help.

"Use my name," he instructed. "Tell everyone you're under my protection. That should keep most from trying anything. Do you have charms?"

Imani nodded her head and pulled a wooden disk on a string from her pocket. "They're expensive, so I only put them on when I sense someone close."

"What the fuck is going on here?" a voice yelled from inside. All of them turned to face the door as a man stinking of body odor and beer emerged. "What the hell? Who broke my door?"

"I'll pay for the damages," Tobias said quickly.

"You better!" the guy raged then pointed a finger at Imani. "And your dinner break was over forty minutes ago. I'm going to—"

"Go ahead and threaten me, Phill. See how that ends for you," Imani said, hopping down to the lower alley.

"Fine, just get back to work. Fight's over and everyone wants to order. And get money for the door from your buddy over there," Phill grumbled before disappearing inside.

Making a wide circle around the three of them, Imani walked to the back door, then paused and looked at Briar. "I work here Wednesday through Sunday, each night. All damn night. Come find me, 'k?"

"I will," Briar promised. "And I'll bring friends. You're not alone anymore."

"That, um," Imani took a deep, shuddering breath. "That would be nice."

Tobias thought he saw a single black, pearlescent tear fall from Imani's eye before she turned to hurry away.

With one arm still around Briar, Tobias reached for his wallet. "Would you pay the barkeep for the door?" he asked Memphis. "I'll walk Briar around the building to get to the car. I don't think I could handle having her in the same room with a vampire right now."

"Or all those nasty humans," Memphis said with an easy grin.

Tobias smiled back. "And I'll be driving home with Briar in the car, like civilized people."

Memphis plucked the wallet from Tobias with a snort. "What fun is that?" he asked, striding away.

The moment he was gone, Tobias picked Briar up and started walking.

"Tobias, this isn't kosher! Put me down."

"Not yet, my heart," he answered. "I was so scared when you left. I was terrified you'd get into an accident and be gone from this life. That I'd lost you before we'd even gotten started. I need to hold you. At least until we get to the car."

She stopped protesting. "I'm sorry I worried you guys."

"Don't be sorry, my love," Tobias told her. "But don't do that again. Rage at me. Declare that you're moving out. I'll help you find a place. We'll go on dates. We'll court. I don't care. But don't storm off like that again. Don't get behind the wheel upset. I don't think either Memphis or I could live with your death, especially if we were the cause."

"I won't," she promised. "Imani helped me figure some things out. I'm willing to give the three of us a try."

There was only one thing Tobias could think to say in response. "I'm buying that vampire her own bar!"

Briar was quiet on the way home. She'd insisted on driving, claiming it would make her feel less guilty about what had happened earlier. Tobias had been tempted to hire a service to drive them back so he could hold Briar in his arms the whole way. But he gave up on that when Briar made her determined face.

Memphis stuck close to them the entire way. He roared up the driveway ahead of them and by the time they reached him, he was off the bike with his helmet hanging from a side mirror. Briar only managed to get her seatbelt off before he was wrenching open the door and snatching her up in his arms.

That's when Tobias realized Memphis had been keeping himself under tight control the whole evening. While Tobias had been a mess and almost ripped open a man's neck who'd gotten between him and the restaurant's front door, Memphis had kept his cool.

The chimera made his living as a bounty hunter and tracker. With his shifter half having better senses than any other preternatural, he'd managed to track Briar the few miles to Pounders, despite heavy evening traffic and being in the middle of a dense urban center.

Tobias had sat impatiently on the back of the motorcycle, holding onto Memphis's waist as they circled around until he'd picked up the scent well enough to follow. Then he'd lose it and have to start circling again. It had been tedious, and Tobias had shouted at him a few times to hurry.

Memphis had responded the same calm way each time. "I'll find her."

Watching the chimera holding Briar, burying his nose against her neck and rocking her back and forth made Tobias appreciate how controlled Memphis had been the entire time. It made the vampire feel a little ashamed of himself.

"Let's go inside," he urged. "I still have Briar's gift and perhaps we could all snuggle on the couch and enjoy a nightcap?"

Briar raised her head from where she'd been snuggled against Memphis. "Gift?"

Her startled expression made him chuckle, relieving much of the tension from earlier. "You don't think I'd shower Memphis with all these gifts and not have something for you also, did you?"

Her brows furrowed. "But you did give me a gift. This jacket, remember?"

"That was an afterthought when I ordered Memphis's vest and jacket," Tobias explained, surprised to realize that was all she thought she was getting. "I have your gifts in the house. If Greg did as I asked, they should all have been set up while we were out."

Tobias opened the front door wide to let Memphis stride through with Briar still in his arms. The chimera stopped suddenly and let out a low menacing sound, making Tobias slam the door and hurry to his side.

Confused, Tobias found Memphis glaring at Greg, who was simply standing at the foot of the stairs, frozen in place. When Greg saw him, his expression turned relieved.

"There you are," he said, edging to the side a bit. "The men you hired finished and left only five minutes ago."

Next to him, Memphis had stopped growling because he had to focus on Briar, who was insisting on being set down. While she negotiated with Memphis, Tobias focused on Greg.

He'd known from the moment he'd hired Greg that the man had romantic views on vampires. But his sycophantic ways hadn't bothered Tobias until now. Greg made Tobias's flock uncomfortable, but Tobias couldn't simply kick the man out after so many years of loyal service. And he didn't seem to want to retire, no matter how generous Tobias made the retirement package. Maybe he could find Greg a position somewhere else.

Was there an internet site he could list Greg and re-home him to other vampires?

"Thank you, Greg," Tobias said, careful to step back so Greg's outstretched hand didn't make contact. He'd never noticed before how much Greg tried to touch him. A hand on his arm. His body pressed close to his as they stood next to each other. Hands on his coat or shirt to straighten garments. None of it was overtly sexual, but with Memphis and Briar in his life, even standing too close to Greg felt wrong.

"What are you guys talking about?" Briar asked, bumping Greg out of the way so she could stand next to Tobias.

Resentment flashed across Greg's face before he managed a polite expression. "Master has arranged a very expensive gift for you. I hope you're appropriately grateful."

Tobias was quick to interrupt the brewing argument. Taking Briar's hand, he tugged her down the hall toward his old office. "Come my, love. I have a surprise for you."

"You didn't need to get me anything," Briar said as she let Tobias lead, Memphis right behind the two of them. "I didn't lose my bike like Memphis did."

"It doesn't work that way," Tobias argued with a grin. "I love you equally so you both get toys. Besides, what kind of vampire would I be if I didn't shower my flock with presents?"

"That's a thing?" Briar asked.

Memphis chuckled behind them. "It's a big thing. Vampires tend to amass wealth, and it's instinctual for them to want to spend it on their flock. Like the human instinct to want to feed people they love."

"That wasn't a thing with my family," Briar muttered. "Tiffany was always telling me to lose forty pounds. I remember we had celery for dinner one day. But thankfully, Tiffany wasn't much into being a mom, so those types of meals were rare."

Tobias stopped at the office door and turned to gather Briar up in his arms. He could tell by the expression on Memphis's face that the chimera had heard the old hurt in her voice as well.

"You're perfect," Tobias insisted as Memphis stepped up from behind to wrap his big arms around both of them.

"Tobias is right," Memphis agreed. "You're one beautiful, bad-ass bitch."

Briar laughed. "I guess I need to be bad-ass to hang around with you guys." Then she shook her head. "Sorry for the self-pity moment. I've been working on getting Tiffany out of my head for a long time and some days I'm better at it than others."

"If you ever hear her, Baby Doll," Memphis said. "You come to us, and we'll drown out her voice."

"Yeah, yeah," she said, pulling away from them and running a knuckle under her eyes. "Let's move on to the part where Tobias reveals what's behind door number one!"

Tobias wanted to insist they talk more about Briar's erroneous belief that she wasn't beautiful, but he caught Memphis's expression and swallowed the words.

He reached behind him and opened the door with a flourish. "Your prizes, my sweet Briar!"

Briar froze as she stared at the contents of the room. Like Briar and Memphis, this was the first time Tobias was seeing the room after ordering everything and arranging for the work to be done. This was one of the reasons it had been so important for him to take Briar and Memphis out for the evening.

All the older furnishings were gone, replaced by a more sleek, modern design. A much larger desk had been installed in the room to replace the original one he'd never bothered using.

Mounted on the wall behind the desk were four large monitors, all hooked to a computer the salesman had assured him was top of the line. He'd also had high-speed fiber optic internet installed and a surround sound system set up. This room would be perfect for gaming, hacking, or listening to music. In short, a room specifically designed to please Briar.

She took one stumbling step into the room. "Is that an Aventum X?"

"I don't know," Tobias admitted as Briar touched the computer tower with reverence. "I asked for the best they had in stock. This one was supposed to go to someone else, but I persuaded them to sell it to me instead."

"Is it a nice computer?" Memphis asked as he joined Briar at the desk.

"Nice doesn't even begin to cover it," she answered, stroking the tower. "The desktop I've got at home is like, um, like a really nice bicycle with only one gear. This system is a crotch rocket powered with jet fuel."

"Sounds dangerous," Memphis said with a grin.

"Just how I like 'em," Briar agreed as she took a seat at the desk. She touched the mouse to bring the system out of hibernation mode, and then started clicking away. She started mumbling to herself about programs and access as she clicked. Before she could get too distracted, Tobias picked up a box that had been sitting on a shelf and set it on the desk next to her.

"I also took the liberty of getting you this," he said.

Her eyes got wide when they locked on the logo. "Is that an Alienware laptop?"

Tobias shrugged. "It is whatever the clerk said was the best they had in stock. I can order you something better if you don't like this one."

Briar grabbed the box and clutched it to her chest. "I like! I like!"

Pleasure filled Tobias. It looked like he'd provided both his flock with gifts they valued.

"Delightful," he declared. He pointed to the couch he'd had brought into the room to replace the delicate, fussy chairs he'd never been fond of. "Would it bother you if Memphis and I sat and talked while you worked with your new computers?"

"Sure," she said, not even looking up as she set the box on the desk and started ripping at the tape and tabs to get it open.

Memphis put his lips to Tobias's ear. "Good job, sweetheart. Outside of sex, I think you found the way to Briar's heart."

Tobias took his hand and led him to the couch. "Hopefully she won't forget about us," he answered with a smile. He sat and drew Memphis down next to him.

"We'll make sure she doesn't," Memphis murmured.

They snuggled close on the couch. Memphis's warm bulk next to him and the sound of Briar mumbling to herself in the background was soothing enough that the last of his tension eased away. He'd give Briar a few hours and then he had plans for the three of them in the bedroom.

Loud banging and shouting broke Briar's focus. Blinking rapidly, she looked up from the laptop to find both Memphis and Tobias getting to their feet with twin expressions of aggression.

"It's almost one in the morning," Memphis growled. "Who the fuck is knocking at your door at this hour?"

"No one that was invited," Tobias said as he marched out of the room.

Memphis was on the vampires heels. calling back over his shoulder. "Stay here."

"Oh, hell no!" Briar said, jogging to catch up with the men as Tobias swung open the door, Memphis right behind him.

With the two of them blocking the door, Briar couldn't see who Tobias was speaking to with intense disdain. "Who are you and what do you want?"

"Let me see Briar!" a familiar voice demanded. "I know she's here."

"Maddy?" Briar called out, tugging at the back of Memphis's vest. He moved slightly so she could see but couldn't get by him.

"Briar!" Maddy called out, tears sparkling in her eyes. "I've been so worried! You only returned a few of my texts and didn't answer my calls. Then Kennedy noticed your car getting towed the other day. He said it had been parked outside the bar since we went to help Mikey. What happened? You said you were going to Santa Barbara."

Briar tried to get past Memphis to comfort her friend. "Don't cry, Maddy! Please don't cry. I can explain everything."

"Maddy, I told you to wait for me!" Mikey boomed, making Briar wince. Standing on her tiptoes, she saw Mikey standing in the driveway with a dozen of his pack around him. He took a sniff, his lip curled up in a growl, and his canines lengthened. "Get away from that door!"

"I found Briar!" Maddy announced. "She's okay."

"Vampire!" Mikey spit the word like a curse. "Get away from them!"

"He's a friendly vampire!" Briar yelled. She heard Memphis scoff, but she didn't think Mikey heard her because he was too busy talking to the pack members with him. She was most worried about Maddy, who had taken a step back and was standing on the first stair.

"Briar, are you mixed up in something?" Maddy asked.

Grabbing Memphis's shoulder to help keep herself steady, Briar met Maddy's concerned gaze. "No more than usual," she answered with a cocky grin. "But I promise, these guys would never hurt me. Mikey's overreacting."

"But is he wrong?" Maddy countered, her expression going from relieved to scared. "About the vampire thing?"

"I'm a vampire," Tobias said, his voice powerful and ominous. "And you will not take Briar from me. She's mine."

"Even if I have to stake you myself, we're getting her away from you!" Mikey yelled out.

Shit, this was getting out of hand! Briar struggled against the wall of man in front of her, trying to get to Maddy.

"No one's going to take me," she wheezed. She needed to work out more. And maybe not smoke half a pack of cigarettes in an evening. Yeah, poor choices had been made.

"They won't take you because we won't let them!" Memphis growled without looking back at her.

This sounded bad. "I just need to show Maddy and Mikey that I'm safe. Let me through!"

"Let me talk to her!" Maddy insisted. "Let her tell me she wants to stay. You could be controlling her mind or something!"

"Thrall!" Tobias said, as if remembering that word after trying to figure it out for a while. "I do have that power."

Giving up on getting past either man, Briar started climbing up Memphis's back. The thick belt and vest provided excellent foot holds. She managed to scamper up and over his shoulder before he had a chance to register what she was doing. Unfortunately, she got her own two feet tangled and ended up falling headfirst once she was over his shoulder.

She tumbled down his chest, but he managed to catch her with a surprised 'umph' sound.

"Briar, what the fuck?" he exclaimed.

She didn't even hear him; her focus was on Maddy. Her good friend's expression had gone blank, and she stood staring at Tobias as if waiting for instruction.

Between her flailing struggles and Memphis's awkward hold on her body, he was forced to put her down or grip her so tight he might cause damage. The moment her feet hit the ground; she was in motion.

She grabbed her friend and she swung her around so her eyes weren't on Tobias anymore. "Maddy!"

Blinking as if coming out of a daze, Maddy's eyes focused on her. "Briar?"

Briar smiled with relief and looked up to admonish Tobias for putting her friend under thrall, but she didn't get the chance.

The world around her exploded into motion.

The world narrowed as the big wolf shifter lunged up the steps and swept both Maddy and Briar up in his arms. Mikey might have been trying to protect Briar, but she wasn't his to look after.

A roar erupted from Memphis's partially shifted throat and jaw. The chimera demanded control. For only the second time his life as a fully adult chimera shifter, Memphis lost the battle to his inner beast.

Ripping through his clothes, he fell to all fours and shifted. The moment the chimera was in control, he charged after Mikey, determined to get their mate back.

The beast was dimly aware of the shouting going on and he felt some stinging impacts to his body, but he ignored all that to focus on Briar struggling in the wolf shifter's arms. He'd rip that shifter limb from limb for touching his mate.

Then something miraculous happened. The wolf shifter let out a pained howl and dropped to his knees, releasing both women. Maddy staggered but stayed on her feet. His mate fell to the ground, landing hard on her butt, shouting at the wolf shifter at the same time.

"Act like an idiot and get a boot to the balls!" she said.

His beautiful, fierce mate had managed to free herself. Excellent, that would expedite ripping the wolf apart!

He was only a stride away and ready to gather for a pounce when his mate saw him, and her eyes went wide. That made him realize he'd need to drag the shifter out of sight before turning him inside out. He wouldn't want Briar to see such a grizzly sight.

To his horror, his mate did something wholly unexpected and terrifying. Scrambling on hands and knees, she placed her body over the downed shifter.

A strong stench of fear came off her as she cried out, "Memphis, no!"

The smell and her cry made him stumble to a halt. Then Tobias was there, picking her up and hugging her to his chest. Concern for both his mates had the chimera rushing to put his body between them and perceived danger.

The wolf shifter got to his feet with a wince. "Fuck Briar, I think you might have broken my dick."

The beast turned to face the wolf, showing his teeth and growling. He felt a delicate hand on his rump. His mate was touching him. He wanted to turn and face her. Give her reassuring licks across the face and purr. But he couldn't take his eyes off the wolf who'd tried to steal her. He contented himself with wrapping his tail around her small wrist.

"What did you think you were doing?" Briar asked. "You don't grab me like that. You know better, Mikey!"

The wolf stood up straight with a wince. "I thought you were a prisoner. I was trying to save you!"

"I didn't need to be saved," Briar answered. "I was perfectly happy where I was. And if I did need saving, I'd do it my damn self!"

The wolf gave her a pained look. "Briar, he's a vampire! He could make you think you wanted to be with him."

"I wouldn't use thrall on my flock!" Tobias protested.

Mikey sneered. "You leeches would do anything to get what you want."

"Don't be specie-ist," Briar called out. "I know most vampires are evil, but not this one. Mine's one of the good ones."

"No such thing," Mikey retorted. "You saw him put Maddy under thrall, right? Took away her will like it was nothing. He could've made her murder you or hurt herself. They can't be trusted, Briar!"

The beast didn't care that some stranger was put under thrall. Nothing was more important than keeping Briar with them. And this wolf called his other mate a leech.

Using his tail to hold Briar back, he snarled and stomped a hoof at Mikey. The wolf shifter cursed and took a step back, herding Maddy with him.

"Memphis, stop that!" Briar admonished, struggling to pull free of his tail. Worried that she'd hurt herself, he released her wrist, but then half turned to make sure his long body stayed between his mates and the angry shifter.

The other shifters had started to gather in a half circle around them. Some were carrying shiny weapons made of silver and others had compact black weapons that smelled of smoke. The beast knew the smaller ones were guns but he didn't need to worry about those. No one had silver bullets. But the sharp, silver-coated weapons were dangerous to both him and his vampire mate.

And all these weapons could be deadly for his little human mate.

It was only because no one was pointing any of those weapons at him, Tobias, or Briar that kept him from going on a murderous rampage.

Briar moved to his head and grasped him with both hands. He followed the pressure until his head was turned to look at her.

"I'm safe," she said, bringing her face close to his.

"Trust me, Briar," Mikey said. "You're not."

Still holding onto his head, his mate rolled her eyes to see the wolf shifter. "Not helping, Mikey," she ground out. "Shut the fuck up unless you're determined to get killed today."

"Vampire," Mikey hissed out. "He. Is. A. Vampire."

Briar turned her head to pin Mikey with a glare. "I. Love. Him."

The moment the words were out of her mouth, she paled. Her hands dropped to her side, and she look down at her feet, whispering to herself. "I love him. I love both of them." Then she rubbed her hands over her face. "I'm so fucked."

Worried that his mate was in distress, the beast rubbed his massive head against her chest at the same time Tobias came up behind her.

"You love us?" he asked.

The beast could feel joy radiating from his male mate. Although still conscious of the wolf shifter quietly growling and the rest of those with weapons still uncomfortably close, the beast did his best to purr. It sounded erratic, like a misfiring engine, but he was proud of being able to make the sound after not having done it since the first time he took control of Memphis when they were young.

Mikey made an exasperated sound. "Briar, that's the thrall talking. You can't really be in love with them."

"Michael Sullivan Mahoney!" Maddy snapped, bringing everyone's attention to her. "Stop it, right now."

"Maddy, he's—"

"No!" she said. The beast approved of her strong attitude with the wolf. He needed to be put in his place. "Do they look like they're trying to hurt Briar? Do they?" she barked out.

"Not right now," Mikey admitted. "But—"

"That's right, they're not," she said, cutting him off again. "In fact, it looks like they're desperate to protect Briar from you."

"The leech put you under thrall!" Mikey said, meeting Maddy's eyes with obvious triumph. "He took away your free will. Is that the kind of guy you want around Briar?"

Maddy's eyes narrowed as she swung her gaze back over to the three of them. The beast felt calmer now that the others had backed off, and Briar was standing secure between him and his other mate. He was able to meet Maddy's angry gaze without feeling the need to growl.

"Did you use some kind of vampire power on me?" she asked Tobias.

He watched the vampire's jaw tighten as he met Maddy's gaze. "I did. But you wanted to take her away. Without her, there is nothing. All I wanted to do was make you go away."

"If you're not hurting her, then I'm not a threat to your relationship," Maddy said, her eyes softening. "I think we should all sit down and talk like civilized people."

A scoff came from Mikey, making Maddy swing her gaze to him. "Shut it," she said, then turned her attention to the crowd. "All of you go wait in the cars," she ordered. When no one moved, she tugged at Mikey's sleeve. "Tell them."

Mikey didn't say anything to Maddy or his people. Instead he looked at Briar. "Prove to me that you're not under thrall."

Briar rolled her eyes. "How do I do that?"

"Walk over to me," Mikey demanded. "Tell the leech and this monster to stay put and walk over here. Then I'll send my pack away and we can talk."

The beast growled; he didn't like that idea at all. Briar petted his head soothingly.

"How do we know you won't grab her and try to run again?" Tobias challenged.

Maddy made an impatient sound and stepped into the space between Mikey and the three of them. "Briar, come on over here. We'll stand together for a minute and talk. Then Mikey can send the pack home, and you can show me all around your new digs."

"The house belongs to Tobias," Briar said as she tried to step around him. Moving his massive body, Memphis blocked her. He trusted Maddy. She smelled of honesty. But he'd never trust that wolf, not after he grabbed Briar earlier.

"Memphis, move your furry butt," she ordered. He didn't and when she tried to walk around him again, not only did he move to block her, but Tobias boxed her in.

"Move back more, Mikey," Tobias ordered. "I'm calmer and can see now that you acted out of fear for Briar, but none of us trust you. You need to be further away."

One look from Maddy had the wolf cursing as he took half a dozen large steps back. "Is that good enough?" he spit out.

"Barely," Tobias answered before lowering his voice to speak to Briar. "Please stay away from your wolf friend. I don't want to hurt him, but if he grabs you again, bad things could happen."

"Don't worry. I think he already learned his lesson when I let my steel toe boots do my talking earlier," Briar said lightly. Then she pushed at Memphis's side. "Come-on, Memphis. You gotta move for me, big guy."

The beast whined and craned his neck around so he could lick a long swath up Briar's arm. His action made Briar laugh even as she wiped her arm off on her pants. "Dude, don't do that."

When she tried to move, he whined again, this time dropping his head and trying for pitiful. He didn't want her moving away from safety, but he didn't want his littlest mate angry at him either.

"Stop that. You're breaking my heart here," Briar said, then pointed. "Look, I'm going to be right there. I won't go any further." When he still didn't move, she started petting his back. "I'm not leaving you. I know I panicked earlier and ran away, but I won't do that again. I'll talk first."

"I don't like this either," Tobias said. "But we need to trust her."

When Tobias reached out and nudged him out of the way, Memphis reluctantly moved. With a loud huff, he sat on his haunches, leaned his bulk against the vampire, and watched their mate stride up to Maddy. The women hugged tightly, and he saw tears in both sets of eyes.

"Maddy is like her family," Tobias whispered to him. "She can't love us if we don't accept the family she created."

The beast understood that but decided he didn't have to like it.

Maddy held her in a tight hug and they both tried to not break down in tears.

"I'm sorry," Briar whispered to her closest friend.

"You should have told me," Maddy whispered back, neither of them letting go. "I understand why you didn't say anything to Mikey. But me, Briar? You kept secrets from me?" Maddy pulled away and held Briar at arm's length. "I'm hurt. Bad. We've never lied to each other. Ever. And then you do this?"

Guilt hit her hard, making the tears she had been holding back flood down her face. "I was wrong. I was so fucking wrong."

She heard Memphis make a growling, upset sound so she whipped her head around to pin him with a hard gaze. "You stay!" she ordered. Both Memphis and Tobias looked pained, but they didn't move, allowing her to focus her attention back on Maddy.

"Will you be able to forgive me?" Briar asked, not sure if she could live without the woman who was closer to a sister than a friend.

"I'm not going to lie. It's going to take me a while to trust you again," Maddy said, tears trickling down her face as well. "But I still love you. You're my Thorny." She took her hand off Briar's shoulder and held it with her pinky out and crooked.

Sniffling and smiling at the same time, Briar hooked her pinky with Maddy's. "Besties," Briar said.

"Besties," Maddy echoed. Leaning down, she put her forehead to Briar's and whispered so quietly it was barely a sound. "Now, tell me the truth; do you need saving?"

"Not even a little," Briar said quickly.

"Good enough," Maddy said with a nod. She dropped her hands away from Briar and tried to wipe tears from her face without doing too much damage to her complicated make-up. "Leave it to you to mess up all my hard work."

Briar sounded a shaky laugh. "What can I say? I like the raccoon eyes look on you."

Maddy snorted and shook her head before turning to face Mikey. "Briar isn't being held prisoner."

Mikey looked like he was about to argue when Tobias called out.

"If you like, we can all sit under the pergola in the backyard," he offered. "We could talk and still maintain enough distance to be comfortable."

Maddy raised her eyebrows at Briar and affected an upper-class accent. "Oh, we could sit under the pergola. How lovely." Then she whispered, "What the fuck is a pergola?"

Briar shrugged her shoulders as Mikey responded to Tobias's invitation. "My people stay while we talk."

"That's acceptable as long as they remain out here," Tobias agreed. "I suggest Maddy and Briar go first and the three of us will follow behind."

"Fine," Mikey said. "Maddy, you and Briar stay close and don't make eye contact with the leech."

Briar caught Maddy's slightly fearful look, so she hooked her arm with the taller woman's. "He won't do anything. A lot happened tonight, and he was worried I'd panic and leave them again."

"Again?"

Leave it to Maddy to home in on that little tidbit. "I might have had a little meltdown this evening and took off with the car."

"It sounds like we have a lot of catching up to do," Maddy murmured as the two of them carefully walked past Tobias and Memphis.

Memphis tried to fall in-step with Briar, but Tobias held him back. "We need to keep showing our support for our mate," he told the chimera. Briar cast him a thankful look and led Maddy around the house.

It turned out that the pergola was a wood frame in the middle of the backyard with awning material stretched across the top and flowering vines climbing up the supports. She wasn't sure if it was the awning or the vines that qualified it as a pergola. Whatever, it was a fancy person set-up and a name to match. She'd noticed it before but hadn't thought much of it until now.

Dressed in pajamas and a robe, Greg appeared at the back door when they were almost to the area. "I heard the commotion, Master Tobias. Should I call the police?"

"Now he wants to call the cops," Briar muttered, casting an aggravated glance over at Greg.

"Who's this guy?" Maddy asked as Greg cast both her and Briar disapproving looks.

"That would be the male-Karen that works for Tobias," Briar explained. "He's supposed to be gone soon. But not soon enough in my book."

Greg must have heard her because his disapproving expression turned into a dark scowl.

Whoops, had she said that a little too loud? She flashed a taunting grin at him.

Stifling the glare, he looked away from her and back at Tobias. "Sir?"

"There was a misunderstanding," Tobias explained. "We're all going to sit here and talk. If you wouldn't mind bringing refreshments for our guests."

"Certainly, I—" Whatever Greg was going to say was lost as he screamed and shrank back in fear. "S-s-sir! There's a monster!"

Briar had gotten so used to Memphis's appearance that it took her a moment to realize that Greg was referring to the chimera. Annoyance made her voice harsh. "That's Memphis. You know him. The big handsome guy? With the beard?"

Greg was shaking his head in denial. "It's . . . it's . . . it's a monster!"

"*He* is my mate," Tobias corrected. His tone must have clued Greg into the fact that Tobias wasn't happy with him.

"Yes sir. Of course sir. I've never seen anything like him before. I was startled." The words and tone were agreeing with Tobias, but his face clearly told a different story. "I'll leave you all to conduct business." With that, he hurried back into the house.

Briar wanted to call out an insult to his retreating back, but Maddy distracted her by pulling her down to sit on a loveseat-sized piece of patio furniture. By the time she was sitting, Greg had disappeared back into the house. At least they probably wouldn't see him again for the rest of the evening.

She looked around at everyone. The furniture under the pergola was set up in a U-shape with the loveseat at the end and chairs on either side. Mikey sat on one of the chairs on her right and Tobias sat on her left. Both men looked uneasy. Memphis stood for a moment before nudging the table in the middle out of the way and laying down at Briar's feet with a grumpy harrumph.

It made Briar smile until Maddy spoke.

"What happened?" Maddy asked. "How did this all start?"

Briar cast Mikey a guilty look. She had more apologizing to do and wasn't looking forward to it. She took a deep breath.

Tobias had to work to keep his body quiet. The remnants of all the power he'd gathered to defend and protect Briar were still raging through his system. It would help if he could touch at least one of his mates. But Memphis was intent on being closest to their most vulnerable member, and he didn't want to antagonize either Mikey or Maddy by putting himself next to Briar along with the chimera.

Maddy leaned over to give Memphis a pet and the male stretched out and nudged her hand with his snout when she stopped, making her ohhhh and giggle. The biker knew how to charm people.

As Briar told Mikey and Maddy about finding him in the basement of the bar and all the things that had happened since, Tobias focused on being calm and controlled.

He listened with only half an ear as he used memories to help tone down his aggression. He thought about the night before with Briar wedged between him and Memphis. The way she sighed, gasped, and writhed as the pleasure became too intense.

The memories were a perfection distraction, and he was able to quiet his power, but he ended up with another issue. A throbbing erection painfully trapped in his pants.

"What's wrong with you?" Mikey's question drew everyone's gaze to him.

Tobias blinked, surprised to find four sets of eyes on him. "Nothing."

"You're wiggling around like a kid," Mikey observed with a deep frown. "Do you need to take a piss, or are you about to go feral?"

"Only wolves go feral," Tobias retorted, tempted to flash a fang at the rude shifter. "Vampires succumb to blood lust. If you're going to be insulting, at least be correct."

"Both of you behave!" Maddy said sharply.

"Why do you hate vampires so much?" Tobias asked, realizing that Mikey's hatred went much farther than the simple wariness everyone had for his kind. "What happened to you?"

Mikey glared at him. "Your kind are all evil bastards."

"Most of us," Tobias agreed, no longer bothered by the wolf's animosity. "But everyone knows that a vampire's flock is sacred. The moment you saw Briar unhurt and saw that I would do anything to protect her, you should have walked away. But you didn't. You insisted on interfering."

That got Maddy's attention. "Is that true, Mikey? Is this stuff about a vampire's flock common knowledge?"

"Yeah," Mikey answered with obvious reluctance. "But he could have still been using thrall, even if she is his flock."

Maddy swept her gaze back to him. "You did use thrall on me. That seems rude, even if I understand why you did it."

"But I'd never use it on Briar," Tobias was quick to point out. "I only used it on Memphis with his permission to control his rut. Healthy flocks aren't formed by using thrall. On top of that, every vampire has to overcome a natural reluctance to use it on a flock member. It's one of the few instincts we have programed in after being turned."

Before she could ask another question, Tobias pinned Mikey with his eyes. "You know enough about us to know a good deal about thrall, but not how a flock truly interacts with their vampire. If I had to guess, I'd say someone close to you was stolen and hurt by a vampire."

Mikey dropped his gaze to his lap and mumbled something even Tobias couldn't hear. Maddy got out of her seat to kneel next to the wolf shifter. "Mikey, what happened?"

"My sister," he whispered.

Briar took a sharp breath. "Emily? The one who died? I thought she, uh, killed herself."

Mikey shook his head, his expression disgusted as he gestured at Tobias. "She did take her own life, but only after what a vampire did to her. He held her in thrall, used her, toyed with her, and then finally let her go. But she was never the same. She drove her car off the PCH about a month afterwards."

There was a collective gasp from Briar and Maddy, but Tobias was too focused to be surprised or stunned.

"Tell me who it was, and I'll end him," Tobias said.

The alpha's eye shot to him, wide with surprise. "You don't know me, and he's one of your kind. Why would you offer that?"

"I might be a vampire, but I know that many of us end up being evil." There was no vampire unity, so he had no problem telling this group the truth. "If we live too long without finding our flock, our humanity disappears. Our empathy vanishes. We become monsters who hurt others for pleasure."

"Hunting another vampire would be dangerous," Mikey pointed out. "I wanted to go after him. Kill him to avenge Emily, but I knew I couldn't win, and he might be so angry at my attempt that he'd slaughter my pack. I couldn't risk it."

Tobias felt a bit of power wash through him. His eyes were probably glowing red, but he couldn't control that. "I'm strong. Probably one of the strongest vampires alive right now. I doubt your nemesis could stand against me."

Mikey smiled for the first time. It was barely there and gone almost as soon as it appeared, but Tobias saw it.

"You mean that, don't you?"

"Without hesitation," he agreed.

"His name was Ryan Elling," Mikey told them, spitting the name out like a curse. "But he's already dead. He took a woman that belonged to another vampire. I guess she was his flock."

"That's surprising," Tobias commented. "Most vampires can feel that someone is a member of another's flock. He might have done it on purpose. Perhaps he realized he was out of control and wanted someone to end him. At least on some subconscious level."

"Whatever the reason, the end result's the same," Mikey said, slumping back in his seat. Maddy stood up and reached for a chair so she could sit next to him, but the big wolf shifter snagged her wrist and pulled her into his lap. She went willingly, snuggling up against him as he talked. "He's long dead, and so is my sister. I'll never get her back, but at least I can try to keep others safe."

"I can understand now why you're so distrustful. All I can tell you is that I'd die before I'd let anyone hurt Briar," Tobias told him.

"What about everyone else?" Mikey challenged.

"I'm not a threat as long as they don't try to hurt my flock," Tobias answered easily. Then he thought of something that might assuage Mikey's worry. "What if I offered you and Maddy unfettered access to my home at any time?"

Memphis growled at the same time Briar spoke up. "Whoa there. I'm not sure what the word unfettered means, but I'm not into having people traipsing through a room when we might, uh, be doing something." Briar pointed at Maddy. "We've shared a house for a couple of years now, and Maddy still has to knock before she comes in."

Maddy laughed. "I learned my lesson within the first week of living with you."

Mikey grinned at the women. "Is there a story here? Something juicy?"

Briar gave him a flat look. "You will not be getting any more information. What happened was between me and Maddy." Then her expression gentled. "You're my family, Mikey, and you're welcome over any time, but you've got to call first. There will be no dropping in unannounced."

"I accept that," Mikey agreed. "And you'll still come hang with the pack?"

"Of course," Briar answered. "Luis's birthday is coming up. I wouldn't miss it." Then she frowned. "But can I bring guests?"

Now it was Mikey's turn to hesitate, glancing first at Memphis lounging at her feet, then at Tobias. He tried to keep his expression pleasant as Mikey eyed him.

"Maybe," he finally said. "But I'll need to talk it over with the pack. Maybe call up to the Annwyl Pack."

"Annwyl Pack?" Tobias asked, confused.

"That pack's alpha is in a relationship with a vampire," Mikey explained. "Talking to her will give me some perspective on how packs and vampires work together." He looked back at Briar. "Don't expect much, but I'll talk to Lobos Gris. Get ready for a bunch of calls after I do."

"That's all I can ask," Briar agreed. "I understand if you guys can't be around me anymore but—"

"Shut your fool mouth," Maddy said sharply. "Family doesn't get rid of family, even if they managed to fall in love with a vampire."

Mikey grinned. "What she said."

Tobias saw the tension ease from Briar's shoulders. He was glad that the alpha was willing to work with him and wasn't rejecting Briar. He didn't like that there would be competition for her attention but knew losing these people would be devastating.

Standing up, Mikey set Maddy on her feet and took her elbow. "We need to go. Almost the entire pack is here, which means there's few people working at the bar."

"And I need to get some sleep, some of us have day jobs," Maddy said. Briar stood up, and the women hugged before Maddy walked off with Mikey.

Tobias got to his feet and stepped behind Briar, wrapping his arms around her.

Memphis stood up, stretched, then shifted back to his human form. He came up behind Tobias and wrapped his arms around the two of them. It felt indescribably comforting to be surrounded by his flock.

"They're leaving," Memphis murmured after they'd stood like that in silence for a while. "I can hear their cars."

"This evening turned out way more eventful than I originally planned," Tobias commented. "All I wanted to do was shower both of you with gifts. Instead, I drove Briar away. Accosted her best friend. And almost murdered a wolf alpha. Not my finest hour."

Briar let her head loll back on his shoulder. "We all made it home in one piece. I learned some important stuff. And no one died. I'm putting tonight in the win column."

Suddenly, Memphis tensed behind him. "Gifts," he whispered brokenly.

Confused, Tobias looked over his shoulder at the chimera. "What?"

"I was wearing my new vest when I shifted!" he cried. "I ripped right through it."

Relief made Tobias grin. "I'll have Frank make you another one."

"Might want to make it an even dozen," Briar added. "Someone likes to shift through their clothes."

"I never had this issue before," Memphis grumbled.

"What issue?" Briar asked with a snicker. "Premature shifting? Don't worry, baby, I've heard it happens to everyone."

Tobias wasn't surprised when Memphis let go of them to grab Briar up and heft her effortlessly over his shoulder. Even with a slap on her ass, she was still cackling with laughter.

"I think someone needs to be taught a lesson about being a brat," Memphis said as he took Tobias's hand with the one not holding Briar steady on his wide shoulders.

Tobias grinned at him. "Challenge accepted."

Briar was so happy that she was sure doom must be on the horizon.

The three of them had been living together for two weeks now, and it had been storybook perfect. When was the other shoe going to drop? When was something going to go irrevocably wrong?

Memphis called his mom, and not only did she cry and say she was happy for him, but she also insisted on talking first to Tobias, then Briar. Briar tried to get out of it, her experience with her own mother telling her that this was a bad idea. But Memphis finally caged her in and forced the phone to her ear.

Within minutes, the woman had Briar calling her Mama Granger. By the end of the hour-long conversation, she was promising to make it to the Granger Family get together in October. She'd freaked out a little after hanging up with the woman, but Memphis had been quick to soothe her with stories of his wild brothers and over-the-top father. If Mama Granger could handle them, nothing could faze her.

Briar had even talked to Lily and confessed that, for the moment, she was living with Tobias and Memphis. Maddy had come by several times so they could hang out. She hadn't heard from Mikey, but that wasn't a surprise. It was going to take some time before Mikey was ready to talk to her again.

It was all starting to feel so normal that Briar was sure something terrible was going to happen.

"Any go-juice left?" Memphis asked as he wandered into the kitchen.

Briar held up her mug and shook her head. "This is the last of it. But I was thinking of brewing another pot."

"I'll get it," Memphis said as he passed her. She was working at the kitchen table, doing a personal project on her laptop. As much as she loved the room Tobias set up for her, sometimes it felt nice to work in other places. Places that were closer to coffee makers.

It was about six in the evening, and she was on her third cup of coffee, but that was their new normal. It hadn't taken much for both her and Memphis to switch around to sleeping most of the day and staying awake at night. She'd done it a lot to begin with, and it turned out that chimera's didn't need much sleep.

When Tobias woke up for the night, they'd all sit down to "breakfast."

"What are you doing?" Greg's high-pitched, outraged voice made her flinch and Memphis growl. "Don't touch that. It's expensive and you might break it."

"It's a goddamn coffee maker," Memphis said but stepped away as Greg came bustling up. The slight man snatched the carafe from Memphis as if it was some kind of priceless vase. "I was making coffee."

"It's not some Mr. Coffee. It's a Concordia, and you shouldn't be touching it," Greg said with a sneer before he got busy with the kitchen appliance. "If you needed coffee, you should've called me. I gave you both my number. I expect you to use it instead of destroying Master Tobias's things because you're impatient."

Okay, maybe things weren't perfect because they were still dealing with Greg.

The little weasel had gotten good at being nice and cordial while Tobias was around, but the moment he was alone with her or Memphis, he turned downright nasty. Neither of them wanted to whine to Tobias, especially since the vampire was working diligently at talking Greg into leaving.

Briar could understand rewarding loyalty and not simply kicking the horrible man out, but if he wasn't gone soon, either she or Memphis were going to do something to him. Something that he probably wouldn't heal from.

Memphis stomped over to the kitchen table and sat down heavily in the chair next to hers, grumbling under his breath.

She scooted her chair closer to him, leaning over and giving him a kiss on the cheek. "Soon," she whispered.

"Not soon enough," he whispered back, then turned his face to give her a proper good morning kiss. Oh yeah, that was how a day should get started.

"Is that really appropriate behavior in the kitchen?" Greg's odious voice was like a bucket of cold water thrown on both of them. They pulled apart, and both turned angry glares on Greg.

The man must have realized he was close to getting the beat down he deserved because he hurried to say, "The coffee should be ready soon. I'm sure you can serve yourselves. Try not to damage anything." Then he fled.

Letting out an annoyed breath, Memphis turned his attention back to Briar. "Any chance I can use your fancy laptop to check my email?" he asked. "I could do it on my phone, but I get annoyed faster on the small screen."

She opened up a browser window without hesitation and slid the laptop over. "Here you go."

As Memphis pecked at the keyboard and grumbled to himself, Briar got him a coffee and freshened up her mug. She rejoined him at the table and unlocked her phone, startled to find a missed call and several text messages from Lily. She'd put the phone on silent to focus on some work and now worried what had happened.

Concerned, she opened up one of the messages only to let loose a stream of cusswords.

Memphis looked up from the laptop, his expression half-amused, half-alarmed. "What's wrong, Baby Doll?"

The sound of a car driving up made her realize that she'd gotten Lily's warning much too late. "I think my mother is here for a visit."

Tobias was descending the stairs when he heard a car pulling up. The sun was low enough that although he couldn't go outside yet; he wasn't trapped in slumber either. With the way the house was situated, he could open the front door this late in the day and not be exposed to the sun, so he strode to the door to greet the new arrival.

When he saw Greg hurrying over, he waved the man off. Greg nodded his head and disappeared back the way he'd come. Briar and Memphis emerged from the direction of the kitchen as he swung open the door. He had enough time to register Briar's horrified expression before a feminine voice cried out with melodramatic fervor.

"Where is my daughter? I demand to see her!"

Tobias saw Briar drop her head into her hands before he turned his attention back to the woman standing at his front door.

She looked to be in her mid-fifties with elaborate make up and a stylish bob haircut without a hint of gray. Her gold jewelry, form-fitting dress, and high heel shoes completed the outfit, making her look like she was heading to cocktail hour instead of a mission to save her daughter.

"Tiffany, I'm fine. You don't need to be all extra about it," Briar said as she came to stand at his side.

"Hey, Briar," a young woman standing behind Tiffany called out. "Sorry about this."

"Hush, Chrysanthemum," Tiffany scolded the young woman.

Tobias could see the strong similarity between Tiffany and Chrysanthemum, but even if he were to stand Briar and Tiffany side by side, he'd be hard-pressed to declare them mother and daughter.

Chrysanthemum frowned. "Mom, I told you we needed to talk to Briar before coming over," Chrysanthemum said in a subdued tone. Tobias got the impression this sister was often railroaded by their mother.

"Don't make that face. It's unattractive," Tiffany chastised before turning her attention back to Tobias. "Who might you be, sir? We've haven't been properly introduced." Tiffany's southern accent was suddenly stronger, and she focused a coquettish smile on him.

"My name's Tobias Becker," he said, holding out his hand to Tiffany. She took it, letting only her fingertips touch his, as if he was supposed to kiss the back of her hand. That motion was too old fashioned even for him, so instead, he gave her fingers a little squeeze and let go.

Tiffany's smile didn't dim. "If I'd known my daughter was spending time with such a distinguished gentleman, I would have put more effort into my appearance before coming over."

He was well aware of the social cue here, so he responded accordingly. "You look stunning, as I'm sure you always do."

"Well, aren't you just the sweetest," Tiffany simpered.

Briar let out an annoyed huff. "As you can see, I'm fine." She waved at the red-faced Chrysanthemum behind Tiffany. "Hey there, Chrissy. Sorry you got roped into driving all the way up here."

Chrysanthemum ignored Briar's comment, her eyes still glued on him. "Is that your boyfriend?"

Briar nodded with a grin. "One of them."

Chrysanthemum's jaw dropped at the same time Tiffany screeched, "One of them?"

With exemplary timing, Memphis stepped out from behind the door to stand next to Briar. "Howdy," he rumbled.

Chrysanthemum was the first to recover. "Hells yeah!"

Holding up her hand, palm out, she extended it over Tiffany's shoulder at Briar. Tobias didn't understand what she was doing until a laughing Briar slapped Chrysanthemum's palm with her own. Tiffany batted at her daughter's arm, making Chrysanthemum stumble back.

"Chrysanthemum, behave like a lady!" Tiffany admonished, then focused her gaze on Memphis, looking him up and down with obvious disgust. "This isn't acceptable."

Briar's expression turned flat. "Not your decision. Last time I checked, I was an adult, and you don't get to say shit about what I do with my life. Not that you cared when I was young, either."

"Don't you take that tone with me, Briar Thorn. I'm your mother and you'll respect me," Tiffany said, pointing a long, manicured fingernail at Briar. "I despaired you'd ever find a man of your own with the way you insist on dressing and acting. Now I find you co-habitating with two men. This is not how I raised you."

"You didn't raise me," Briar shot back before looking over to her sister. "You want to come in and see the house, Chrissy?"

"I would," Chrysanthemum said, excited until Tiffany caught her eye. "Or I guess not?"

"*We* will be coming in," Tiffany said and turned a high-wattage smile on Tobias. "From what I can see, you have a lovely home, Mr. Becker."

Tobias stood there, slightly stunned. Tiffany had managed to insult Memphis, demean both her daughters, and then expected him to welcome her into his home?

"You must be under the mistaken impression that I want you in my house," Tobias said evenly.

Tiffany gasped and put a hand to her throat. "Mr. Becker!"

"Lay off the southern belle routine," Briar said dryly. "No one here is going to buy it."

"Let me take Mom home, and then I'll come back," Chrysanthemum offered. Tobias got the impression that she was the peacemaker of the family.

"No need," Tobias said then called out for Greg. The man appeared instantly, telling Tobias he'd been listening in. "I need you to drive this woman home."

Greg's expression didn't change. "Of course, Master Tobias. I'll fetch the Rover." One glance at the crowded front door made him turn on his heels and head for the side door to get to the garage.

"Well, if that's how you're going to treat a good, upstanding, Christian woman, then I want nothing to do with any of you," Tiffany huffed. "What the three of you are doing is immoral and against God. It was Adam and Eve, not Adam, Eve, and Steve."

"Putting aside that juvenile and asinine comment," Tobias said, "I would think a mother's first inclination would be to care about her daughter's happiness and safety."

"I do care," Tiffany protested. "Lord knows I've tried my best to clean her up and make her pretty, despite the fact that she looks like her father and insists on dressing so badly. But there's only so much I could do, and my task was impossible when she refused my best efforts. All my daughters, except for Chrysanthemum, were stubborn children, but Briar Thorn was always the worst."

Could this woman even hear herself? Briar was gorgeous because of her skin color, not despite it. Before Tobias could open his mouth to tell this woman to leave his property, Memphis spoke.

"I feel bad for you," the big man said softly. "And I pity the lonely life you will always have."

"How dare you!" Tiffany hissed as the last of her façade bled away. "How dare someone like you feel bad for me?"

"You think appearance, style, and clothes make the person. You think wealth is equal to happiness," Memphis said with a sad shake of his head. "But you couldn't be more wrong. Money makes us comfortable; friends and family make us happy."

"That's something poor white trash would say," Tiffany fired back, running her eyes up and down Memphis.

Tobias knew he was perilously close to losing his temper and judging by Briar's expression, she was right behind him. But Memphis wasn't bothered and simply put an arm around both his mates. The weight of the chimera's arm grounded Tobias, allowing him to rein in his rage.

Memphis's soft tone never changed. "Briar's told me about you. About how you always looked for the storybook marriage. Always searching for a man who would take care of you and make all your worries go away. But that's not how it works."

"Oh really?" Tiffany said, her voice dripping with sarcasm.

"Yes, really," Memphis said as if explaining something rudimentary to a child. "The three of us are all in this together. Caring for each other. Strong when the others are struggling. Accepting when we are weak. Forgiving when we transgress. And most important, open to each other. Vulnerable. I've seen Tobias at his weakest, and it made me love him more. I've seen Briar at her most insecure and it was my privilege to convince her that our relationship was worth the risk. In return, both of them have seen me at my most violent and were never scared I'd hurt them. You can't buy that with money. You can only earn it with reciprocity."

Tiffany gaped at him, probably thrown by his eloquence. Tobias had to admit, even he was surprised by the poetry in Memphis's words. Briar was looking up at him with a big grin and a suspicious wetness in her eyes.

"You really feel that way?" she asked.

"With all my heart, Baby Doll," Memphis said.

"You can't love two people equally," Tiffany protested. "It doesn't work that way."

"Why am I not surprised you'd have a view like that, considering you obviously played favorites with your daughters?" Memphis commented casually. "These two are my heart and because of that, I'd do anything for their happiness. Has anyone ever felt that toward you?"

"Oh, snap," Chrysanthemum muttered, making Tiffany swing around to glare at her.

"You keep your mouth shut!" Tiffany raged in a tight, low voice. "Men have loved me. They would have stayed but someone always ruined it. You were such a fussy baby that you drove your father away. He would be with us now if it wasn't for you!"

Chrysanthemum shrunk back as if Tiffany had hit her and dropped her eyes to her feet. "Sorry, Mom," she mumbled.

"And that's the last time you will talk to her like that," Briar announced, stepping past Tiffany to take Chrysanthemum by the arm. "Come on Chrissy, come inside."

"Chrysanthemum, don't you dare!" Tiffany called as Briar tugged her sister past her mother and into the house. Tiffany tried to grab Chrysanthemum's free arm, but Tobias moved to stand between them as Memphis stepped aside to let them pass.

Greg was in the Rover, idling in the driveway next to an older model Nissan Versa.

"There is your ride," he said with contempt as he pointed Tiffany toward the vehicle. "Or you can walk but make no mistake that you are not welcome on my property any longer. If you choose to stay, I will have Memphis forcefully remove you."

"If he touches me, I'll call the police," she threatened, digging a cell phone out of her handbag with a shaking hand.

"If I have to move you, you won't be able to," Memphis said. The sentence was delivered so emotionlessly that it took a moment for Tiffany to register what he'd said. She paled and stepped back, stumbling a little on her high heels.

"Animals," she hissed before turning and walking on unsteady feet to the Rover.

It was satisfying to watch her refuse to meet their gazes as Greg backed up and turned around.

"I can't believe Briar had that for a mother," Tobias grumbled, looking up at Memphis.

"I can't believe Briar didn't murder her in her sleep years ago," Memphis responded, making both men laugh.

"Let's go meet some of our new family," Tobias said. He could hear Briar and Chrysanthemum talking in low tones in the kitchen.

Memphis nodded, his expression going from disgusted to pleased. "Yeah, let's show her how real family treats new members."

Tobias couldn't have said it better himself.

"You know that thing that Tobias wants to do to us?" Briar asked.

Memphis looked up from his phone, trying to figure out what his littlest mate was talking about. "You mean from that porn you were watching?"

Briar blushed a bright red and sputtered. "I told you Maddy sent that to me. I didn't go out looking for it!"

He gave her a slow grin. "When we found you, you'd watched 20 minutes of it by yourself and were turned on as hell." Briar opened her mouth, probably to deny it, like she had at the time, but Memphis shook his head. "Don't lie. I could smell your lust."

Slapping both hands over her eyes, she groaned. "Don't say stuff like that!"

"Why?" Memphis asked with a chuckle. "It's both true and delectable. You smell fucking amazing all the time, but especially when you're horny."

Briar dropped her hands into her lap and tried to look serious. "Changing the subject now," she declared forcefully. "I was wondering about the soul sharing thing."

Memphis sobered. "He's waiting for you to ask. He's terrified he'll scare you off, so he won't even bring the subject up unless you do."

"Oh," Briar said, setting her coffee mug down with a loud clink. "I didn't realize."

She went quiet, and Memphis watched her face go through some complicated emotions before she finally asked, "But he still wants to, right?"

Someone was feeling insecure. Putting down his phone, Memphis pushed his chair away from the table and reached out to pluck Briar from her seat and snuggle her in his lap. Because it was such a common impulse for both him and Tobias, Briar had gotten used to it over the last few weeks and didn't even flail.

Snuggling against him, she sounded a soft sigh. "Did I fuck this up beyond saving?"

"Of course not," Memphis answered. "But you did make both of us cautious."

"Well, shit." That was obviously not the answer she wanted to hear, but he wasn't going to tell her lies.

"Baby Doll, we both love you unconditionally," he promised, rubbing his hand in a circle on her back. "But neither of us is going to push for anything from you. We're simply happy that you moved some of your stuff in here."

When she spoke, her voice was barely a whisper. "What if I might be ready?"

It took effort, but Memphis kept himself calm and seated instead of standing up and twirling Briar around with joy. He was proud of how he managed to only tighten his arms around Briar a little in reaction to her statement.

"Ready to claim us?" he asked, keeping his tone light.

"I thought it was the vampire who claimed his flock?" Briar asked, sitting up so she could look into his face.

"The vampire is the one with the power to share souls, but it's the flock who gets the final say," Memphis explained. "I knew you were my mate the moment I heard your voice. I knew Tobias was also meant to be my mate when I walked into that basement and could smell the two of you. Tobias knew you and I were his flock the moment he met us. That's why he was able to keep his instincts in check and not hurt you."

Briar's mouth turned down. "So the two of you have been waiting for me to get with the program?"

"No, we've been waiting for you to be comfortable," Memphis countered. "Vampires tend to be overly cautious when creating their flock because once it's done, it can't be undone. It's forever, Baby Doll, and he'd never want you to resent him later. You could hold off for a month, a year, or a decade, and he wouldn't complain. We'd both wait for you because you're worth our time and effort."

She dropped her gaze to her lap, fidgeting with one of her nails. "So he meant it when he said I could go back to living with Maddy and the three of us could date?"

Memphis wanted to growl at the idea, but he took a deep breath before speaking. "We both meant it. You going back to Maddy's would be depressing as hell, but we're willing to do whatever it takes."

When she looked up, her smile was huge. "I love you so much," she said, wrapping her arms around his neck. "It hurts sometimes. And it's scary, but it's also amazing."

Relieved, he hugged her tight. "So you think you might want to become a proper flock member soon?"

She nodded her head against his neck, her breath warm on his skin as she talked. "I have a few more questions for Tobias, but yeah, really soon. He said something about a ceremony?"

Memphis felt tension he hadn't known he was holding release from his shoulders. "I think it's called an Alighting Ceremony, kind of a flock version of a wedding. You stand in front of a few friends, say a few words, give each other gifts, then we go off and he does the soul thing. When we come back, we're all holding hands to show we're joined together."

"That sounds nice," she murmured. "We could—"

Suddenly she straightened up, almost hitting him in the jaw with her head. "I don't have a gift!"

He chuckled at her concern. "I'm sure we can figure something out."

She grinned at him. "I mean, I don't have it now, but I have an idea. There's this place that sells antiques. Maddy and I were trying to sell some dishes I had that turned out to be worthless, but they had a display case full of antique watches. I want to get one of them and have it inscribed for Tobias."

"That sounds like a great gift," Memphis agreed, already wondering what he was going to get Tobias. What do you get a rich vampire with very particular tastes? "Maybe I could go in on it with you?"

She crossed her arms over her chest. "No way, you have to come up with your own gift."

Memphis tapped his phone on the table to check the time. "Tobias won't be up for another few hours. I could take you over to the shop on the back of my bike. Then I could look around and see if there was anything else there that Tobias might like."

Briar nearly vibrated with excitement. "Tobias said I wasn't allowed to ride on the back of your bike until we were flock. Something about me being too fragile."

Memphis scoffed. "I'm not going to let anything happen. Besides, you've got both pants and a jacket with the reinforced armor in them from Frank and that full-face helmet I picked up. Between me and that gear, you couldn't be much safer."

"It's not me you need to convince, it's Tobias," Briar said.

Leaning forward, Memphis whispered, "I won't tell him if you don't."

"Deal!"

With her arms wrapped around Memphis's waist and the Road King vibrating between her legs as they barreled down the 101 freeway, Briar was in heaven.

The sun hung low in the sky to their right and the wind whipped around them as Memphis effortlessly maneuvered around cars and trucks. Briar had to admit that she was glad for the leather outfit and helmet. She'd have worn the leather anyway because who wouldn't want to wear such a bad ass outfit, but it was also great protection against the elements.

She felt like they were flying. After this, there was no question that she was going to be getting a motorcycle of her own. Maybe she could talk Tobias into riding on the back. He could snuggle up to her like she was doing now with Memphis. The vampire wouldn't like it, but he'd be willing to do it because it made her happy and he loved her.

They both loved her. And she loved them back. And they were going to make it all permanent.

That thought was equal parts exciting and terrifying.

Talking was impossible, so when she saw the exit they needed, Briar tapped Memphis's side and pointed. Without hesitation, he moved over several lanes and got off the freeway. She pointed again at the base of the offramp. It didn't take long before they pulled into a spot right in front of the antique store.

Swinging off the bike, Briar stepped back to give Memphis room to drag the kickstand down with his heel and swing his long leg off the bike.

"What'd ya' think?" he asked as he pulled off the small half helmet he'd worn.

Briar was still fumbling with the clasp of her full-face helmet when Memphis brushed her hands away and undid it for her.

She tugged the helmet off and grinned at him. "I want one!"

"I thought that might be your reaction," he said with a chuckle. "But don't be in too big of a rush. I like it when you ride behind me."

"Yeah, that was fun too," Briar agreed.

She took his hand in hers and led him into the store. The place was jam packed with display cases and shelves full of items. The same guy who'd talked to her and Maddy was there behind the counter. He looked up as they entered, his gaze polite even though she and Memphis probably looked like extras from a biker movie.

"I'm afraid I'll be closing in twenty minutes," he warned them. "You're welcome to browse until then."

Briar led Memphis up to the counter the man was standing behind. Leaning over, she started examining the contents of the case. "Last time I was here, you had a pocket watch. It was silver with filigree and a matching chain and pocketknife."

The man smiled warmly. "Ah, yes, I remember you now. You and your lovely friend had those dishes. I do still have that piece." He reached for a set of keys on a table behind him. "Wait here, and I'll grab it."

He returned with the watch on a velvet-lined tray. It was just as Briar remembered it. And the price was still as high, but if there was any time to splurge, it was now.

"That's perfect. I'll take it," Briar said as she dug out her wallet.

"Is this a gift?" he asked. "I have a lovely wooden box I could put it in."

"Yes and yes," Briar agreed. "I also wanted to get it engraved. Do you know where I could do that?"

He beamed. "Certainly! I can do that here." He pulled out a colorful pamphlet and flipped it open. "These are the fonts I can do. For that watch, I would suggest this one or this one. I can have it done by tomorrow if you like."

"That works," Briar agreed as she picked a font and wrote down what she wanted him to put on the watch. It was only when she was handing the form back to him that she noticed Memphis was staring at something in a nearby display case. "Found something interesting?"

"I want to see this ring," Memphis said without looking away.

The man went over and opened the case from the back, pulling out a tray of rings and setting them down next to the watch. Memphis pulled out a ring from the center and showed it to her.

It was a man's ring with a crest. It looked like something a European royal would wear. It was so detailed that Briar had to lean over to make out what the animal in the crest was, and then her breath caught.

"Is that a chimera?" she whispered, looking up at Memphis with wide eyes.

He nodded his head, looking equally stunned. "I've never seen anything like it."

"Isn't it a unique piece?" the man said cheerfully. "I found it at an estate sale last week. I haven't had a chance to trace the crest yet, but it's probably from a made-up lineage. Most crests are from Americans desperate to find some kind of nobility or royalty in their family line, so they go to charlatans that will make up stories and family crests for them. Still, it's a lovely piece."

"I'll take it," Memphis said without letting go of the ring. He looked over at her. "This is meant to belong to Tobias. I can feel it."

Briar nodded her head. "The ring, the watch, you, and me; we're all meant to belong to Tobias."

Fisting his hand around the ring, Memphis pulled her into a tight hug. "Yes. Now and forever."

With the crescent moon visible and the last of the light from the setting sun making the world look soft and golden, Memphis felt an intense sense of contentment wash over him. With Briar pressed against his back, and her arms wrapped around his waist, the only thing missing to make this moment perfect was Tobias. But they would be home soon, and they'd be able to share the good news with their third partner.

Memphis knew it would be a relief to both of them when Tobias shared his soul with Briar. As the only human in their triad, she was frighteningly fragile. It wasn't only the paranormal community he worried about, but the various maladies all humans could suffer from. Being tied to Tobias meant she wouldn't succumb to any sneaky human diseases.

Not to mention his little shit-starter liked to find trouble, and once she had the increased endurance, strength, and resilience of being part of the flock, he'd breathe easier.

Although it was nearly impossible to tattoo a vampire, maybe Briar and he would go out for matching tats after the Alighting Ceremony.

Quinn, mate to the Alpha of the Annwyl Pack. was a budding artist and the last time Memphis visited, he'd seen some of his artwork framed at the house. He should talk to Quinn about coming up with a design for their flock, and maybe he could get it put on something to give Tobias.

But not a ring. He already looked forward to giving Tobias the ring he'd found at the antique store. It had felt horrible to leave it behind to get engraved along with the pocket watch, but he'd wanted to personalize it. He and Briar would pick them up tomorrow and he wasn't sure either of them could wait until the ceremony to gift the items to Tobias.

Memphis came to a stop at a red light. With both feet down to steady the two of them, he put the bike in neutral and looked over his shoulder at Briar. She let go of him to flip open her visor. Grinning, she opened her mouth to talk, but never got a chance to utter a word.

The revving of an engine was his only warning before a vehicle impacted them, sending both him and Briar flying.

Instinctively, he reached for Briar and managed to get an arm around her before they hit the ground. Because it all happened so fast, he wasn't able to shield her from much of the impact.

By the time they stopped tumbling, she'd been ripped from his hold. Angry and scared, Memphis stood up and swept the area for Briar. There was a car on top of what was left of his bike and bits and pieces of his brand-new Harley littered the area.

All that barely registered for him as he found Briar in a crumpled heap next to a parked minivan. He staggered to her side, only realizing one of his legs was badly injured when it had trouble supporting his weight. Ignoring the pain, he dropped to Briar's side and gently rolled her on her back.

"Baby Doll," he whispered as he unlatched the helmet and gently worked it off her head.

She was breathing but didn't open her eyes. He could smell blood but wasn't sure where it was coming from. Her heart was beating strong, but she could be bleeding out and the leathers would be covering it up. He needed Tobias. The vampire could share souls, and she'd be able to pull from Tobias and himself to heal.

His hands were shaking as he fumbled in his jacket for his phone. Pulling it out he saw it was nothing but a broken bit of technology. Shit!

Looking up he saw that they were in a deserted area with nothing but empty buildings around them. Figures appeared from the gloom, and Memphis realized this hadn't been an accident.

Standing up, he whipped off his helmet and sent it flying at the closest figure. The helmet disappeared into the large shape, telling Memphis that he was facing down golems. Creatures made of magic and mud. Impossible to hurt and difficult to defeat.

His beast demanded they shift, and Memphis was ready to give his body over to his animal side when three of the figures rushed at him. They held a net between them. His claws were emerging as the net covered him. The magic in the net was so damn powerful that it forced back his beast and knocked him on his ass.

"NO!" he screamed as the net wrapped tightly around him. He was unceremoniously picked up between several of the golems. Briar was roughly lifted by another one and the two of them were carried to a nearby cargo van.

He was tossed in first then Briar was dumped on top of him. The creatures closed the van door and then one of them got in to drive. Unable to get his hands free, he couldn't even steady her for the rough ride.

One sharp turn sent her tumbling headfirst into the side of the van and then into his bulk. Her eyes fluttered open, and she groaned.

"What's going on?"

"Trap," Memphis whispered to her. "I'm sorry Baby Doll. I didn't see it coming."

Briar blinked at him, as if she couldn't quite understand what he was saying. Then anger set in. "Asshole hit us."

"Yes, a car hit us."

Her eyes focused on the net holding him helpless. "What the fuck?" Her voice was tight from pain. She moved her arm, slowly and with obvious pain, but she managed to get one of the pockets of her jacket unzipped. She pulled out a folding knife and opened it with a flick of her thumb.

Gods above, he loved this woman.

Her movements were slow and uncoordinated as she tried to cut the net. Memphis wasn't surprised when the knife did nothing. This thing needed to be broken the same way it was made, with magic.

The van came to a screeching halt, sending Briar tumbling to the front. The knife flew out of her hand and slid to a stop next to him.

Briar groaned. "I think I'm hurt."

"I know, Baby Doll," Memphis whispered. The driver didn't look at them during their interaction. Unless Briar tried to escape or attack it, the golem wouldn't deviate from its orders. Small blessings. "Do you have your phone?"

"Maybe," Briar said as she slowly sat up. She was panting and sweating by the time she got her other pocket unzipped and pulled out a broken phone. Although he wasn't surprised at the state of her phone, a wave of frustration went through him.

"Maybe I could try with the knife again," Briar said. "Or I could . . ." Her voice started fading, then she slumped over.

"Briar!" Memphis shouted, frantic with worry. "Baby Doll, open your eyes for me." He wiggled and rolled his body until his head was near hers.

"I'm going to get you out of here," he promised, touching his forehead to hers. The magic in the netting zapped her, making her body twitch. Cursing himself, he pulled back.

The back door to the cargo van swung open, and he was cruelly pulled out of the van by his ankles and dumped on the hard concrete ground. Standing over him were more golems and one familiar human.

"I'm going to enjoy this," Greg smirked.

Briar's brain kept trying to shut down on her. She fought to stay awake but wasn't sure how long she could keep conscious. She was distantly aware of being carried and then roughly dropped onto a hard floor. That was enough to make her cry out.

"Goddamnmotherfuckingsonofabitch!"

"Foul-mouthed trash," a familiar voice hissed. She forced her eyes open and saw Greg staring down at her with his usual contempt.

"Does this mean I finally get to beat you up?" she asked. It was a struggle, but she managed to sit up against a wall. It caused a lot of pain but made her feel less vulnerable. "Because I've been waiting for an excuse."

Greg crouched down next to her, then casually slapped her. There wasn't much she could do but take the hit. She hurt everywhere and was pretty sure if she tried to hit him back, she'd black out.

"Coward!" Memphis yelled. She heard struggling. Looking past Greg, she saw Memphis, red faced from fighting the net and glaring. "You're really fucking brave, hitting a hurt woman."

Greg laughed as he stood up. "Point of correction, I hit a corpse," he answered gleefully. "At least she will be once the Vedmak gets here to break both your bonds with Master Tobias."

Briar felt as confused as Memphis looked. "Break our bonds? Is this to get back at Tobias?"

Greg frowned for the first time. "Don't be stupid, why would I want to hurt Master Tobias?"

"Hurting us is going to hurt him, limp dick!" Memphis growled.

Greg's expression turned sanctimonious. "I've already thought of that. The Vedmak should be able to break the bonds without damaging Master Tobias. He assured me all my beloved vampire will feel is a little discomfort, and then I can kill both of you without worrying about hurting him. See, I've thought of everything."

Briar finally understood. "You're in love with him. You think that after we're gone, he'll love you back. No going to happen, asshole!"

"Of course he will. If he could love trash like you, then he must be able to love someone worthy like me. And no one will ever love him more than me!" Greg hissed at her. "All he needs is another little push to realize I'm perfect for him."

"Another little push?" Briar asked with a sinking feeling. "When was the first push?"

Greg shot her a frustrated look. "When I was supposed to rescue him from the spell anchor. If it had been me, he would've realized he loved me back. I had it all arranged."

"Arranged?" Briar whispered. She couldn't speak any louder now, not with the pain in her chest making it nearly impossible to breathe.

"Do you really think Sheridan could have pulled it off without me? The man was incompetent. The only reason the restaurant was flourishing was because of Tobias."

"You did it?" Memphis asked. Briar was sure the horror on his face was reflected on hers too. "The person he trusted the most had him poisoned?"

"I didn't want to, but it was necessary. And it turned out to be easy to talk Sheridan into it. He owed a lot of people a lot of money. The man had a gambling problem that only took a little digging to find," Greg explained, his eyes lighting up with delight. "I convinced him to poison Tobias, but not kill him. That I would take care of that, and then he'd own the restaurant free and clear. I provided him with the silver-laced blood. I'm the one who bought the spell anchor. The only thing Sheridan had to do was put Master Tobias in the basement. Then I could have shown up and set him free. Afterwards, Master Tobias would've seen I was worthy to be a member of his flock."

"But you left him there," Briar accused. "You left him there for ten years!"

Despite the lack of volume to her voice, Greg flinched, and his pale face turned mottled red. "That's not my fault," he screamed at her. "Sheridan wasn't supposed to put him in some secret room. And how was I to know that the man I hired to execute Sheridan to cover up my tracks would show up that night? Nothing went right! Nothing!"

"You had Sheridan killed," Briar said, putting the last puzzle piece together. "That was all part of the plan. A person to pin all the blame on and you would be the hero. Except you weren't because you were dumber than Sheridan."

The taunt hit the mark. For a moment, Greg looked so apoplectic that he might've been about to have a seizure. "You bitch!"

He drew back a foot and kicked her in the thigh. It hurt but at least he hadn't aimed for her torso or head.

"Try that with me, asshole!" Memphis raged, thrashing around for a few moments.

Greg's smile turned malicious as he watched Memphis's helplessness. "I'm looking forward to killing her in front of you," he sneered as he pulled an embroidered handkerchief from a pocket and dabbed at his face. Apparently, kicking a girl when she was down was hard work for him.

"Not happening," Briar gritted out. Not because she thought she could fend Greg off, but because she was pretty sure she was going to be dead before he ever laid a hand on her. The pressure in her abdomen was intense and the way her vision kept wavering was a strong indicator she wouldn't be conscious much longer.

"As I was saying," Greg continued, ignoring her comment. "Master Tobias wasn't supposed to be hidden away. That secret room wasn't part of the plan. It was a stupid idea Sheridan must have come up with on his own. He was only supposed to keep Tobias in the basement, and the next day Green would have killed him and made it look like a drug deal gone wrong. Then I would arrive to free Master Tobias, and he'd realize how much he loved me. But Green messed up and disappeared, Sheridan was dead, and Tobias was hidden away." He calmed as he explained it to them. "But it's all going to work out now. And this time, nothing will go wrong because I'm not putting my trust into anyone else. I'm overseeing every aspect."

"You couldn't have known we would be at that stoplight today," Briar protested. Guilt hit her as she realized she was the reason they were stopped there. She hadn't been paying attention and made Memphis get off the freeway too early.

"But I knew because I'm the one who slipped a compulsion spell on you before you two left. It brought you right where I needed you to be."

"Compulsion spell? But—" Briar started to say, then knew. "The coffee. It was in the coffee you gave me. I knew you were being too nice."

"You're not as clever as you think, are you?" he taunted. "This time, I left nothing to chance." He tugged on a piece of twine around his neck, pulling a wooden disk out from under his shirt. "I also bought the golems last week when I first formed this plan," he said showing them the disk. "They obey only me and are nearly indestructible. Perfect worker bees that will follow my instructions. No one will wreck my dreams a second time."

"Tobias will never want you. You're a bas—" Her diatribe was cut short by a bout of coughing that left her breathless and wincing.

Greg's confidence didn't falter as he sneered down at her. "He'll want me, I know it. And I have to say, you both did me a huge favor by leaving during the day while Master Tobias was sound asleep."

Memphis growled. "You're delusional."

Greg smiled down at Memphis. "I assure you, I'm not delusional, merely impatient to earn my reward after so many years of love. Master Tobias will make me his flock, and we'll build an empire together." He sneered down at her. "And I'll make sure he never comes into contact with riffraff like the two of you again. We will mix with only the best of society."

Memphis's expression was grim. "You need to run. Tobias will find out about this, and he'll rip you apart."

"I assure you, he'll never know," Greg said as he pulled out his phone. "Ah, the Vedmak is on his way."

He left the room without another glance at them, the door shutting loudly behind him. Six golem guards remained behind, not that there was much she or Memphis could do anyway. The chimera wasn't getting out of that net any time soon. And she wasn't going to last much longer.

"I think this might be the other shoe," she whispered before giving up on staying conscious.

Tobias was disappointed to wake alone, but not surprised. Still adapting to his nighttime routine, Briar and Memphis were often up before him. Looking forward to starting the day, he hurried through his shower and dressed in one of his new bespoke suits.

He couldn't wait for his flock to see him. Although both of them might tease him about his clothing, he knew they both found it sexy and enticing. Memphis went so far as to call his outfits wrapping paper because he loved to take them off.

Practically jogging down the stairs, he called out, surprised when no one answered. He checked the kitchen, Briar's office, and systematically checked the entire house, but they were nowhere to be found.

With a growing sense of unease, he pulled out his phone and tried calling each of them. All his calls went directly to voicemail.

A quick check in the garage showed two vehicles missing, one of his cars and Memphis's motorcycle. Had they both gone somewhere? Why didn't they leave him a note? Maybe they'd talked to Greg, and he knew where they were.

Heading back into the too quiet house, he called out, "Greg?"

No answer. Where could Greg be? He was always home and considering how often he tried to get Tobias by himself, if

Briar and Memphis left, it would make sense for Greg to stay behind to garner Tobias's full attention.

He tried Greg's phone. It rang but then sent him to voicemail.

A strange apprehension made him walk to Greg's room. He knocked on the door but got no answer. He shouldn't let himself into the man's room, it was a serious breach of trust. But something didn't feel right.

After spending precious minutes standing outside the room debating with himself, he went in. He'd apologize to Greg later.

The moment he walked in, he realized he'd never been in this room after Greg moved in. The door had always been closed, and Greg had never invited him in. The reason was obvious now.

There were pictures of Tobias everywhere. Some of them photographs and others were drawings. Many of them were in expensive frames and hung artfully on the walls. Feeling a little sick, Tobias went to the desk and pushed papers around. A few were contracts or bills, but most were more drawings. His face stared back at him a dozen times over.

Tobias forced himself to critically examine several of the drawings. They were all flattering, even going so far as to leave out the small scar he had on his forehead and the blemish on his neck. They were also romantic, the type of art one might draw or have commissioned for a lover.

A sick feeling washed over him. Greg was in love with him but had never told him. Instead, he'd become the perfect servant, making himself indispensable. Even going so far as to continue in his role all the years Tobias was missing. Greg had lived a life of unrequited love, probably waiting for Tobias to notice his unwavering loyalty and love him back.

And then Tobias came home with two new lovers in tow. There was no question in his mind that Greg would want to get rid of Briar and Memphis, but was that the reason they weren't answering their phones?

Good god, this felt like a plot right out of a Stephen King novel.

Still hoping that he was alarmed for no good reason, Tobias called Maddy, hoping that Briar's best friend might have some insight he didn't.

"Have you seen or talked to Briar recently?" he asked the moment she answered the phone.

"Not since yesterday," Maddy answered. "Should I be worried?"

It could all be innocent, but Tobias doubted it. "Yes. I can't find her or Memphis, and they're not answering their phones. There's something wrong, I know it."

"Let me call Mikey," she said before hanging up. Before he could get a good panic going, Maddy called back.

"I've got Mikey on the line with us," she explained.

The alpha was all business. "What do you know?"

Tobias explained the little he knew, including that Greg had a sick obsession with him and might have done something to his flock.

"You got Memphis a brand-new Road King, right?" Mikey asked.

"Yes I—" Tobias stopped talking as he realized the significance of Mikey's question. "I installed tracking on the motorcycle so it couldn't be stolen again!" he nearly shouted into the phone.

He hung up on them and opened the app on his phone that would track the motorcycle. Unfortunately, that created more questions than it answered when the map displayed the vehicle parked in an area of new construction. The tracking app indicated the motorcycle hadn't moved for the last hour.

He took a screen shot of the location and set it to both Mikey and Maddy before heading back outside. He needed to get down there fast. Taking a car would force him to drive the circuitous route through the mountains before he'd reach the closest freeway but flying would get him there quicker.

Tucking his phone into a pocket he rushed outside. Once he was clear of the house he closed his eyes and focused on the hawk form he'd worked so hard to perfect over a century ago.

Vampires can learn to shift into an animal form, but it takes years of study. Even after they've managed to successfully shift, they don't have an animal side to their soul to take over. Without any instincts, they had to learn how to fly from scratch. No matter how much they practice, it always required intense concentration.

As he felt his body change, he opened his eyes to see the world turn sharp and defined. With a screech of impatience, he launched into the sky, almost careening to the ground in his eagerness.

Silently cursing, he forced himself to focus on ascending. All the time he'd spent in the sky while living here for almost an entire human lifespan, gave him an excellent mental map of San Diego. It didn't take him long to find the location.

Landing was a little rougher and he nearly tripped on the ground as he shifted back to his human form. Mikey rushed out of some nearby shadows and caught him before he went tumbling. Considering the alpha's bar, The Downward Dog, was only about five miles from this location, he wasn't surprised the wolf got there first.

"Maybe you should leave animal forms to the shifters," he grumbled.

Tobias pulled away from Mikey, too worried about his flock to bother trading barbs with the wolf. "That's Memphis's motorcycle," he said, hurrying over to the wrecked machine.

"Yeah, his and Briar's scent are all over the place," Mikey explained. He pointed to a spot of asphalt with twin lines of tire marks extending out a few yards. "I think they were put into a vehicle there."

Kidnapped. His flock had been hurt and abducted. Briar could even be dying!

His mind stopped working for a moment as he stared blindly at the marks on the road. How was he going to find them? They hadn't shared souls yet, so he didn't have any kind of tangible link with them. They could be anywhere.

"I've got a guy coming," Mikey said. "He's the best I know. He should be able to get enough of Memphis's aura off the bike to track him."

Tobias lifted his gaze to the wolf. "Anything," he croaked. "I'll pay him anything. We need to find them. Save them. I can't . . . they can't," he choked, unable to finish. He felt tears gathering in his eyes.

"I know," Mikey answered quietly, and for the first time, Tobias didn't sense any animosity coming off the alpha. "We'll get them back. No one hurts pack and gets away with it."

But they weren't pack. They were his flock and he'd failed them. If he got them back safe and sound, he promised he'd make sure they were always safe.

If he didn't get them back, he wasn't sure he wanted to survive another night.

The sound of another motorcycle pulling up drew Tobias out of his dark thoughts. Looking over, he saw Mikey waving to direct the rider to them. Unlike Memphis and his massive Road King, this guy was riding a taller, adventure bike. From his few conversations with the chimera about motorcycles, Tobias knew this kind of machine was for riding many different types of terrain.

Pulling to a stop next to them, the guy pulled off his helmet and hung it on a mirror before swinging his legs off the motorcycle. The man had dark brown skin and black hair cut so short that it was only a layer of thick bristles. He was as tall as Mikey but not as broad. Moving with powerful grace, he stepped up to grab Mikey's hand and do a half hug with their hands locked between them. His bright, light brown eyes shown with curiosity as he greeted the alpha.

"Heya, Mikey. What's so urgent?"

"I need your help, Danzig. Some of my people were abducted," Mikey explained.

"My flock," Tobias added. "A human woman named Briar and a chimera shifter named Memphis. This was Memphis's motorcycle."

Danzig's eyes widened a little. "And you can't track them yourself?"

"We weren't official yet," he admitted. He wished he hadn't been so honorable and waited for Briar to agree. He wished he'd forced the issue. When he got them back, he'd share souls, no matter how much she protested. She'd forgive him eventually. Probably.

"Right, okay," Danzig said with a nod. "This Harley belonged to the chimera, right?"

"He and the human were riding it earlier," Mikey elaborated.

"Okay, both of you step way back," Danzig ordered. He and Mikey took a few steps back, but Danzig shook his head. "Much further."

They ended up standing against temporary fencing while Danzig circled the wrecked motorcycle. As he watched the man, Tobias realized he'd never seen an aura like his before.

"What is Danzig?" he asked Mikey.

"Jörmungandr," the alpha said without taking his eyes off the man.

"A world serpent?" Tobias asked, shocked. "I thought they'd gone extinct."

Mikey shrugged. "There aren't many left, but they aren't extinct. Danzig and his brother Marduk moved here a few years ago. They ended up at the Downward Dog and Izzy struck up a conversation. The next thing I knew, they were hanging out with us all the time and lending a hand when we needed it."

"So they're pack now," Tobias stated. "Are there any actual wolves in your pack besides you?"

Mikey snorted. "A few."

"Okay, I've got them," Danzig called out. He started for his motorcycle, but Tobias stopped him.

"Where are you going?"

"I've got a feel for the chimera's aura so I'm ready to start tracking them," Danzig explained, then pointed to the bike. "And I am not doing it on foot."

"Shift," Tobias demanded.

"I'm a Jörmungandr," he stated, incredulously. "We don't do speed. We're protectors, guardians. The bad guys come to us. We don't chase them down."

When the Jörmungandr focused on him and his expression turned concerned, Tobias knew his eyes hadn't only turned red, but were probably glowing.

"I'll carry you," he explained. "I can carry you and fly low so you can pick up their auras. It'll be faster."

Danzig nodded his head thoughtfully. "That might work. What's your animal, vampire?"

"Hawk," Tobias said, then hurried to assure Danzig. "But I'm highly skilled. I've had my hawk form for over a hundred years."

Danzig smirked. "Don't worry. I'll make sure you don't drop me. But just so you know, if you shift in flight by accident, I'll make sure you end up under me when we land."

For a moment, Tobias wasn't sure if Danzig was threatening him or flirting with him. After examining the man's face, he decided it was both.

"My flock's at stake," Tobias reminded him. "I won't accidently shift."

Danzig sobered. "Right, sorry. Old habits." He looked over to Mikey. "This guy really belongs to Briar?"

"Yeah," Mikey said. "She's his flock. You can feel it when the two of them are touching. You know I wouldn't say it if it wasn't true. Fucking vampires." There wasn't much heat in his curse.

"Okay then," Danzig said with a nod and then turned to Tobias to give instructions. "I don't know how much you know about my kind, but I can control the size of my shifted form. I'm going to go as small as I can. That means I'll only be about a foot long. Do not grab me with your claws. I'll wrap around your feet and hold on. I'm tracking auras, not smell, so you don't need to get super low. I'll point with my tail what direction I need you to go. I'll tap to tell you to land. Got it?"

Tobias nodded. "Help me retrieve my flock, and I'll give you anything."

"Getting Briar back is thanks enough," Danzig said, then abruptly disappeared. His clothes fell empty to the ground, pooling on top of his sturdy motorcycle boots.

Next to him, Mikey jerked, then hurried to the pile of clothes. "Damn it, I hate it when he does that."

As the wolf shifter got there, the shirt started moving. Mikey went down on one knee next to the clothes and carefully lifted the shirt. A shiny golden snake slithered out of the item of clothing and wrapped around Mikey's arm.

"A little warning would've been nice," Mikey muttered as he stood up and carried Danzig over to Tobias. "Shift then hop up on my arm and let Danzig curl around your legs."

Tobias did as instructed, the shift coming more naturally to him this time. Careful not to dig his claws into Mikey, he kept his wings out for balance as the Jörmungandr got himself situated.

It was a horrible feeling to have a shifter this powerful wrapped around his weaker bird form. He had to fight his instinct to fling off the serpent shifter.

"He's settled," Mikey said. "I'm going to give you an assist." With that, the wolf shifter hurled the two of them into the air. Tobias pumped his wings hard to gain some altitude, then circled the area. The Jörmungandr kept his middle secured around Tobias's legs and hung his head down searching the ground. Tobias flew in whatever direction he looked at and soon they were following a distinct path through the streets of San Diego.

Hang on my loves, Tobias thought. *I'll be there soon. I won't let you down.*

It was a horrible feeling to have his beast suppressed. Memphis could barely even feel the chimera he shared his body with. His magic was so inhibited that he felt numb. If he was kept in this net long enough, he'd probably weaken and maybe even die.

Despite how dire his own situation was, all he could think about was Briar. She was slumped against a nearby wall, eyes closed and breathing shallow. He hadn't taken his eyes off her, worried that if he wasn't watching, she'd die.

"Baby Doll?" he called out. "I need you to open your eyes for me. Just give me a flutter, okay?"

Nothing.

Despair engulfed him, making his voice rough. "Briar Thorn, I need you to fight!" he demanded. "You're my tough, bad-ass bitch. You can't give up. What's that poem you quoted to me? The one about fighting. If you don't wake up and tell me, I'm going to make some shit up."

He could swear he saw an eyelid twitch. He started speaking more frantically. "I think it starts with talking to the night. Something like, 'Hey, nighttime, I'm not ready to die yet.'"

Briar's eyes half opened as her lips tried to grin. "You mean the Dylan Thomas poem?"

Relief made Memphis's voice shaky. "I don't know, maybe? Do you remember it, Baby Doll? Could you recite it for me?"

She blinked slowly a few times before speaking. "Do not go gentle into that good night, Old age should burn and rave at close of day; Rage, rage against the dying of the light."

She stopped talking to give a shallow cough, her eyes closing again.

"That's the one," Memphis said quickly. "Rage, Baby Doll. I need you to rage against the dying of the light because if you leave me, there will be no light left."

Briar didn't open her eyes again when she spoke; her voice was so soft he could barely hear her. "You need to promise me something."

"Anything," he agreed. "Anything Baby Doll, as long as you keep talking to me."

"I'll try," she sighed. "But you have to promise to take care of Tobias, Maddy, and Lily for me. They are the people I love the most outside of you."

He couldn't hold back his tears any long. "No, Briar, you're not leaving me. You're ragin', remember? You're not givin' in. What's that other line? The one about not going outside? Tell me that one. Please, Briar, please talk to me."

He couldn't tell if she coughed or laughed, maybe a combination of both, before she spoke. "'Do not go gentle into that good night.'"

He could feel the tears pouring down his face. "That's it, Baby Doll. Keep ragin'. Keep fightin'. Don't fucking go gentle into that good-goddamn-night."

She made another wheezing sound but didn't respond.

"I almost feel sad for the two of you," Greg said as he walked into the room. "It's really too bad you stole my vampire. Otherwise you could have gone off and lived a perfectly mundane and uncivilized life together."

Memphis wanted to scream obscenities at Greg, but he was too concerned that Briar didn't respond to the man's taunts with some kind of scathing commentary.

"Break the girl's bond first," Greg ordered as another person came into the room. The guy was scruffy with a long, unkept blond beard, messy hair pulled back into a ponytail, and eyes so light blue they looked white. His black and oily aura meant this had to be the Vedmak.

"Don't you touch her!" Memphis yelled as the Vedmak crouched down next to Briar. Neither man acknowledged him as they studied Briar.

"She won't live much longer," the Vedmak said.

"Then break her bond before her death hurts my master," Greg urged.

Memphis thrashed in the net as the Vedmak put his hands on Briar. The man framed her face and tilted her head. She didn't react to his touch. Not even a fluttering of her eyes.

"I can't feel a bond," he said. "But she's human. I don't deal with them much."

"Could it be because she's almost dead?" Greg asked, making Memphis howl in rage and pain.

The man shrugged, uncaring that a woman was dying in front of his eyes. "Possible. I've never broken flock bonds before. All my knowledge is academic, not practical."

"Fine," Greg said and pushed at the Vedmak. "Then do that one first."

Casting Greg an annoyed look, the Vedmak dropped to both knees and turned to face Memphis. Although he was only an arm's length away, there was nothing Memphis could do. The Vedmak put two fingers through the mesh of the net and laid them on him. The netting sparked. The Vedmak drew back with a hiss the Vedmak.

Memphis grinned with malicious glee. That touch had hurt him too, but it was worth it if it caused this guy pain.

"I can't do anything with that net there," he complained, shaking out his hand.

"I can't take the net off," Greg said with a nervous chuckle. "You'll have to figure out how to work around it."

The Vedmak frowned. "There is no working around it. I can't even see his aura with that net surrounding him."

Greg made an impatient sound. "Well, figure it out. That's what I'm paying you for."

The Vedmak swept his gaze over Memphis, his expression considering. "I could put him under my control. It will cost you extra, but it should work."

"Fine, whatever you need to do. Just do it quickly. I want to get back to Master Tobias," Greg said, a sick smile spreading across his face. "I need to be there to comfort him."

The Vedmak leaned in close until his nose was almost touching the net stretched across Memphis's nose. "You said he's a shifter, correct?"

"Yes, yes. He's one of those things."

"This will be a pleasure," the Vedmak cooed. "Look at me, Memphis."

"Fuck you," Memphis growled. Then he felt it. The Vedmak was doing some kind of thrall, trying to control him like a vampire. It felt strong but different. He tried to move his eyes away but found he couldn't.

"There it is," the Vedmak crooned. "Fall into my will. What I want, you will do."

Memphis wanted to spit in the man's face but couldn't even blink. Fuck, this man had to be the most powerful Vedmak he'd ever met. Not that he'd met many. The descendants of Rasputin tried very hard to stay in the shadows, especially from wolf shifters. They were almost universally hated by all shifters, but wolves seemed to have an especially strong hereditary hatred of them.

The Vedmak didn't break eye contact as he spoke to Greg. "You can remove the net now. I have him under control."

Without comment, Greg moved to Memphis's other side and pulled out a willow tree branch and ran it down the side of the net. The magic gave and the net fell away.

Several things happened at once. Memphis felt his beast rise up, unaffected by the hold the Vedmak had on his human form. As that happened, the Vedmak's eyes widened in fear.

"He's a fucking chimera!" he screamed and scrambled back.

"Why—" Greg started, but he was cut off as Memphis's beast tore free. The nature of his animal/human relationship meant the Vedmak could only control one of them at a time. No longer restricted by the net, the chimera inside was free to take over, shoving Memphis's human form inside and breaking the Vedmak's magic.

Standing tall, the chimera roared with rage. It was time for some men to die!

Memphis was alive and roaring so loud that Tobias didn't need Danzig to point him in the right direction. Swooping low, Tobias flew through a set of wide-open doors in an industrial building that looked like it was still under construction. He tried to land but ended up tumbling because Danzig was still wrapped around his legs.

The moment the world serpent let go, Tobias shifted back to his vampire form. He scrambling to his feet and sprinted in that direction where he heard fighting. He was vaguely aware that Danzig had changed size, but Tobias didn't have the attention to spare as he did a mad dash through an area full of building materials into a reinforced room at the far end of the building.

Skidding to a halt, he took a precious second to take in the scene around him. The first thing he saw was Briar, eyes closed and unmoving on the floor. Then Memphis standing over her, roaring and snapping his tail at the circle of golems trying to get to him.

As his gaze swept the room, he caught sight of a man he didn't recognize. The guy was focused on Memphis, holding out his hands and mumbling something. Tobias recognized what that man was immediately. Once you met a Vedmak, you never forgot what their oily auras looked like.

The chimera was holding off the golems so Tobias focused on the Vedmak. One lunge took him across the room.

Crashing into the Vedmak, he took them both to the floor. The magic he'd been gathering fizzled and snapped in the air around them.

Although he caught the Vedmak by surprise, the man didn't hesitate to start fighting back. He punched out a fist, catching Tobias in the face at the same time he called out in Russian; sending a jolt of magic through the vampire.

Gasping from the pain, Tobias tried to keep his hold on the Vedmak, but his fingers stopped working, allowing the man to struggle out of his hold. Staying on the ground, he reached out and grabbed the Vedmak's ankle, pulling the man back down.

Magic hit him again, but it wasn't as strong this time and Tobias was able to pull the man under him.

"I was only hired to do a job!" the Vedmak screamed. "Don't kill me. I can work for you."

"You took this job," Tobias growled. "You hurt my flock. No mercy."

With that, he wrenched the man's head aside and bit into his neck. He drank down several mouthfuls, feeling the Vedmak magic warm his insides at the same time the man's oily aura slid against his own.

Killing him this way would take too long. With a violent motion, he pulled his head back and ripped the man's throat out. Blood sprayed everywhere as the Vedmak grasped his hands around his neck, trying to staunch the flow.

Tobias didn't bother watching the man die. He could hear fighting behind him, so he got to his feet and turned, unprepared for the sight before him.

Danzig had gone from a small, golden-scaled snake no bigger than a foot long to a massive beast that filled the room. He'd coiled his body around Briar, flinging golems away with his tail and biting them in half with his massive, fanged mouth. Memphis was leaping on the golems ripping them apart with his massive jaw and articulated tail.

None of the golems stayed down for long.

The problem was that a golem can't be killed, not with violence anyway. The magic link they had with whoever made them or owned them had to be destroyed. Once that charm or fetish was broken, they would turn back into the pile of mud and clay they'd been formed from. He needed to find whoever was controlling the golems before the nearly indestructible creatures wore the three of them down.

Even more terrifying was that Briar hadn't joined in the fight. She must be gravely injured to remain hidden within Danzig's coils.

"Master Tobias! What are you doing here?"

Tobias swung around to find Greg stumbling to a halt, staring at Tobias with wide eyes. Although dressed in his normal business casual attire, he held a shotgun in his hands. Then the man saw Danzig.

"What is that monster?" he screamed, bringing the shotgun up to his shoulder and pointing it at the world serpent.

Tobias was close enough to fling an arm up and knock the barrel of the gun high before Greg squeezed the trigger. The blast was deafening in the room as a chunk of ceiling rained down. Greg staggered back from the recoil but didn't fall on his ass. He hit the wall behind him, breaking unfinished drywall and sending up a cloud of fine white dust.

While Danzig had been distracted by Greg, one of the golems managed to get a hold of the serpent's neck. Despite throwing his head around, Danzig couldn't get the golem off. To get free, the world serpent would need to move enough to leave Briar unprotected by his coils, but if he didn't move, he'd be choked to death.

Memphis was busy with three other golems and there were two more rapidly gathering themselves back together to attack again.

"We need to find out who's controlling the golems!" Tobias yelled to Greg, but when he turned his desperate gaze back to the man, he found himself looking down the barrel of the shotgun.

"It's full of silver shot," Greg informed him stonily. "Even a vampire as strong as you won't survive that to the head."

Cold rage washed over Tobias. "I trusted you."

"You ruined everything," Greg spit out. "It was supposed to be me. It was always supposed to be me." He nodded his head in the direction of Memphis's roaring form and sneered. "Me, not them. I'm the smart one. I'm cultured and refined. But you refused to see me as your flock."

"The vampire doesn't pick their flock, fate does," Tobias said as he tried to edge a little closer to Greg. If he could get within arm's reach of the gun, he'd be able to snatch it from Greg.

As if sensing his intentions, Greg stepped back without taking his aim off Tobias. "Fate should have picked me," Greg insisted. "I spent decades making myself perfect for you."

"Decades?" Tobias echoed. Had Greg really been with him that long? Time passed differently for creatures that lived as long as vampires did. All the drawings in Greg's room came back to him. This man had built a whole world around the idea of becoming Tobias's flock. How had he missed this level of obsession?

"Decades!" Greg repeated, his eyes going wild. "I'm almost fifty now. I was a boy of twenty-two when you first hired me. Do I mean so little to you that you don't remember that?"

"I'm sorry," Tobias said. There was no chance he'd be able to talk Greg out of his fantasy. His only recourse was to play along and get Greg to let him get close. "I should have seen you sooner."

"You should have!" Greg yelled, then seemed to pull back and compose himself. "But now it's too late. I can tell you won't forgive what I've done here. I'll need to start over with another vampire."

Tobias saw his time was up. Greg tightened his hold on the shotgun and Tobias lunged. A gray shape impacted the wall near Greg, making the man flinch as he pulled the trigger. Tobias's roar was drowned out by the blast of the gun as he tackled Greg. He ripped the gun from the man's hands and effortlessly broke it in two. Then he saw the wooden disk around Greg's neck. He reached out and grabbed the disk, easily snapping it in half.

The powerful spell bound to the disk exploded, knocking him on his back. For a brief second, there was no air in the room, only magic.

When he'd been tossed away, the two pieces of wooden disk had landed next to Greg. A tight ball of pure power engulfed Greg. The spell was centered on those bits of wood so all the magic holding the golems together tried to find balance by gathering there.

Tobias watched Greg scream in agony as he was burned to ash by the disintegrating spell. It was a horrible way to die but fitting that he was killed by the magic he'd used to hurt others.

With the threat gone, he needed to get to his flock but when Tobias tried to stand, he found he wasn't able. Looking down, he saw a gaping hole in his abdomen. It appeared Greg's shot hadn't missed him entirely.

"Tobias!" Memphis, naked and shifted to his human form, was kneeling next to him.

"Silver," Tobias croaked. He couldn't get anything else out, but it was enough for Memphis to understand. The chimera was bleeding from several wounds and the right side of his face was badly battered and his lip split.

With infinite care, Memphis cradled Tobias's head and presented the vampire with his neck. "Drink," he begged.

Even though he might be dying, he couldn't do it. Taking Memphis's life blood while he was wounded was anathema to his instincts. As if sensing his reluctance, Memphis said the one thing that would guarantee Tobias's compliance.

"Briar needs you," Memphis said, his voice cracking. "She's dying, and she needs your soul. Drink from me, sweetheart, and save our third. I can't do it alone."

Tobias sank his fangs into Memphis, letting the chimera's powerful magic-laced blood fill his mouth.

The shotgun blast had been powerful, and so close that it sent the shards of silver straight through his body. Only a few beads lingered in him, but with Memphis's blood, his body was able to push the poison out and begin healing at a rapid pace.

The moment he felt he'd had enough, he pulled from Memphis's neck. When he opened his eyes, it was to find

Danzig standing over him. The shifter was also in his human form, naked, and cradling Briar's limp body.

Tobias made an inarticulate sound of distress and held out a shaky hand for his littlest flock member. Danzig knelt and set Briar in Memphis's lap.

"Save her," Memphis begged, drawing both of them against his bigger body. "I can't live without both of you."

Tobias didn't waste time talking. Resting a hand on Briar's pale face, he felt for her soul. Her body was barely clinging to life, and her soul was already half detached from the corporeal world.

It took all his focus to gently nudge her soul to fully attach back to her body. Then he pulled out a piece of his soul and carefully transferred it to Briar. Starved for life, her soul latched on to his, eager to attach to something so full of vitality.

Once he was sure her soul was stable, he eased a piece free from her and pulled it into himself. He felt her body sigh into the bond between them.

"Her heartbeat is getting stronger!" Memphis said, and Tobias felt moisture on his face. Looking up, he saw his proud, strong chimera weeping from relief.

They weren't out of trouble yet. Between still healing his own body and supporting Briar's, he was stretched to the limit.

"Need you," Tobias said.

Memphis took Tobias's hand and pressed it to his bloody, bruised face. "Take me."

Because he was depleted, and Memphis was in better shape than him or Briar, Tobias wasn't as careful when he exchanged souls with the chimera. The big man sucked in a breath but other than that, he didn't react. The moment their bond snapped into place, power and strength flowed into Tobias and through him into Briar.

"You saved us," Tobias murmured to the chimera.

Memphis shook his head, even as his eyes started to lose focus. "We all saved each other."

Then he slumped over. Tobias could feel Memphis's body through their link; strong, healing not only itself but working overtime to help both Tobias and Briar.

"Don't leave us," Tobias begged Danzig as his eyes shut.

"You and your flock are safe," Dazing promised as unconsciousness swept over Tobias.

Kneeling next to the three unconscious people, Danzig checked pulses and examined auras. He could tell the vampire had well and truly made the chimera and human his flock because their auras were saturated with his vampire magic.

He was happy to note that all three had strong heartbeats and their auras were looking healthier by the second. After a good long sleep and a meal, they'd probably be back to normal.

But now he was faced with a slight dilemma. He was naked, with no phone, and had three unconscious people who needed to be gently transported to a bed someplace safe.

Running a hand through his hair, he grinned ruefully down at the snoozing trio. "I don't suppose any of you have a phone?"

Briar came awake slowly, her brain feeling oddly fuzzy. It reminded her of the few times she'd taken edibles. The last time she did, her brain had felt foggy for two days straight and she'd sworn off all marijuana products.

Had she slipped up and ate something she shouldn't have? And, oh damn, was she hungry!

Opening her eyes, she found Memphis's grinning face close enough to her that she could've licked him.

"You're awake!" he whispered excitedly.

How much had she imbibed to end up asleep long enough to worry Memphis?

"Morning?" That one word made her realize how dry her throat was.

"I'm going to sit you up," Memphis said as he gently lifted her and placed her against a soft mountain of pillows. The world swam a little. Man, whatever she consumed must have been top shelf and strong.

"I heard you talking. Is she awake?" Tobias asked as he came into the room.

Despite her muddled brain, she was starting to realize something must have happened. Had she been sick?

"What did I eat?" Damn, her voice sounded rough. Had she been throwing up? Both men gave her quizzical expressions, so she elaborated. "Did I eat something that made me sick?"

"No, my heart, you weren't sick. Not in the way you think," Tobias said as he took a seat on the bed next to Memphis. "What's the last thing you remember?"

"Um, Memphis and I took his motorcycle out to, uh," she paused, unwilling to give up the surprise of the gifts she and Memphis had found. "Shop. We went shopping. And we were heading back home." The memories trickled in slowly. Snuggled up to Memphis on the back of his Road King. The thrill of zooming through traffic. The joy of finding Tobias the perfect present.

The satisfaction of knowing that she'd made a choice and feeling in her heart the choice had been the right one.

Suddenly, the memories flooded back to her.

"Greg!" She nearly screamed. "Fucking Greg tried to kill us!" She frantically reached for Tobias's hand. "He wants to be your flock. He's deranged."

"Shhh, easy," Memphis soothed as Tobias cradled her hand in both of his.

"Greg's dead," Tobias assured her. "He can't hurt you."

Relief made Briar feel a little dizzy. "I was dying," she stated slowly. "Memphis was in that magic net, and I was dying."

"I saved you," Tobias said. "Please don't hate me."

"Hate you?" Briar asked. "How could I hate you for saving my life?"

"I had to make you my flock so your body could pull from mine," Tobias explained, his expression pained. "It was the only way. I know I promised to wait. I swore to you that I wouldn't do it without your permission, but I couldn't let you die."

She smiled at him. "Oh, that's not a problem." She pointed at Memphis. "We'd decided to be flock that day. That's why we were out shopping. We were getting you a present."

Memphis looked chagrined. "I'm sorry Tobias, I didn't think to tell you that she'd agreed. I didn't realize you felt guilty."

Tobias blinked a few times, then grinned. "So you're both mine with no regrets or resentment that will surface later?"

"We're all yours, sweetheart," Memphis agreed.

"One hundred percent yours," Briar added with a smile. "I hope you're up for a wild ride."

As she spoke, Briar felt a strange sensation go through her. It was like a warmth flooded her chest. She absently rubbed across her collarbone.

Memphis reached out and wrapped one of his big hands around Tobias's hand. Now there were two layers of hands holding hers.

"That's us you're feeling," he said softly. "That warmth is our love. And we can feel yours too."

She took a moment before saying anything. She wanted her words to match her heart. "I've never felt so perfect in my life."

Lexington Granger stood on the fringes of the crowd watching everyone hug and congratulate his brother Memphis and Memphis's mates: Briar and Tobias.

The bar they held their Alighting Ceremony in, The Dapper Dog, was a brand-new bar opened by a local wolf pack. The place was almost wall to wall with people, most of them wolf shifters but with a smattering of pixies, gargoyles, and other preternatural creatures. There was even a world serpent here.

From what he'd heard, Alighting Ceremonies were supposed to be a few close friends, but not this one. Between the families, packs, and friends of Briar and Memphis, there was no getting around inviting almost a hundred people.

It didn't escape Lex's notice that very few of the partygoers tried to make conversation with him. He'd long since lost most of his brothers to the dance floor. His father had commandeered a guitar and was slaughtering a country song, while his mother was busy gushing over Briar. Out of all his family, he was the only one who remained by himself, not mingling with the happy throuple or mixing with the rest of the guests.

Part of him felt guilty. He was the one dark spot in the party, standing stiffly against a wall while people danced, talked, and laughed in front of him. If he could, he'd join them, but happiness seemed like a foreign concept to him.

"Hey, you're Lex, right?" a tall human woman asked him.

He nodded his head once. "Yes."

Her grin turned wry. "And that answers my second question," she declared. "I was going to ask if you were enjoying yourself."

He tried to smile back, but he knew it fell flat. When had he forgotten how to get along in polite society? "It's a nice party."

"You don't strike me as the party type," she said. "I'm Maddy, a friend of Briar's from way back. You know, she would understand if you wanted to leave. Briar's not one to hold a grudge or anything. I don't know your brother Memphis as well, but he strikes me as a pretty understanding guy too."

Irritated, Lex didn't try to hide his scowl. "Eager for me to leave and stop messing up the vibe?"

Maddy tilted her head, her expression turning sympathetic. "I'm eager for everyone to be comfortable in their own skin, and you're not. You look on edge, and if you hold that beer any tighter, you'll probably break it."

Her words made him realize he was gripping the bottle with too much force. Grimacing, he set it down on a nearby table, then crossed his arms over his chest.

"I'm fine," he mumbled.

"Go on, get out of here," Maddy urged gently. "Briar said you're staying the week, so you'll have plenty of time to spend with your brother and new in-laws in small groups later. That will be more meaningful for both you and them anyway."

As much as he hated to admit it, she had a point. Not only was he uncomfortable, but he was acting like a black hole, sucking in the joyful party energy. He didn't mean to, but it was obvious by the way people were keeping at least ten feet away from him.

He'd flown straight to San Diego from his last job. A job that not only hadn't gone as planned but also made him question if there was any justice in the world. Now he was bringing that energy to a happy event. It wasn't fair to Memphis or his mates.

"You might be right," he admitted to Maddy. "Tell Memphis to call me later, and we'll get together."

"Sure thing," Maddy agreed and then held out her arms. "You want a hug before you go?"

Her offer made Lex grin. The tough talking, shit-kicking Briar and this well-spoken, sharply dressed woman didn't seem to have much in common at first glance, but he could see they both were kind, caring souls.

He folded her in a quick hug, careful to keep his chimera strength in check. "You best go chat with that wolf over there," he said as they separated. "He's scowling something awful."

Maddy looked over and grinned. "That's Mikey," she said. "He doesn't like it when I hug other people."

Lex gave her a little nudge in the wolf shifter's direction. "Off you go."

Once she was back in Mikey's arms, Lex worked his way out the door of the bar. Outside was as lively as inside, and he was forced to do a few two-steps to keep from bumping into people. Someone had finally taken the guitar away from his father and a real band had started up.

The night was young, the alcohol was flowing, and happiness was in the air.

Feeling restless and grumpy that he couldn't simply relax and have a good time, Lex pulled out his phone. He knew exactly one person in San Diego that wouldn't be at this party; A sloth bear shifter named Mac.

He often worked with Mac and maybe the shifter would be up for getting a drink with him someplace quiet where they could get smashed in peace.

Or someplace full of assholes where he could pick a fight and not feel guilty. Both were equally appealing.

"Lex?" Mac answered the phone after only one ring. There were loud traffic sounds around him. "You need me?"

"Wanna grab a drink? I'm in San Diego," Lex said.

"Abso-fucking-lutely," Mac agreed without hesitation.

"Give me a place, and I'll meet you there," Lex said, feeling a surprising amount of relief hit him now that he was going to meet up with Mac.

"I'll text you the address. Meet you there in about twenty. If you get there first, get me a whiskey and order anything you want for yourself, but only one," Mac instructed, then hung up.

Far from being upset at Mac's order, Lex let out a little sigh of relief and made his way to his rental car.

Out of all the men and women he'd worked with over the years, his favorite had always been Mac. Unlike most sloth bear shifters, Mac was a reasonable guy and slow to anger. That quality along with his quick wit and fast reflexes made him an invaluable member of the team.

The added bonus was that he'd always felt comfortable around Mac. The sloth bear never acted like Lex's long silences were an affront or left Lex guessing about what to do in any given situation. Mac always told him straight out what to do and what to say. It was invaluable, especially when they were meeting with clients.

Lex might know how to work any type of gun or how to navigate in desert, forest, or jungle, but give him a social situation, and his hands got sweaty, and his heartbeat kicked up. Mac might not be the best tracker, but his social skills and patience with Lex made him priceless.

A real smiled curved his lips as he followed the directions on his phone. Drinking with Mac meant the beer would taste better, and the strange tension that had been building in his chest since he'd gotten to the Alighting Ceremony would finally ease.

He ended up in a bar called Pounders and his assessment of it as a dive bar from the parking lot held true as he entered the establishment. One sniff told him the place was full of humans, including the old guy behind the bar slinging drinks.

There were only a handful of men, most of them gathered around an old, battered pool table talking smack to each other. Judging by the collection of empty glasses, they'd been at it for a while.

Doing as he was told, Lex sat at the bar and ordered himself a beer and the best whiskey they had for Mac.

"Best? Nah, you'll get what I got," the old guy grumped before going off to pour their drinks. His attitude almost made Lex smile. This wasn't the type of place to have expensive whiskey, the choices were probably cheap or cheaper. Thankfully, shifters were immune to rotgut.

Just as the guy was setting the drinks down, strong arms wrapped around his chest and lifted him off the seat. There weren't many who could lift a full-grown chimera shifter, even in human form, but Mac was built like a tractor and could probably pick one up too.

"I missed you!" Mac said, and Lex went limp and let the sloth bear swing him around a few times.

The cranky bar man slapped the dirty bar top as he shouted at them. "Hey, I don't want any of that gay shit around here."

"Fuck off, Phill," a female voice said before either Mac or Lex could lay into the guy for being a homophobe. "Use that language again and I'll introduce your teeth to my knee."

Everyone turned to take in the stunning woman as she opened the bar pass-through and joined Phill. Her hair was done in braids, the magenta extensions hanging all the way to her waist. She casually swept a mass of braids over her shoulder as she gave Phill a challenging look.

"I don't pay you to threaten me," Phill answered as he backed off.

"That's just one of the many bonuses I get," she said to his retreating back; then she turned her gaze to them. "Are you guys good? You don't gotta leave if you don't want to. No one's gonna harass you while I'm here."

Lex was stunned into silence by her beauty. Judging by the way Mac went still, he was sure the sloth bear was affected as well.

Her flawless dark skin and bright brown eyes were stunning to begin with but throw in the small swell of her breasts framed by the deep cut of the tank top and the tight jeans that perfectly outlined her generous hips and ass and Lex wanted to fall to his knees in front of her.

That's when he realized Mac was still holding him in the air. The sloth bear must have figured that out too, because he unceremoniously dropped Lex to his feet.

Because he had to get his balance back, Mac beat him to the bar top. Leaning over, the sloth bear reached out to grasp one of the woman's hands.

"You're by far the most gorgeous woman I've ever met, please say you'll go on a date with me!'"

The woman graced him with an arched eyebrow but didn't tug her hand away.

Not to be outdone, Lex hurried to the bar and grabbed the woman's other hand, ready to beg for her attention too.

The moment their skin met; a strange jolt went through him. The way both she and Mac jerked meant they felt it too.

Then heat filled him and the smell of this woman and Mac filled his nose. His inner beast roared with triumph and demanded he act. It took all his willpower to remain still and only hold onto the woman's hand and not reach out to drag her across the bar.

He wanted to throw her over one shoulder and Mac over the other. He wanted to run until he found a safe place to act as a den, then he wanted to claim them both until they screamed from pleasure.

"Mine," Lex whispered. His eyes narrowed as possessive feelings flooded him. His gaze bounced between Mac and the woman. "You're both meant to be mine."

How had he not realized Mac was his mate? They'd known each other for almost a decade.

And this stranger was looking at him with fear, but he had to make her understand she was in no danger. She smelled like a human, so he might have to explain everything to her.

As if to prove his earlier assessment wrong, she ripped her hands away from them with strength a human shouldn't have.

"Stay the fuck back," she hissed and fled. She was startlingly fast and speed-vaulted over the pass-through before Lex even realized she was running away from them.

"I'll follow her. You go out the front and circle the building. Meet me in the alley so we can box her in," Mac ordered as he rushed after the woman. "Don't grab her. We need to corner her and talk only."

Lex obeyed without question. He sprinted out the front door and around the building. By the time he got to the back alley, all he found was Mac standing there looking frustrated and bewildered.

"Where did she go?" Lex asked, slowing his pace and sniffing, trying to catch her scent.

"Vanished," Mac growled. "She smelled human earlier, but no human is that fast."

"And I could only smell her when we were touching," Lex remembered. "How is that possible?"

Mac ran a hand through his hair. "It's got to be a charm. She's probably using it to hide, and now we've scared her."

"We'll find her," Lex promised. There was no way he was going to let one of his mates wander around unprotected.

He scanned the uneven, double-wide alley, trying to figure out a likely escape route. Their best bet would be to go back in and interview Phill. It would probably only take a bribe to find out what he knew. But that might not get them far. He had a suspicion that Phill probably didn't know much.

The chimera he shared a body with beat at him, demanding release. He wanted to hunt their mate as much as he did. His skin itched, and he was half tempted to unleash his beast, despite the potential repercussions of letting it loose in a dense urban area.

Then Mac was there, pulling him into a hug. Breathing in Mac's scent, he let the sloth bear comfort him. "It's you too. You're mine too."

"I know," he said simply, his voice soft. "And you're mine. And we have a third. I never expected to have you, let alone another partner. I guess dreams do come true."

"But we don't even know her name," Lex mourned, feeling frustrated to have found and lost his mate so quickly. This had to be a record.

"We'll find her," Mac promised. "We'll find her and keep her safe. The fates wouldn't have spun our threads like this if we weren't meant to weave them together."

Dear Readers,

Thank you for reading *A Hacker, Vampire, and Chimera Walk into a Bar…*. (Longest darn title ever!) If you want more of the Ours Evermore Series, Lex, Mac and Imani's story is published: *When Darkness Meets Dawn.*

I hope you enjoyed *A Hacker, Vampire, and Chimera Walk into a Bar…* enough to leave a review! As an indie writer without the support of a publishing company, I need all the help I can get. Your good reviews keep me writing.

Go to my website to find all the important links: free novellas, social media, and signed paperbacks:

www.rkmunin.com

Cheers,
Rye

Other books by RK Munin

-Science Fiction-

Hissa Warrior Series
Rescuing Halin (Mian and Halin)
Buying Tiran (Mara and Tiran)
Tempting Selon (Lara and Selon)
Defying Kilan (Deena and Kilan)
Healing Mavito (Raleen and Mavito)
Claiming Yopin (Mouse and Yopin)
Teasing Woken (Safena and Woken)
Defending Revin (Kamaril and Revin)
Trusting Warik – Coming soon

Human Pets of Talin Series
Loving Captivity (Sora and Searin)
Escaping Captivity (Lakin and Dalt)
Negotiating Captivity (Nalia and Derani)
Fighting Captivity (Zia and Palforma)
Tender Captivity (Jinna and Holian - This is a novella you
can get for free by signing up for my newsletter)
Craving Captivity (Lasha and Tamerin)
The Twelve Nights of Halloheen: A holiday mashup
novella (Isla and Tisuran)
Stealing Captivity – Coming soon

Origins (A Human Pets of Talin Series)
Creating Captivity (Ari and Bazium)
Gossamer Chains (Rain and Hesarium)
Golden Cages – Coming soon

-Paranormal /Urban Fantasy-

Ours Evermore Series
Two Wolves for Soren (Soren, Kalli, and Quinn)
A Hacker, Vampire, and Chimera Walk into a
Bar….(Tobias, Briar, and Memphis)
When Darkness Meets Dawn (Imani, Lex, and Mac)
Tag, You're It (Novella)

Kidnapping Their Third (Cora, Pike, and Kimble) –
Coming soon

Alpha Series
Alpha Mage (Emma and Kade)
His Alpha Mage (Avery and Jason – Novella)
Alpha King (Cathleen and Lazlo)

New Clan Series
Stray Wolf (Steph and Eli)
Lost Lion (Maeve and Cyrus)
Reluctant Cervid (Tavi and Donovan)
Broken Thorn (Sabina and Theodosius)